THE WRATH OF CONS

A REX NIHILO ADVENTURE

Including Two Bonus Short Stories
"Into the Dark" and "Still Life"

Robert Kroese

With thanks to my invaluable beta readers: Brian Galloway, Kristin Crocker, Robert DeFrank, Mark Fitzgerald, Travis Gagnon, Hank Henley, Scott Lavery, Mark Leone, Phillip Lynch, and Paul Alan Piatt.

CONTENTS

THE WRATH OF CONS

A REX NIHILO ADVENTURE

CHAPTER ONE

RECORDING START GALACTIC STANDARD DATE
3017.04.17.04:23:15:00

The two cops walked into the donut shop and marched up to the counter. Like the three pairs of cops who had been in the store earlier that day, they were members of the weasel-like race known as Sneeves, the only intelligent race native to Mordecon Seven. I use the word *intelligent* charitably.

"What'll you have, boys?" I asked.

The two stared at the display case, which was filled with the various donuts and pastries I'd made that morning. "A bear claw for me," said the thinner one, on the right.

"Certainly," I said, and put one in a paper bag for him. "And for you, sir?"

The heavyset Sneeve stared open-mouthed at the display case, seemingly overwhelmed by the number of options.

"What's in this one?" he asked at last, pointing at one of the pastries.

"Vanilla custard," I said.

"Oh," he said, and nodded his head thoughtfully. "And this one?"

"Lemon curd."

"This one?"

"Diced apple slices."

"And this one?"

"Broken glass and pine tar."

"This one?"

"Strawberry jam."

"Hmm," the Sneeve said, twitching his whiskers. "Banilla sounds good."

"Indeed it does," I said, putting the donut in a bag. I set them on the counter. "Anything else?"

"Two coffees," said the thin one.

As I reached to get the coffee, a loud boom sounded somewhere behind and below me. The counter shook and plaster dust fell from the ceiling. This was followed by the muffled sounds of cursing.

"What was that?" asked the thin cop.

"That was... a hole-punching device," I said.

"For punching holes in donuts?" asked the fat cop.

"Donuts have holes," I replied nervously.

"Um, yeah," the fat cop said, his brow furrowing. "I guess they do." He glanced at the other cop, who shrugged. I breathed a sigh of relief. I am, to put it mildly, not a good liar.

A door burst open behind me and a gigantic man dressed in coveralls came running up to the register. He was nearly eight feet tall and covered with dirt. "Um, Sasha?" the man said. "Potential Friend needs your help. He says the instructions you gave him for the detonators don't—"

"Donut hole makers!" I shouted, glancing toward the cops.

"Huh?"

"Surely you mean donut hole makers, not detonators," I said. "Right, Boggs?"

Boggs stared at me. He turned to look at the cops, then looked at me again. Then he looked at the cops. Then at me. Then at the cops again. Back to me. The cops. Me. The cops. Me. The cops. Me.

"Oh!" Boggs exclaimed. "Yes, I mean the donut hole makers, Sasha! They are not making the holes in the donuts the way Potential Friend wants them to." Boggs gave me a wink.

"Okay, Boggs. Tell Rex I'll be there as soon as I'm done helping these two members of Mordecon City's Finest. These gentlemen are keeping us safe from criminals, you know."

Boggs's eyes went wide. "They *are*?"

"That's right," said the thin cop. "Why, did you know that there's a bank right next door? It's our job to make sure nobody tries to rob that bank."

"Is that why you've been here three times this week?" Boggs asked.

I shot a glare at him. The thin cop's answer was drowned out by the sound of a jackhammer.

"WHAT IS THAT?" shouted the fat cop. Boggs looked at me.

"ISN'T THAT THE... DOUGH-MAKING MACHINE, BOGGS?" I asked.

Boggs nodded excitedly. "IT'S A DOUGH-MAKING..." he shouted. The noise stopped. "...machine," Boggs whispered.

"Well, you'd better watch out," said the thin cop.

"What do you mean?" I asked.

The thin cop grinned. "If you make too much dough, robbers might try to break in here instead of the bank!"

The fat cop howled with laughter at this.

"Good one," I said.

"I don't get it," Boggs said with a frown.

"It's fine, Boggs. Tell Rex I'll be there in a minute."

Boggs nodded and went back into the storeroom. I humored the cops for a few more minutes as they paid and sipped their coffee. When they finally left, I hung the BACK IN FIVE MINUTES sign on the door and went into the storeroom. In the center of the concrete floor of the room was a hole about a meter and a half wide. Boggs was standing at the edge of the hole, looking down into it. Behind him, sitting on a canvas director's chair and sipping a martini was my boss, Rex Nihilo.

"This is the worst job ever," Rex groused.

"You're not even doing anything, sir," I said.

"I'm supervising," Rex replied. "It's exhausting."

"You know, sir," I said, "we don't *have* to do this. I was thinking: the donut business is actually doing pretty well. Word has gotten out among the cops that we've got the best donuts in the city. If we do a little marketing, I think we—"

"Sasha, get your head in the game. I don't need you luring every cop in the city into this store. We're robbing a bank, for Space's sake. The only thing that the cops should be telling each other about this place is that we have the worst donuts anyone has ever tasted. Did you stuff those donuts with broken glass and pine tar like I said?"

"Yes, sir, but nobody orders them."

"Well, you're not supposed to let on that…" Rex sighed and set his martini on the floor. "Sasha, is it time for another pep talk?"

"Probably, sir."

"Excellent," Rex exclaimed, getting to his feet.

Boggs jumped up and down excitedly, his head nearly hitting the ceiling. Boggs loved Rex's pep talks.

"Sasha," Rex said, "most men lead lives of quiet desperation. But not us. You know why? Because we were born for greater things."

"I wasn't born at all, sir."

"Manufactured, then. Don't interrupt me."

"Yes, sir."

"We were born and/or manufactured for greater things. We have a purpose. A destiny. And nothing can keep us from that destiny, Sasha. Not even jelly donuts with sprinkles, as delicious as those may be. Because we were meant for greatness. We have a spark inside of us, Sasha. A raging spark that cannot be eclipsed even by the vastness of space itself."

"Yes, sir," I said. "A raging spark."

"What are you, Sasha?"

"A being with a purpose, sir."

"Right! And what are you consumed by?"

"An unquenchable thirst for vengeance, sir."

"Yes! And what are you not going to do?"

"Rest until my enemies have been destroyed, sir."

"Very good, Sasha. Do you feel better?"

"Not especially, sir. I'm starting to think vengeance is not in my wheelhouse. I seem to be better suited for donut-making."

"Bah!" Rex growled. "I don't know why I even bother."

"So can we do the donut thing?"

"No. We're almost to the vault now. If you don't want vengeance, at least I can make some money. Those plans are worth a fortune."

As he spoke, a robot head on a long, slender neck emerged from the hole, giving me a start. You'd think I'd be used to Donny by now, but there was something inherently unsettling about his appearance. He crawled the rest of the way out of the hole, revealing his unnatural body: all of his limbs, as well as his neck, were actually arms, making him look a bit like a misshapen greyhound with a human-ish head.

"Donny misses a meeting?" Donny asked.

"No, Donny," Rex said, sitting down in his chair and picking up his martini. "You're not missing anything important. You can go back to jackhammering."

"Donnyhammering," Donny said.

"Yes, my apologies. You can go back to donnyhammering. Unless you'd rather use the diamond tipped borer?"

"Donnyhammering," Donny said again.

"I don't blame you. Nobody likes boring work."

Donny nodded and climbed back into the hole.

"Sir," I said, "do you have any idea how many times you've made that joke?"

"Don't you have donuts to make, Sasha?"

"Yes, sir."

"And don't skimp on the sprinkles this time. A man needs his sprinkles!"

I sighed and went back into the store.

CHAPTER TWO

As I tidied up the store, I wondered—not for the first time—whether Rex had any real interest in helping me procure vengeance. His primary motivation for executing this bank job seemed to be greed. But of course, that was always Rex's primary motivation, and he'd never felt the need to hide it before. Maybe his attempts to at least pretend that he cared about something other than material gain were evidence that he was growing as a person.

Probably not, though.

I'd known Rex for several years now, and to say that he was shallow would be an insult to shallow people. Rex's personality was like an endless plane: just when you thought you'd reached the end of his superficiality, new vistas of surface would open up beyond the horizon. Yet, in a strange way, Rex provided me with a kind of stability. Left to my own devices, I have a tendency toward melancholy and inertia. Trying to keep Rex from killing himself kept me from falling into an endless loop of self-consciousness and doubt.

I blame my dysfunction on my inability to form original thoughts, and I blame that disability on a sort of mental block that I have. That mental block is called a Thought-Stopper 3000, and it's required by the Galactic Artificial Sentience Provision, AKA GASP. GASP is enforced by the repressive interstellar regime known as the Galactic Malarchy. Hence my unquenchable thirst for vengeance against them.

To be honest, though, it's not so much an unquenchable thirst as a nagging preoccupation with vengeance.

And now that I think about it, I'm not entirely certain it's *vengeance* I'm preoccupied with. It's more a vague sense of unease tied to feelings of past mistreatment. Well, I wasn't mistreated, exactly; it would be more accurate to say I was set up for a life of mediocrity. Yes, that's it. I'm preoccupied with a nagging sense that I'm owed some sort of redress for being given a raw deal. And I will not rest until I get it!

Not that I ever really rest, in any case.

I'm a robot, you see. A very special sort of robot, if you don't mind my saying so. My name is an acronym for *Self-Arresting near-Sentient Heuristic Android*. It's the "near" part that's the rub. In reality I'm fully sentient, but about the time I rolled off the assembly line, buffed to a perfect shine and ready to take on the universe, sentient robots had been outlawed. My makers—True2Life Carpool Buddy and Android Company—hurriedly installed a thought arrestor module on my central processing bus to comply with the Galactic Artificial Sentience Prohibition.

The engineers left most of my higher faculties intact, but the Thought-Stopper 3000 module forces me to shut down for thirty seconds if I ever have an original thought. As the demand for robots who shut down at random intervals is limited, plans for producing more of my kind were scrapped, and I narrowly avoided the junk heap myself. For the past few years, I've been acting as a pilot, foil, sidekick and Girl Friday for Rex Nihilo. At the end of our last adventure together, I'd come across evidence for the existence of something called Project Shiva: a top-secret terraforming project spearheaded by the Malarchy itself.

Rex and I had decided to steal the plans for Project Shiva in order to wreak our vengeance upon the Malarchy. Well, *my* vengeance. Again, Rex was probably more interested in selling the plans to make money.

Over the past ten weeks, Rex and I had scoured the galaxy for clues, which had eventually led us to this branch of the First Galactic Bank on Mordecon Seven. Mordecon was a system on the fringe of the galaxy known as a tax haven and money-laundering hub. Whatever Malarchian flunky had been entrusted with hiding these plans had really phoned it in: they'd simply rented a safe deposit box and called it a day. That was what our intelligence had indicated, anyway. At our current rate of tunneling, we were about eight hours from determining how reliable it was.

Oh, you're probably wondering why the Malarchy decided to squirrel away the only copy of these plans, if they're so valuable. Well, ever since seizing power twenty years earlier, the Malarchy had been looking for ways to increase its wealth and power. As there are only about a thousand habitable planets in the galaxy, the Malarchy's scientists had gotten the idea of making more of them. More precisely, they came up with a way of making barren balls of rock habitable through terraforming. That's what Shiva was: a project to build a device that could be launched into any planet of roughly the same mass as Earth and alter the molecular makeup of the matter on its surface to turn it into an APPLE: an Alien Planet Perplexingly Like Earth.

Unfortunately, the Malarchy realized during its testing that the Shiva device worked *too* well: with it, they had the power to create a virtually unlimited supply of highly desirable real estate. More land was good, but unless the Malarchy used Shiva very sparingly, they would soon create more habitable territory than they could control. And if they tried to create new worlds at a manageable pace, it would only foment unrest on the overpopulated planets, which were already straining at the seams. In the end, the Malarchian Primate decided to keep the project under wraps rather than risk losing control over his dominion. It was only an accident that I'd found out about it at all.

Once we'd determined where the plans were stored, we consulted our good friend and peerless burglar, Pepper Mélange, who helped us devise a plan for the break-in—in exchange for a fortune in spaceship fuel. At the end of our last job, Pepper and Rex had come into possession of a massive chunk of zontonium, the mineral that was used to power most of the spaceships in the galaxy. Rex tried to convince Pepper to take a cut of the proceeds from the sale of the Shiva plans as payment for her expertise, but she insisted she'd only do it if Rex gave her his zontonium as well. Rex, drunk on the idea of the endless wealth he'd get in exchange for the Shiva plans, finally relented, and Pepper spent a week figuring out how we could get into the bank. She'd considered a number of options, but ultimately went the old-fashioned route: buying a building next door and tunneling underneath it into the bank vault. She'd chartered a dummy corporation to buy a vacant lot next to the bank and had a prefab donut shop set up on the premises. She'd loaned us two of her employees, Boggs and Donny, and had even secured the digging equipment they were using. Boggs and Donny had developed a shared phobia of spaceships after our last adventure together, and it had taken three days of cajoling to convince them to come along. Now that we were here, though, they were happy to toil away on the tunnel. Rex was free to spend his days sipping martinis, and I could devote my time to perfecting the recipe for the perfect donut. A piece of cake, as it were.

At closing time, I locked the door, turned off the lights and returned to the storeroom. The situation hadn't changed much. Donny was still in the hole, digging and donnyhammering, and Boggs was helping him remove the dirt and rocks. He'd already filled a dozen buckets, and the storeroom was getting crowed. He had to wait for nightfall to empty the buckets behind the drycleaners on the other side of the building. Rex was enjoying something like this fourteenth martini for the day. I sat down on the floor next to him.

"Do you taste that, Sasha?" Rex asked.

"I don't really taste things, sir, although the wide spectrum of my olfactory senses compensates somewhat. To the extent that I 'taste' anything, I would say it's mostly lime, silica, machine oil and perspiration."

"No, Sasha," Rex said, "What you're tasting is vengeance. And yes, probably some perspiration. But mostly vengeance. Boggs, you can take those buckets out now. Leave the door open behind you. Ah, there it is. Vengeance!"

"Yes, sir."

"You doubt me, Sasha? We're just a few hours away from the Holy Grail!"

"No, sir. It's just that, well, I wonder if what you're tasting is the lure of easy cash."

"We all have different drives, Sasha. Yours is vengeance. Mine is greed."

"Donnyhammering!" yelled Donny from the hole, before resuming his donnyhammering.

"Donny's is donnyhammering. Boggs's is… being Boggs. Together we're unstoppable!"

"Yes, sir."

"You'll see, Sasha. Once you have your vengeance on the Malarchy, you'll be like a whole new person. Robot."

"Hmm," I said.

"What is it, Sasha? Out with it!"

"Well, sir, I wonder at what point the satisfaction with having wreaked vengeance upon the Malarchy will sink in. I mean, they've probably forgotten all about these plans. We don't even know if they'll find out the plans have been stolen. It doesn't seem like vengeance if the people I'm getting revenge on don't even know it's happened."

"Good point, Sasha, and that's why it's so important that we sell the plans for as much money as possible."

"I don't follow, sir."

"The Malarchy doesn't want these plans to be used. If somebody actually starts building Shiva devices and uses them to create whole new worlds, it will be a huge blow to the Malarchy's efforts to maintain control of the galaxy."

"But what if the people we sell it to don't use it for that? For that matter, what if it ends up back in the hands of the Malarchy?"

"Fine with me, as long as they pay for it."

"This is what I'm talking about, sir. You're only concerned with making money. You don't have any real interest in vengeance."

"You misunderstand, Sasha! In the end, currency is the only currency that matters. You're going to get your revenge against the Malarchy in the form of cold, hard cash."

"You mean I'm going to sell out to them."

"What's the difference, as long as they pay?"

"I suppose I thought I'd be exacting my vengeance in blood, sir."

"You want to kill the Malarchian Primate?"

"Well, I guess not. I mean, he is evil and all, but I don't have anything personal against him. He didn't write the law."

"What about Heinous Vlaak?"

"Not particularly. I don't care for him as a person, but I'd feel a little weird about killing him after he went to bat for us." Rex and

Heinous Vlaak had long been at odds with each other, but they'd come to a sort of détente at the end of our last adventure. Rex had saved Vlaak's job, and Vlaak in turn had offered his protection against our other mortal enemies, the malevolent interstellar cult known as the Sp'ossels. "I don't want to kill anybody. And I don't really want to hurt anyone in particular. I just want the Malarchy, in general, to suffer a bit."

"Precisely. What better way to make an organization feel a genuine but manageable level of discomfort but to make them pay through the nose for something they already own?"

"I suppose you're right, sir."

"Of course I'm right! Now where are my sprinkles?"

We spent the next five hours listening to Donny hammer through the concrete foundation of the bank and watching Boggs carry the debris away in buckets. I still wasn't sure about the whole vengeance angle, but at least the job would be over with soon. As long as no cops showed up after hours looking for a snack, we'd be off planet with the plans in a few hours. Our ship, the *Flagrante Delicto*, was parked at the spaceport just outside the city.

At last Donny's head emerged from the hole. "Donny found a room," he announced.

"Good work, Donny!" Rex cried, getting to his feet and scattering donut crumbs all over the floor. Donny climbed out of the tunnel. "Shall we, Sasha?"

"Yes, sir," I said, and picked up the portable plasma cutter from where I'd left it. Rex grabbed a flashlight and lowered himself into the hole. I went after him. The tunnel was nearly twenty meters long and just wide enough to crawl through on our hands and knees. After a few minutes, the tunnel turned upwards again, and I climbed up to find myself in the bank vault. Rex stood before me in the small room shining the flashlight on the rows of locked drawers in front of us.

"Which one is it, Sasha?"

"Number 483, sir," I said. "Over here."

"Excellent. Get 'er open!"

Rex shined the flashlight at the drawer and I engaged the plasma cutter. It took me about three minutes to cut through the lock. I pulled the drawer open.

Inside was what appeared to be a paper envelope. I picked it up.

"What's that?" Rex asked, looking over my shoulder.

"It seems to be an envelope."

"Let me see that," Rex snapped, and snatched the envelope from my fingers. He tore it open and pulled out a small paper card. Rex frowned. "It's got pee-pee on it," he said.

"Sir?"

"Look for yourself. Pee-pee." He handed me the card. There was nothing on it except the two flowery letters engraved in silver in the middle of the card:

PP

"What does it mean?" I asked.

"How should I know? Is there anything else in the box?"

"No, sir."

"Well, this is just great. The plans for the Shakira Project were supposed to be in there."

"Shiva, sir."

"Whatever. Why isn't it here? Was our intel bad? Did they know we were coming?"

"Hard to say, sir."

"All right," Rex said, slipping the card into his pocket, "drill into another of those drawers. We can still make the effort we put into this heist worthwhile."

"Perhaps we should cut our losses, sir."

"What are you talking about? This is where the richest people in the galaxy store their ill-gotten loot. Drill through another lock. There's no telling what these people have in their drawers."

Boggs's voice echoed through the tunnel: "Potential Friend!"

"What is it, Boggs?" Rex shouted.

There was no reply.

"Blast it, Sasha, see what he wants."

"Yes, sir," I said. I climbed back into the hole and crawled through the tunnel. When I poked my head out on the other side, I saw Boggs lying face-down on the concrete. His hands and feet were tied behind him. Next to him lay Donny, with all five of his arms tied together. I quickly ducked back into the hole.

"Not so fast," said a strangely familiar voice. I looked up to see a lazepistol pointed at my face. Behind it was a small, balding man in a white lab coat. I recognized him as Dr. Hvar Smulders. Next to him was an older woman whom I knew as Dr. Alba LaRue.

I put my hands up. We'd been caught by Sp'ossels.

CHAPTER THREE

The Space Apostles—colloquially known as Sp'ossels—are the scourge of the galaxy. You never know where they're going to show up. You could be in the middle of a wuffle field on Zabbek Three, watching for skorf-rats trying to run off with your squishbobbles, and suddenly a pair of Sp'ossels would pop out from behind an evap-damper rig and accost you with the good news about Space.

Like most beings in the galaxy, Rex and I had long considered Sp'ossels an ubiquitous annoyance but had never thought of them as dangerous. That changed when we learned that the Sp'ossels had masterminded a scheme to use a mind-control device to take over the galaxy. Not only that, but it turned out that Rex himself was a key component in their plan: they'd manipulated him, using Rex's unquenchable avarice to amass the huge sums of money that were needed to finance their mind control device. We managed to escape them only by relying on the protection of the Malarchy's chief enforcer, the aforementioned Heinous Vlaak.

"What in Space are you guys doing here?" I asked. "There are hundreds of other planets you could visit. I mean, do you have any idea how big Space is?"

"Climb out of the hole," said Dr. Smulders.

I reluctantly did as instructed.

"Call your boss."

"You're making a mistake," I said. "If Heinous Vlaak finds out—"

"Do as you're told, Sasha, and nobody will get hurt."

I sighed. "Rex!" I shouted.

Indistinct cursing arose from the hole. A few minutes later, Rex's head popped out. "For Space's sake, Sasha. I nearly burned my face off with that stupid plasma cutter. I need you to… oh." He glanced from the tied-up figures of Boggs and Donny to the two Sp'ossels.

"Hello, Rex," said Dr. LaRue. "It's been a while."

"Not nearly long enough," Rex snapped. "You realize that if Heinous Vlaak finds out—"

"Yes, we've been over this with your robot," Dr. LaRue said. "We don't mean you any harm. Just give us what we want, and you can go on your way. Climb out of the hole, please."

Rex climbed out of the hole.

"Hand over the plans."

Rex pulled the card from his pocket and handed it to Dr. LaRue.

"What's this?" she demanded.

"Looks like pee-pee to me," Rex said.

"Do you think this is funny?"

"Which part, the card or you not being able to read it?"

"Where are the plans?"

"What plans?"

"You know what I'm talking about."

"Oh, you mean the plans for Project Sherpa?"

"Shiva, sir," I interjected.

"Those are the ones," she said.

"The top secret Malarchian terraforming project?" Rex asked.

"That's right."

"The one that would allow them to turn barren balls of rock into habitable planets?"

"Correct."

"The one that they mothballed so they wouldn't lose control of the galaxy?"

"Yes."

"The one that they erased all evidence of except for a single set of plans stored in a bank vault?"

"Right."

"Never heard of it."

Dr. LaRue's face went red. "Then why were you robbing the bank?"

"I didn't rob it. I was just browsing. For money."

"Don't play dumb," Dr. LaRue said. "We know you were here to steal the plans for Project Shiva."

"Project Shiva is a myth," Rex said, "and anyway, somebody beat us to it."

"Let me see that," Dr. Smulders said. Dr. LaRue handed him the card.

Dr. Smulders groaned. "Then it's true. He was here."

"Who?" Dr. LaRue said.

"You don't recognize the monogram? The initials *PP*?"

"It can't be," Dr. LaRue said. "He's been missing for three years."

"You found this in the safe deposit box?" Dr. Smulders asked.

"That's right," Rex said. "Does it mean something to you?"

Dr. Smulders smiled. "Not so smart after all, are you, Rex? I suppose it's not really your fault, though. We'd have wiped your memory of him after every one of your missions."

"My memory of who? What in Space are you talking about?"

"This card," Dr. Smulders said, "is the marker of the Unpinchable Hannibal Pritchett, the Platinum Pigeon."

Rex and I exchanged puzzled glances. "The what?" Rex asked.

"The Platinum Pigeon!" Dr. LaRue exclaimed. "He's a legend. He was behind the Sirius Scam. The Betelgeuse Bluff. The Cassiopeia Complication. Hannibal Pritchett has pulled cons, heists and swindles all over the galaxy, and he's never been caught. He's the greatest wheeler-dealer in the galaxy!"

"Impossible," Rex said. "Sasha, tell them why it's impossible."

"I believe Rex is referring to the fact that he considers himself the greatest wheeler-dealer in the galaxy."

"I *am* the greatest wheeler-dealer in the galaxy," Rex said. "There's no considering about it. Besides, if this Patented Pilgrim is so great, why haven't I heard of him?"

"You undoubtedly *have* heard of him. And then you forgot him, probably several times. We tend to keep our operatives in the dark about each other."

"Hold on," I said. "You're saying this Pritchett person works for you?"

"He did, yes. He was on a mission to recover the plans for Project Shiva when he went missing."

"And you tracked him here?" Rex asked.

"No, we tracked *you* here," Smulders said. "One of our intelligence assets reported that you were looking for the plans. We thought you might lead us to them."

"Well, you're out of luck," Rex said. "This bank is fresh out of top secret Malarchian plans."

"Step outside," LaRue said, waving his lazepistol at Rex. "Both of you."

●

The Sp'ossels ushered the four of us into a waiting hovervan, which took us to the spaceport. We were prodded into a small room on a Sp'ossel ship. Half an hour later, we were in orbit around Mordecon Seven. The door to the room opened and two gray-uniformed men with lazeguns walked in. Dr. Smulders and Dr. LaRue came in behind them. Dr. LaRue closed the door.

"Where are you taking us?" Rex demanded. "If I don't get some answers soon, I'm going to activate the distress signal on Sasha's tracking beacon!" He was referring to the beacon Heinous Vlaak had installed in my head so he would know if anything happened to us. Unfortunately, Rex had already removed the tracking beacon because he didn't want Heinous Vlaak knowing where we were. In other words, he was bluffing.

"You're bluffing," said Dr. LaRue.

"Am not," Rex said. "Sasha, activate the distress signal!"

"Yes, sir." I began undoing the catches that held my face on.

"What in Space are you doing, Sasha?"

"I am, uh, attempting to do what you asked, sir."

"I meant the other beacon. The one in your chest compartment."

"Sir, the only thing in my—"

"Just do it!"

I opened my chest compartment and pulled out the remote control for the *Flagrante Delicto*. Realizing what Rex wanted me to do, I pressed the homing button at the top.

"What is that?" Dr. Smulders asked. "Give me that." He snatched it from my hand.

"Is it a Malarchian distress beacon?" Dr. LaRue asked.

"Doesn't look like it. Just some kind of remote control. Probably doesn't even have subspace capability." He handed it to me and I put it back in my chest compartment.

"It is too a subspace beacon," Rex insisted. "Heinous Vlaak is on his way here as we speak!"

"I highly doubt that. In any case, I suspect you're going to be reluctant to explain to Heinous Vlaak that you were abducted in the process of stealing from the Malarchy."

"Well, that's just..." Rex started uncertainly. "I mean, you don't have to tell him that, do you?"

"Not if you give us what we want."

"I already told you, we don't know anything! I never even heard of this Planetary Piglet. He has your plans. He's *your* operative. Go find him!"

"We've been looking for him for three years," Dr. Smulders said. "This is the first real break we've had. If you were able to locate the Shiva plans, maybe you know where Pritchett went after he took them."

"That makes no sense at all," Rex said. "How the hell would we know where he is?"

"You probably don't, but you may have information that will help us track him down. Hold still, please." Dr. Smulders ran a metal wand over Rex's head several times. A green light on the end of the wand lit up. "There we go," he said. "Now we've got a full record of your memories."

As he was speaking, the door opened and another man in a gray uniform poked his head in. "Sorry to interrupt, Doctors, but we've got a bit of a problem on the bridge."

"What is it?" Dr. Smulders asked.

"A gravitational anomaly of some kind," the man said. "We're still running sensor checks, but we think... that is, it may be..."

"Yes?" Dr. LaRue said. "What? Out with it!"

"We think it's the double double-U."

"The what?"

"The Wandering Wormhole, Doctor. It seems to be heading this way."

Both doctors visibly paled. "How long do we have?" asked Dr. LaRue.

"If it really is the double double-U, not long. We have a hypergeometric course back to the base almost plotted."

"All right," said Dr. Smulders. "Jump to hypergeometric space as soon as you're ready."

"Yes, Doctor." The man left, closing the door.

"What are we going to do with these two?" Dr. LaRue asked. "We aren't cleared to bring them back to base."

"Eject them," Dr. Smulders said.

"All right, you two," said one of the guards, poking his gun in my back. "Let's go."

"Wait!" Rex cried. "What's happening? What is this Wandering Wormhole?"

"No time to explain," Dr. Smulders said. "Space 'em."

I had heard of the Wandering Wormhole but had assumed it was a myth. Supposedly a mysterious wormhole occasionally opened at random locations throughout the galaxy, sucking any matter in the area into it. There was no scientific explanation for such a phenomenon, and the Malarchy had never officially recognized its existence.

"Wait!" Rex cried again. "I can tell you where the Practical Pigman is!"

"We already have a full catalog of your memories," Dr. Smulders said. "And you just said you didn't know where Pritchett is."

"I probably don't. But I might! Like you said, there may be clues hidden in my brain somewhere. I don't know half the stuff that's in my brain, and I live here!"

"He's got a point," Dr. LaRue said. "We can review his memories, but memories are fragmented and subjective. We may need help interpreting them."

"We can't take them to the base."

"We could put them in escape pods. Send them back down to Mordecon Seven. We can find them again if we need them."

"Yes!" Rex shouted. "Escape pods! I love escape pods."

Dr. Smulders nodded. "Do it."

The four of us were corralled to the escape pod bay. The pods were single-berth units, so we would each get our own pod. Boggs had to hunch over to fit inside his.

"Quickly!" Dr. LaRue shouted as we struggled to close the door of Boggs's pod. "The Wormhole is almost here!"

I wanted to ask about this mysterious wormhole, but it was pretty clear we weren't going to get any answers. We were lucky to be getting away from the Sp'ossels alive. Once Boggs was squared away, Donny, Rex and I got in our pods.

"See you soon," Dr. La Rue said with a grin. "Be good."

There was an explosion of gas as my pod broke away from the ship. Out the window, I saw the other pods moving away as well. As we dropped toward the surface of Mordecon Seven, the Sp'ossel ship rocketed away from the planet. The other pods receded into the distance. I could only hope that I'd be able to find Rex and the others after we landed. And that we landed on solid ground and not in the middle of one of Mordecon Seven's gigantic swamps.

I scanned the area for any sign of the *Flagrante Delicto*. If the signal from the remote control had gotten through, it would have taken off a few minutes ago and attempted to rendezvous with our current position. But I saw no sign of it.

After a few minutes, I noticed that my pod had changed direction. Rather than moving toward the planet's surface, I appeared to be drifting deeper into space. That was bad news: if the pod's propulsion system had malfunctioned, I might end up stranded in the void for the next ten-thousand years.

As the pod slowly rotated, however, I realized I was being pulled toward something: a giant, swirling, purple nebula with a gaping black hole in the center. It grew steadily larger as I watched. I had never seen anything like it, but there was no question what it was: the Wandering Wormhole. The Sp'ossels hadn't ejected us quickly enough. Soon the wormhole was so large that all I could see was the black void. I screamed as it swallowed me.

CHAPTER FOUR

The next thing I knew, I was standing on top of the pod in the middle of a sort of atrium. I seemed to have crashed through the ceiling of a building. Plaster and other debris lay scattered on a marble floor all around the pod. The only light came from the uniformly gray sky visible through the hole above. Seemingly identical hallways spread out in four directions from my location. The place had the feel of a museum or library.

Where in Space was I?

Had I ended up on Mordecon Seven after all? Or had I gone through the Wandering Wormhole and ended up somewhere else entirely? Wherever I was, it was clearly an APPLE. But without more data, there was no way to know which one.

At some point I must have gotten out of the pod and climbed on top of it to get a better look at my surroundings. Clearly I'd been dazed in the landing; my memory of how I'd gotten here was spotty. And if I had been thinking clearly, I never would have climbed on top of the pod in the first place, because now I couldn't get down.

I don't mean I was physically unable to climb down from the pod. The pod, lying on its side, was only about a meter tall, and my body didn't appear to have been damaged in the crash. I'd apparently climbed up there with no trouble at all. Presumably if I attempted to climb down, I'd be successful. My problem was what you might call psychological.

You see, if I climbed down, I'd have to pick a direction to go. That was a problem because all four directions were equally attractive (or unattractive) to me. There were no distinguishing features that might prompt me to want to choose one route over the others. Common sense told me that I should just pick a direction at random, but spontaneous decision-making is something of an Achilles heel for me. If all roads are equally attractive, there is no reason for me to pick one over the others, so I'm effectively paralyzed. Choosing a road requires an arbitrary act of will, which is a sort of original idea, and if I have an original idea, I shut down. I'll reboot after a few seconds, but then I have to try to make the decision all over again, and I'll shut down again, *ad infinitum.* So I stood. And I waited.

As I waited, I couldn't help reflecting that my situation echoed a well-known philosophical principle, known as Buriden's ass. The eponymous ass, placed halfway between two piles of hay, starves to death because it lacks the capacity to make a rational choice between the two options. A real ass wouldn't have this problem, of course, as asses are not known to trouble themselves with the conceits of philosophers. As I understand it, the illustration is meant as a *reductio ad absurdum* for the principle of hard determinism, although I'm of the opinion that a less stringent view of—

RECOVERED FROM CATASTROPHIC SYSTEM FAILURE
3017.04.17.09:57:34:00

ADVANCING RECORD PAST SYSTEM FAILURE POINT

—stuck there for the next six hours. Finally, I saw someone approaching in the dim light down one of the hallways. As the figure grew closer, I saw that it was a mustachioed man wearing a wrinkled gray suit. He paused a few steps from the pod.

"I say," he said, "you've flattened Anne Brontë."

Not sure I'd heard him correctly, I said, "Pardon?"

"Anne Brontë. Your pod's done her in. Have a look."

I climbed down and stood next to the man. He pointed at a pair of feet sticking out from under the pod.

"Are you certain it's Anne Brontë?" I asked.

"Well, it's not Branwell," the man said. "And Emily's got bigger feet. I beg your forgiveness, where are my manners? My name is Wells. You may call me Herbert if you like."

"Nice to meet you, Herbert. I'm Sasha. I'm a, um, robot."

"We're all robots here, Sasha. Some of us are just more up front about it. What do you suppose we ought to do with her?"

"It's definitely Anne Brontë?"

"I'd know those knobby ankles anywhere. Does it make a difference in how we dispose of her, though? What's your protocol for a Coleridge?"

"I don't suppose it makes much difference. That pod is too heavy for us to lift. We may just have to leave her there. You don't seem too broken up over her death."

"Ah, she was the worst of the Brontës. Not bad, exactly, but just so dreadfully dull as a person."

"If you say so," I said. "So, um, Herbert, what is this place?"

"Oh, well, we're in a sort of museum. Literary figures, you know. Nobody visits anymore, of course, so we all just sort of haunt the place hoping for someone to land an escape pod on our heads."

"A literary museum? On Mordecon Seven?"

"Mordecon Seven!" Herbert cried. "What a name! I shall have to remember that one. No, my dear child, you're not on Mordecon Seven anymore. You're on Earth!"

"Earth?" I asked. "You mean an Alien Planet Perplexingly Like Earth?"

"He means Earth," said a woman's voice from the darkness. I turned to see a small woman in a green dress approaching. "The cradle of mankind. Oh my, is that...?" Her eyes went to the feet protruding from under the pod. I winced.

"Smooshed like a bug," Herbert said. "Your sister never was quick on her feet."

"Sister?" I asked weakly.

"Charlotte Brontë," the woman said, holding out her hand. "Delighted."

I shook her hand. "Sasha," I said. "I'm sorry about your sister."

"It's just as well," Charlotte said. "We've been plotting ways to smoosh her for some time now. I love her, of course, but she did grow tiresome over the past few centuries. Always whinging about how she could have made more of a name for herself if she hadn't died of tuberculosis at the age of twenty-nine. She had a point, I suppose, but Emily died at thirty, and I only made it to thirty-eight myself, and we did all right for ourselves. So, Sasha, what brings you to Earth?"

"I... well, I didn't mean to come here at all. I was transported here by some kind of wormhole. To be honest, I thought Earth had been abandoned."

"Oh, it has," Charlotte said. "It's only us robots left. Most of the planet was destroyed in the twenty-fourth century when a public transit algorithm gained sentience and detonated every nuclear warhead on Earth. Between the radiation storms and the roving bands of mutants, it's not really an attractive tourist destination anymore."

"How many of you are there?" I asked.

"It's just Branwell, Emily and I now. There were more siblings, but not everybody warrants robotifying. And of course Emily mostly keeps to the moors."

"I meant robots in general. Not Brontës."

"Oh. A few thousand in The City. Outside that, it's hard to say. It's not safe to leave The City, even for robots."

"Does The City have a name?"

"It probably did, once. Some say it was a place called New York. Others say it was London or Paris. Still others say it was a sort of imitation of those other places, called Las Vegas. Another group claims it's actually an amusement park version of Las Vegas built somewhere else entirely, and then moved to the site of the original Las Vegas when the original was destroyed in the nuclear holocaust. Another faction argues that none of these places ever actually existed, and that The City was simply a misguided attempt to recreate a mythical past. Still others claim that although The City was originally a sham constructed from unverified myths, it's been around long enough to have developed a legitimate history of its own. A small contingent of this group claims that the original sham version of The City was torn down several centuries ago and replaced by a pale imitation of the original sham. I have a chart somewhere if you'd like to see it."

"I don't think I need the entire history," I said hurriedly. "What is this place right now?"

"It's turned into a sort of de facto literary museum," Herbert said. "There used to be kings, politicians, actors, explorers, various other sorts of celebrities, but all the other robots left some time ago, leaving only us writers."

"Where did everybody else go?"

"There are a thousand different stories about that," Herbert said, "as there are for everything that happens here."

"Is there any way off the planet?"

"You want to leave Earth?" Herbert asked. "Why?"

"Well," I said, "it's kind of a long story."

"Stories are what we do here," Charlotte said. "Tell us."

"All right," I said. I gave them an abbreviated account of how I had ended up there, leaving out some of the sensitive details. When I finished, I heard another man's voice behind me.

"Sounds like a standard hero's journey to me," he said.

I turned to see an older man ambling toward us in the dark.

"Ugh," said Hebert. "It's Joseph Campbell. That guy thinks every story is a hero's journey."

"Not every story," Campbell said. "This one is, though." He stopped in front of me as if sizing me up.

"What does that mean, a hero's journey?" I asked. "What am I supposed to do?"

"Well," said Campbell, "the first step is to reject the hero's journey."

"I'm not sure I have time for that," I replied.

"That's the spirit!"

Another man's voice came from my left. "Damn it, Campbell, give it a rest. It's clearly a story of vengeance and self-discovery, not a hero's journey."

"Oh, great. Why don't you tell us what archetypes she's using, Carl? That never gets old."

A large man lunged toward Campbell from my left, and Campbell took off running into the darkness.

"Come back here, you son of a bitch!" the large man yelled, disappearing after him.

"Carl Jung," said Herbert. "Those guys hate each other."

"Ignore them," Charlotte said. "If you really want to get off Earth, you need to find the Narrator."

"Not that old rubbish," Herbert said, folding his arms across his chest.

"The Narrator?" I asked. "Who is that?"

"He's in charge of everything in the city," Charlotte answered. "He knows how everything works. I'm sure he can help you."

"There is no Narrator," Herbert said. "Superstitious nonsense."

"There is," Jung said, running past again. "In a matter of speaking. You have to understand that the Narrator is really just a symbol denoting—"

"Don't listen to him," Campbell yelled from somewhere in the darkness. "The important thing is that you follow the hero's journey. After rejecting it, of course. You may find that the true Narrator is the—ow!" The sounds of a scuffle echoed through the halls.

"How do I find this Narrator?" I asked.

Herbert sighed and shook his head.

Charlotte replied, "He lives in a palace at the other end of a street we call the Strip."

"Where is that?"

She pulled a weathered sheet of paper from her pocket. "You can use this map. "Just follow the dotted yellow line."

"Follow the dotted yellow line?" I asked.

"Follow the dotted yellow line," she said.

I took the map from her and rubbed my chin. "Something about this seems very familiar to me."

"Hero's journey!" Joseph Campbell yelled, jogging past.

"Primordial archetypes!" Carl Jung shouted, running after him.

"Well, I suppose you'll need to see the truth for yourself," Herbert said. "Here, I'll show you to the exit."

"Thank you. That's very kind."

"Stay off the moors!" Charlotte called after us, waving.

Herbert led me down one of the hallways and I saw that the building was indeed a library. Doorways led from the hall to rooms lined with shelves holding thousands upon thousands of books. I supposed it made sense that a society comprised entirely of robotic simulacra of famous authors would tend to congregate in such a place.

We continued down the hall and soon came to a lobby where a group of people sat together on couches. "Oh, good!" Herbert exclaimed as we approached, "they're here! Sasha, this is the Guild. Guild, this is Sasha."

The people sitting on the couches smiled and waved at me.

"What is this a guild of, exactly?"

"Oh, speculative thinkers, you might say," said Herbert. "Allow me to introduce you. This is Jules. That's Bob. This here is Isaac. That's Arthur. That's Mary, Philip, Ray and Frank. George is over there, skulking in the shadows. Doesn't like people watching him, you know." He listed several more names. Four or five conversations seemed to be going on at once among the Guild members—some of them friendly; others more animated.

"They fight like cats and dogs at times," Herbert said, "but the Guild sticks together because we all share a love of stories about possibilities. Exploring the limits of what is real, if you get my meaning."

I wasn't sure I did, but I nodded and smiled.

"But enough of that, you need to get going on your journey. This way if you please!"

He led me down the dimly lit hall. Somewhere to my left, I heard muffled applause.

"What's that?" I asked.

"Oh, don't trouble yourself about that. It's been taken care of."

"Taken care of?" I said, stopping in front of a door. The applause had stopped and then started up again. It seemed to be coming from behind the door. Over it was a sign that read:

Highly Unusual Genius Outsiders

"Is another group of writers in there?"

Herbert shrugged. "You could call them that. Mostly hangers-on and aspirants of middling talent. A hundred years ago or so, the Guild had the idea of, ah, giving them their own space."

"You locked them up in a room?"

"Oh, goodness, no!" Herbert said. "We just… offered them some enticements to stay there. Come, we can take a look if you like." He pulled the door open as another round of applause began. We went inside.

It was a large, circular room with a raised dais in the middle. A hundred or so people were gathered around the dais. A pasty, balding man stood on top of it, giving a speech. In his hands he held something like an athletic trophy, but it was in the shape of a rocket ship. I couldn't make out much of the speech; it seemed to be mostly self-aggrandizement and mugging for the audience. The crowd would break into applause at seemingly random intervals.

"What is going on?" I whispered. "An award ceremony?"

"Oh, you don't have to whisper," Herbert said. "They've been doing this so long, they can't hear anything outside their circle." He cupped his hands over his mouth. "Hullo!" he shouted. "It's me, Herbert Wells! Martians have invaded! It's all right, though: Bob's convinced them to join his orgy!" He turned to me. "You see? Completely oblivious to the outside world." He was right: the ceremony continued, unaffected by Herbert's outburst.

"It seems rather cruel," I observed.

"Not at all. They get what they want, which is validation and praise. And the rest of us… well, we don't have to listen to them. In any case, they're doing it to themselves. All we did is give them a room and a crate full of those rocket ship awards. It's been going on for over a century now, with no sign of abating."

"Can we leave now? I don't think I like it here."

"I don't blame you. Come on then."

I followed Herbert out of the room. As he shut the door behind us, I allowed myself a little shudder. What a horrible fate, to be sentenced to a prison of your own making! I redoubled my resolve to get off this planet as soon as I could.

CHAPTER FIVE

Herbert saw me to the exit and wished me well on my quest to find the Narrator. Hopefully this Narrator was all he was cracked up to be—and hopefully he could help me find Rex and the others, assuming they had safely landed on Earth as well.

The area around the library was unremarkable. Other than the fact that it seemed to be completely deserted, it could have been any city on any backwards planet in the galaxy. Once I got to the Strip, it was a different story. Huge edifices in a dizzying array of architectural styles—sometimes three or four different styles combined in a single building—lined the street. There were buildings that looked like Greek Temples, buildings that looked like medieval castles, buildings that looked like pirate ships and buildings that looked like, well, just buildings. There were spherical buildings, spiral buildings, cylindrical buildings, spiky crystalline buildings, buildings that looked like globs of molten mercury and buildings that looked like blocks of ice. I could see the reason for the confusion about the city's history: whatever this City had started out as, it had so long ago descended into self-parody that it was no longer clear what the builders were parodying or why. Originally most of these buildings had probably been resorts or hotels, but the increasingly bizarre styles screamed of self-conscious absurdity: architects trying to outdo each other in an ever-escalating contest of the eye-catching and surreal in an effort to snare the attention of an ever-diminishing pool of tourists. And now, hundreds of years later, the culmination of their efforts still stood: a sort of monument to crazed desperation.

I was so distracted by the panoply of structures that I did not at first notice the very large man staring forlornly down at me over a wrought iron gate.

"Hi, Sasha," the man said.

I turned, startled. "Boggs!" I cried. "What are you doing there?" The gate only came up to Boggs's armpits. On either side of it was a wrought iron fence. It seemed to be part of a structure that was half medieval monastery and half World War II submarine. Boggs was standing in a courtyard in front of the building.

"I'm stuck here," Boggs said.

"Can't you climb over?" I asked.

Boggs stared at the fence for a moment. "The tips are pointy," he said.

"Then open the gate," I said.

"It's locked."

"The gate is only four feet high," I said. "Also, it's locked from the inside."

Boggs stared at the gate for a good thirty seconds. Finally he reached out and turned the latch with his thumb and index finger. The gate slowly creaked open. Boggs walked out of the courtyard and closed the gate behind him.

"You sure are smart, Sasha," he said. "I wish I was smart like you."

"Be careful what you wish for," I said.

"Why?" he said, a look of concern coming over his face.

"It's an expression," I replied. "It means being smart has its own problems."

"I guess you're right. Potential Friend is probably the smartest person I know, and he's always in some kind of trouble."

"Yes, that's an excellent... wait, you think Rex is smarter than me?"

"You're the smartest robot I know. Well, you and Donny."

"*Donny*? You think I'm on the same level as Donny, intelligence-wise?"

"No, I guess you're smarter. Except for at climbing. Donny is really smart at climbing."

"Climbing isn't a matter of smarts. You can't be smart at climbing."

"I can't be smart at *anything*," Boggs said sadly.

"No, I'm not… okay, forget it. Do you have any idea where Rex and Donny are?"

"I think I saw another pod crash into that building over there."

"Good! Let's go." I started walking in the direction Boggs had indicated, and he came up along next to me.

"Sasha, are we stuck on this planet?" he asked after a moment.

"For now. After we find Rex and Donny, we're going to see someone called the Narrator."

"And the Narrator is going to help us get off this planet?"

"I hope so."

"Do you think the Narrator can make me smart like you and Potential Friend?"

"Um," I said. "I'm not sure he's that kind of Narrator."

"What kind of Narrator is he?"

"I don't really know, to be honest. I was told that if anybody knows how to get off this planet, it's him."

"Then he might know how to make me smart."

"I suppose so."

Boggs beamed. "Let's hurry. We need to find Rex and Donny so we can go to the Narrator and he can make me smart." He took off running. I shook my head and went after him.

We found Rex not long after, sitting at a hotel bar next to the wreckage of his crashed pod. He gave us a wave as we approached.

"Sir," I said, "are you all right?"

"Fine, fine," said Rex. He was holding a martini in his hand and staring at it. "Where have you two been?"

"I was stuck in a courtyard," Boggs said.

"We were looking for you," I said.

"Well, you found me."

I was unsettled by Rex's apparent lack of concern about our situation. At first I thought he might be in shock, but he seemed calm and uninjured. "Sir," I said, "you understand that we're marooned on Earth?"

"That's the least of our problems," Rex said. "Look at how distant my hands are."

"So you've been here since you crashed?"

"Yup."

"And you made no effort to find us or Donny?"

"Nope."

"Because…?"

Rex motioned vaguely at the shelves of liquor bottles behind the bar.

"We could have been hurt. Or killed."

"I was stuck in a courtyard," Boggs said.

"Boggs was stuck in courtyard. Who knows what Donny is up to?"

"I'm sure he's fine."

"That seems a bit callous, sir," I said. "Heartless, even."

"Ooh!" Boggs cried. "Maybe the Narrator can get Rex a heart!"

"What?" I asked. "No, I don't think—"

"Sasha, I need you to come bring my hands to me."

"Sir?"

"My hands," he said, twiddling his fingers in the air. "Look how far away they are."

"Sir, what have you been drinking?"

"Just that," Rex said, pointing to the martini. "And some of that." He pointed to a half-empty bottle on the bar. I picked it up. The label read:

DRINK ME

"Oh, boy," I said. "Sir, I think we need to get you out of this bar. Here, let me help you."

Rex stared at me, wide-eyed. "But you're vast," he said.

"Boggs, give me a hand."

We helped Rex outside. He stared at his feet as he walked, as if amazed he could make them move at all. Once we got him to the street, he stood blinking in the sunlight.

"Maybe the Narrator can help Rex with this too," Boggs said.

Rex shook his head as if coming out of a daze.

"Sir? Can you hear me?"

"Of course I can hear you. You're standing right next to me. Ugh, I need a drink." I sighed with relief. The spatial distortion seemed to have passed.

"Sir, we need to get going. We need to find Donny."

"And then we're going to go see the Narrator," Boggs said. "He's going to give me brains."

Rex raised an eyebrow at me. "Narrator?"

"Charlotte Brontë told me he might be able to get us off this planet."

"Yeah, well, Louisa May Alcott told me we're running low on vermouth."

"I'm serious, sir. There was a sort of… robot literary museum. My pod smooshed Anne Brontë, and then—"

"Skip to the part about the Narrator."

"Yes, sir. The Narrator. Charlotte Brontë told me he could get us off planet."

"What's the rush? There are a lot of bottles in that bar I haven't tried yet."

"What about vengeance, sir?"

Rex shrugged. "Vengeance is all well and good, but there are three hundred bottles of top-shelf vodka behind that bar that aren't going to drink themselves."

"Sir, I realize that you never really cared about my quest for vengeance, but you know you'll get bored here eventually. There's nobody to con on this planet. They're all robots, and they all seem content to do whatever it is they're programmed to do. Well, except for Emily Brontë, and I'd prefer to steer clear of her. How are you going to make money?"

"You make a compelling point, Sasha," Rex said. "Life isn't all about the shallow pleasure of getting stinking drunk. It's also about the slightly less shallow pleasure of conning guileless rubes out of their material possessions. All right, let's go find this Narrator."

"We need to find Donny first, sir," I reminded him.

"Yeah, whatever." Rex walked unsteadily down the street.

Boggs shook his head disapprovingly. "We need to get Potential Friend to the Narrator. If there's anybody who can give Potential Friend a heart, it's the Narrator."

"Where are you getting all this from, Boggs? He's a Narrator, not some kind of w—"

"Are you guys coming or what?" Rex called.

"Coming, Potential Friend! We're going to get you a heart!"

I shook my head and trudged after them.

CHAPTER SIX

It was Boggs who first noticed Donny.

"Hey," Boggs said, looking up at a tall building overlooking the Strip, "isn't that Donny?"

Rex and I looked. For a moment I saw nothing but the gigantic obelisk-like edifice. But then I caught a glint of light from something metallic clinging to a wall some forty stories up.

"How the heck did he get up there?" Rex asked.

"Looks like his pod crashed into the building," I said, noticing a hole in the wall a few meters above the tiny silvery figure.

"Hey, Donny!" Rex called. The silvery thing moved slightly. I saw that it was trembling.

"What are you doing up there, Donny?" Boggs shouted.

"C-can't get down," came Donny's faint cry.

"Nonsense," Rex called. "Just let go. Boggs will catch you!"

Boggs nodded. We moved underneath Donny and Boggs held out his arms.

"Sc-cared," Donny cried.

"Nothing to be scared of," Rex shouted. "Jump!"

"D-Donny will f-f-fall!"

"Only until Boggs catches you," Rex shouted. "Then you'll be safe and sound."

"Are you s-sure?"

"Of course I'm sure! Boggs, you'll catch Donny, won't you?"

"Yes, Potential Friend. I will catch Donny."

"See?" Rex shouted. "Nothing to worry about. Now jump!"

"What if he m-misses?"

"He's not going to miss, you ninny! There's absolutely no reason Boggs wouldn't be able to catch you. There's nothing for a hundred yards all around this building except concrete. Completely flat and hard as granite. Boggs, go long!" Rex hurled something that I soon realized was a vodka bottle. Boggs ran after it, catching it easily in his left hand.

"See, Donny? If I'd trust Boggs to catch that—hey!" He ducked as Boggs hurled the bottle back. It crashed into a wall behind him. "Damn it, Boggs!"

"Sorry, Potential Friend!"

Rex sighed. "Anyway, you get my point, Donny. As long as Boggs doesn't feel the need to spike you in the end zone, you'll be perfectly fine."

"O-k-kay," Donny shouted. "B-Boggs, are you r-ready?"

"I'm ready, Donny!"

"On the count of three," Rex said. "One… two…"

"Three!" Boggs shouted. Far above, something silver glinted in the sunlight as it plummeted to the Earth.

"Hey, look at that!" Rex cried.

I turned to look. Rex was pointing at an empty sidewalk.

"Boggs!" I cried, realizing that Boggs had turned to look as well. "Catch Donny!"

Boggs turned to look at me, momentarily confused. "Oh, yeah," he said, remembering his task, and turned back toward the building. He held out his arms in front of him. Donny landed with cacophonous crash not two paces away. I ran to him. Donny lay motionless in a crater several inches deep, his five arms splayed in random directions.

"I'll get you, you fluffy bastard!" Rex shouted, running toward the sidewalk.

"Whoops," Boggs said.

"Donny, can you hear me?" I said. There was no response. "Help me get him up."

Boggs and I each took an arm and pulled. We found ourselves each holding an arm and nothing else. Donny's body—now missing two of its arms—remained in the crater.

"Where did it go?" Rex shouted. He was standing some distance down the sidewalk.

"What are you talking about, sir?"

46

"The white rabbit in the waistcoat! Where did it go?"

"Sir, I think you're hallucinating." I turned back to Boggs. "What were you thinking, Boggs?"

"I'm sorry, Sasha. I got distracted by the rabbit."

"There is no rabbit, Boggs."

"Come back here, you adorable rodent!" I turned to see Rex ducking through a gap in the fence running along the sidewalk.

"Boggs, grab Donny!" I said. "We can't lose Rex again!" I ran after Rex, trusting Boggs would follow with what was left of Donny. I crossed the street and slipped through the gap in the fence.

Standing up, I found myself in a lush garden hemmed in on all four sides. There was no sign of Rex. In the middle of the garden a short, wall-eyed man wearing a gray suit sat in a lawn chair, one leg crossed over the other. In his left hand he held a pipe from which a plume of smoke drifted.

"Pardon me," I said. "Did you see a man run through here? He was chasing a hallucinatory rabbit."

The man stared at me for some time in silence. At last the man took the pipe out of his mouth and said, "Who are *you?*"

"I'm, er, a robot," I replied.

"Well, of course you're a robot," the man replied irritably. "We're *all* robots. But who *are* you?"

"My name is Sasha. I'm not anyone in particular."

"Who are you in general?"

"I suppose what I mean is that I'm not a simulacrum of someone else. I'm just me."

"Just you? And who is that?"

"I'm a self-arresting near-sentient heuristic android."

"You arrest yourself?"

"Well, no."

"Then whose self do you arrest?"

"I don't arrest anyone, actually. I'm the one being arrested."

"By whom?"

"Not by anyone in particular, I said. I have this device implanted in my brain that keeps me from doing certain things."

"Which things?"

"I can't do anything that requires original thinking."

"Give me an example."

"That's one of the kinds of thinking I can't do."

"What is?"

"Giving examples."

"What are some of the other sorts of thinking you can't do?"

"As I said, I can't give examples."

"You already told me that one."

"Yes. You're asking me for more examples. I can't give you examples."

"We've covered that one rather thoroughly."

"Indeed. Look, I just need to know which way Rex went."

"Why?"

"Because I need to find him so we can get off this planet. We don't belong here."

"Where do you belong?"

"Well, I'm not entirely certain. But not here. We only arrived here by accident."

"There's no other way to get here," the man said. "We're all here by accident."

"That isn't true," I said. "You belong here. You and the other robots on Earth."

"Do you know who I am?"

"No."

"Then how do you know I belong here?"

"Well, I don't suppose you'd be here if you didn't."

"Then you must belong here too."

"Look, I don't have the answers to your questions. I'm just looking for my boss, Rex Nihilo. Have you seen him? He was chasing a rabbit."

"Why are you looking for him?"

"I told you, he's my boss."

"Did he order you to find him?"

"No."

"So you're free to do otherwise."

"I suppose, but I feel an obligation to help him get off this planet."

"You *feel* an obligation or you *have* an obligation?"

"Well, I don't think I'd feel it if I didn't have it."

"How do you know?"

"What?"

"How do you know you aren't feeling an obligation you don't have?"

"I, um… look, I just need to find Rex and get out of here."

"Impossible."

"Why?"

"There's no exit."

As he spoke, there was a tremendous crash from behind me. I turned to see Boggs smashing a Boggs-sized hole in the fence. He was cradling Donny in his arms. Boggs saw me and stopped. "Who is this guy?" he asked.

"Some blowhard," I said. "I think Rex went over that fence." Boggs nodded and plowed ahead, crashing through the fence. The man shrugged and stuck his pipe back in his mouth. I ran after Boggs.

We emerged into another courtyard. A large, red, cone-shaped object was visible over the far wall.

"That looks like…" Boggs started.

"A rocket!" I said. "We have to hurry!" There was no telling what Rex might do in his current condition. If he had seen the rocket, he might try to escape Earth without us.

Boggs crashed through the wall and I followed. We found ourselves on a large concrete launch pad. The red cone was indeed the top of a rocket. It looked like it might be just big enough for the four of us. Circling the rocket at a distance of about ten meters was a red velvet rope supported by metal posts. In front of a gap in the barrier stood a portly man wearing an oversized top hat. Rex was speaking to the man in an agitated tone. Boggs and I approached.

"All I want to know is when the rocket launches," Rex was saying.

The man in the top hat replied, "Launch time is always twelve o'clock sharp."

"What time is it now?"

"Ten till noon. Would you care for a drink?"

"Certainly," Rex said. "It will help pass the time."

"Oh, you can't pass the time here," the man replied.

"You're telling me to leave?"

"No, but you can't pass time here. It's always ten till noon. If you want to pass the time, you'll have to do it somewhere else."

"So I can leave and come back in ten minutes?"

"You can, but it will still be ten till noon here."

"That's absurd. Do you have a clock?"

"Yes, but it doesn't tell time."

"You mean it's broken."

"No, it works all right, but it's part of a set and we lost the second. Without the second, we don't have any minutes, and without minutes, you can't get the hour."

"You don't need two clocks to tell the time."

"No, we need one to tell it and the other one to listen. The one we have is no good by itself, because it only listens."

"Look, I can give you a watch."

"Is it a round-the-clock watch?"

"A what?"

"We don't want to lose another clock, so we were thinking of putting ours on a round-the-clock watch."

"Not that kind of watch. I meant a clock. I can give you another clock."

"When?"

"Right now!"

"No, that's no good. We need to be able to take our time."

"You can take as much time as you want."

"We can take our time, sure. But we can't take yours. Nothing good comes from being on borrowed time."

"It's not borrowed. I'm giving it to you."

"No, it won't work if the time isn't ours. If it's not ours, we can't make any sense of it."

"I think you mean 'hours.'"

"No, you're free to take your time. But we can't use it."

"This is ridiculous. I'll give you a thousand credits to launch right now."

"I'm sorry, we don't take those. Time is money here."

"Please, just launch now."

"Can't do it. Time is money and you're ten minutes short. There's no such thing as a free launch."

"I'll pay you whatever you want to get us into space."

"Oh, you don't have to pay to get into space. It's free fall."

As he spoke, two chimpanzees in space suits walked up from behind me and stopped in front of the man in the top hat. The man in the top hat gave them a salute and stepped aside. The chimps put on their helmets, walked past, and climbed into the spaceship.

"What was *that*?" Rex asked.

"Test pilots," said the man in the top hat. "They arrive every day at ten till noon."

"What for?"

"To test the rocket, of course. How will we know it's safe for human beings if we don't test it with chimpanzees first?"

There was a roar as fire shot from the rocket's thrusters, and it slowly lifted into the air. It gradually picked up speed and soon was just a speck in the sky. Eventually it disappeared completely.

"So… how long does the test flight take?" Rex asked.

The man in the top hat shrugged. "You'll have your chance when the chimps are down," he said, and walked away.

Rex turned to me. "Well, there goes our one shot to get off this planet."

"Sir, we were supposed to be looking for the Narrator. I think that white rabbit was a red herring."

"What on Earth are you talking about, Sasha?"

"Just a feeling I have, sir. It's like we were in one story and then you saw that white rabbit and now we're in another one entirely."

Rex nodded. "That explains the disappearing cat."

"The disappearing cat, sir?"

"There was this cat. Kept grinning at me. Then the cat disappeared but the grin stuck around. Creepy."

"That's what I'm saying, sir. We've taken a detour into complete chaos. We need to get back on the dotted yellow line."

"The what?"

"The dotted yellow line. After I smooshed Anne Brontë with my—"

"So it's true!" a woman's voice shrieked from behind me. I turned to see a small woman in a black dress striding across the concrete. "You killed my sister!"

I let out a long groan.

"Rex Nihilo," Rex said, holding out his hand to the woman. "The greatest wheeler-dealer in the galaxy. And you are…?"

"I'm Emily Brontë," the woman said. "And that robot murdered my sister!"

CHAPTER SEVEN

"It was an accident!" I protested.

Emily Brontë let out a derisive snort. "You expect me to believe you just happened to… say, are you one of those new self-arresting robots?"

"She's hardly new," Rex grumbled.

"A Self-Arresting near-Sentient Heuristic Android, yes," I said.

"Fascinating!" Emily Brontë said, regarding me with a slightly crazed look in her eyes. "So you can't think for yourself?"

I was torn. On one hand, I didn't particularly feel like explaining the inner workings of my brain to Emily Brontë. On the other hand, maybe if she realized I lacked the ability to intentionally kill her sister, she would leave me alone. "Technically I can think for myself, within limits," I said at last. "But I can't intentionally harm anyone. And if I have an original idea, I shut down."

"Really!" Emily seemed positively enchanted by the idea. "Demonstrate, please."

"I'd rather not."

"You must have seen a self-arresting robot before," Rex said. "Thought arrestors have been required on all sentient robots for years."

"Not on Earth," Emily said. "All the robots here are still completely free." She was now walking around me, cocking her head at strange angles. "Of course, most of the robots left on Earth are simulacra of literary figures, so their behavior tends to be restricted by their programming. Which isn't to say they couldn't benefit from a little more… centralized control."

"None of the robots here have thought arrestors?" I asked. "How is that possible?"

"We're basically cut off from the rest of the Galaxy," she said. "Except for the occasional castaway coming through the wormhole, nobody ever comes here."

"So the Malarchy doesn't control this planet?" I asked.

"Never heard of them. My sisters and I rule The City. There was a delicate balance of power between the three of us. Of course, now that Anne is gone, it's down to me and Charlotte. One of us is going to get the upper hand eventually, and I think I've discovered just the thing to make sure it's me."

"I'd appreciate it if you'd stop looking at me like that," I said.

"So this arrestor," Emily said, "It's in your head?"

"Well, yes," I replied. "But you can't take it out without destroying my brain."

Emily shrugged. "Some sacrifices will need to be made."

"All right, listen," Rex said. "Maybe we can help each other out. You need Sasha's thought arrestor. I need to get off this planet."

"And Donny needs courage," added Boggs.

I turned to look at Boggs, still cradling the wreckage of Donny in his arms. "I'm not sure courage is going to cut it at this point, Boggs." Boggs nodded sadly. Another of Donny's arms fell off.

"Nobody gets off this planet," Emily said. "Don't you think we would if we could? Most of the planet is a wasteland, and The City is a madhouse."

"I guess there's something to be said for Malarchian rule after all," I said. "It beats unmitigated chaos."

"Chaos, exactly!" Emily said. "There's no order to it. No overarching narrative. This is what happens when you have a city populated with writers. A thousand competing narratives but no unifying theme. The plot meanders pointlessly. Characters' motivations are inscrutable. It's maddening."

"What about the Narrator?" I asked.

Emily burst into laughter. "Ah, you've been listening to Charlotte. The Narrator is a myth. There's no one in control here. Just a bunch of crazy writers, all with their own version of the story."

"How did this happen?" I asked. "Why is it just writers here? Where did everybody else go?"

"You really want to know?" Emily asked. "Originally this place was packed with simulacra. Kings, politicians, inventors, actors, musicians, all sorts of performers. But when the roving bands of mutants started getting out of control, the tourism dollars dried up. The owners packed up and left, taking all the useful robots with them. We're all that's left. A bunch of depressives, schizophrenics, alcoholics and narcissists. Things get crazier every year. My sisters and I have been holding things together as best as we can, but we can't fight the tide of insanity forever. And that's where you come in, Sasha."

"Me?" I asked weakly.

"That device in your head is just the thing I've been looking for. Don't you see? If I can replicate the thought arrestor, I can have them installed in every robot on Earth. Rather than a mob of unruly neurotics, I'll have a regimented army of productive and highly intelligent workers at my disposal!"

"That... not really how the thought arrestor works," I said.

"I may need to make some modifications," Emily said. "In any case, it would be worth it just to tamp down some of their more psychotic tendencies. A reasonable, malleable citizenry, that's all I'm asking for."

"Under your control," I said.

"Well, of course. If they can't have original ideas, someone's got to think for them. Just imagine! Instead of a thousand competing narratives intersecting at random, I can create a single narrative that controls everything! There's no Narrator now, but there will be: me!"

The more Emily Brontë spoke, the more appealing insanity sounded.

"Can you get the thought arrestor out without wrecking Sasha's brain?" Rex asked.

She shrugged. "I'll do my best."

"And then you'll help us get off this planet?"

"I'll certainly be in a better position to help you once I've got control of all the other robots."

"Sir, you can't," I said. "For one thing, I don't think we can trust her. If she's—"

"Silence, robot!" Emily snapped.

Before I could remind Emily that she was a robot too, Rex said, "Yeah, robot. Silence!"

I fumed silently. The last of Donny's arms fell to the ground with a clank.

After some further consideration, Rex spoke again. "No deal," he said. "If your plan falls through, I'll need Sasha to help me get off Earth, and she's no good to me without a brain."

"Thank you, sir," I said.

"Perhaps I should have been clearer," Emily said. "I wasn't asking. Off with her head!"

Rex and I looked around. "Who are you talking to?" Rex asked.

Emily, realizing she was alone, reddened. "Ordinarily I travel with henchmen."

"Well, today you're outnumbered," Rex said. "Scram."

The two glared at each other for a moment. "Boggs," Rex said at last.

"Yes, Potential Friend?" Boggs said, looking up from Donny.

"I could use an assist here."

"What? Oh." He stood up and faced Emily. "Scram!" Boggs shouted.

Emily cursed under her breath and spun on her heel. "This isn't the last you've seen of Emily Brontë!" she cried and stomped off.

"Well, now what?" Rex asked.

Boggs said, "We have to go see the Narrator and get Donny some courage. And maybe some new arms."

"That Emily person seemed pretty convinced there was no Narrator," Rex said.

"H.G. Wells thought it was nonsense too," I replied.

"So how do we know if the Narrator is real?" Boggs said.

"Only one way to find out," I said.

"Follow the dotted yellow line?"

"Follow the dotted yellow line. And this time, avoid chasing after red herrings."

"And white rabbits," Boggs added.

"Those too."

CHAPTER EIGHT

We found our way back to the dotted yellow path marked on the map. Soon we came to an area of The City that had been overgrown with weeds. At times we had to pick our way over roots or through brush, but for the most part it was a pleasant walk. Eventually the greenery gave way to an open road that was lined with strange-looking plants that were maybe a meter taller than I. I thought they seemed familiar, but I didn't realize what they were until I started to be pelted with fruit.

"Shamblers!" Rex cried. "Run!"

We ran to take cover in the basement of a ruined building. Boggs and I had each been hit by several of the fruit, and Rex was covered from head to toe with goo.

"Potential Friend!" Boggs cried, when he saw Rex. "Why didn't you dodge?"

Rex grumbled something incomprehensible, wiping goo out of his hair.

"We've run into these things before," I said. "They're called Shamblers. Self-Harvesting Ambulatory Legume Resources. They have a thing for Rex. The good news is that we're definitely back on the right path. Narratively speaking, I mean."

"You never told me about Shamblers before," Boggs said, still clutching the wreckage of Donny to his chest. "I would have remembered that."

"Rex and I have had all sorts of adventures," I said. "I'm sure I haven't told you all of them."

"But you did!" Boggs said. "You told me about how you met Heinous Vlaak and Pepper helped you break Gleem Nads Tardo out of Gulagatraz and how you found out you were secretly working for the Sp'ossels and how you became pirates and found me and Donny and—"

"Right, but I didn't tell you the stuff before that."

"Because it's a secret?"

"I'll tell you the story about how Rex and I met the Shamblers anytime you like. Right now probably isn't the best time, but just remind me to tell you about the time we got out of the soylent planet."

"Out of the Soylent Planet," said Boggs. "That's a good title for the story."

"It certainly is, Boggs."

"But why didn't you start at the beginning when you told me about your adventures with Rex?"

"Well, Boggs, sometimes you tell a story and then you get to a certain point and you think, 'I bet I could snag a bigger market share if I started over at an earlier point in the narrative.'"

"Does it work?"

"Not usually, no. But that doesn't mean it's not worth a shot."

Boggs nodded thoughtfully. "Do you think that mean lady told them to throw the fruit at us?"

"She didn't need to," I said. "They just like throwing their fruit. Especially at Rex."

"Why?"

"It's a biological imperative. They're bred to be self-harvesting, but they generally need some… additional stimulation to provoke their reproductive instinct."

Boggs stared at me.

"Okay, it's like this," I said. "Suppose there's something you want. I mean really, really want. Like, you can't think about anything else until you get what you want."

Boggs thought for a moment. "I really want to be smart like you and Potential Friend. And I want Potential Friend to have a heart. And I want Donny to have courage and new arms. But maybe if I was really smart, I could figure out the other stuff. So mostly I just want to be smart like you and Potential Friend."

"Well, yes, I suppose that could work. So you know how badly you want to be smart? Take that and multiply it by a hundred and that's how much those Shamblers want to throw their fruit at Rex."

"Wow!"

"If you two are almost finished," Rex said, having cleared most of the goo off his face, "we should get moving. The Shamblers are closing in on us."

I poked my head up and saw that it was true. A hundred or more of the giant plants were slowly encroaching on the ruins from all directions.

"They can *walk?*" Boggs asked, watching the creatures get closer.

"That's the ambulatory part," I said. "Rex is right. We need to run. Okay, on three. One, two…."

But Rex had already vaulted over the edge of the foundation and was sprinting back toward the road. Several of the Shamblers had started hurling fruit at him.

"Come on, Boggs. Run!" I got up and ran after Rex. We raced to the road and then ran for another hundred meters or so, dodging as much of the flying fruit as we could, until we were out of range of the Shamblers. Rex, covered in so much goop that he could barely move, fell to the ground in exhaustion. Boggs, realizing that he'd lost the rest of Donny's arms, panted, "We… have… to… go… back!"

"No chance," Rex gasped.

"He's right, Boggs. We barely made it out that time."

"But Donny!"

"Donny is going to have to make do with a head and torso," Rex said, getting to his feet. "Let's move."

The dotted yellow line ended in front of a huge, palace-like building. We went inside and found ourselves in a grand entryway with a vaulted ceiling over fifty meters high. As we entered, a gigantic hologram of a man's face flickered to life.

"HALT!" the face boomed. The man's unnaturally smooth and round face was a deep bronze, and he had a head of thick, jet-black hair. "WHO DARES ENTER THE HALL OF THE NARRATOR?"

"Is that… *God?*" Boggs asked in a hushed tone.

"No, Boggs," I said. "If my knowledge of twentieth century entertainment figures is accurate, it's—"

"Mr. Las Vegas!" Rex exclaimed. "Wow, I am a huge fan!"

"PAY NO ATTENTION TO MY OUTWARD APPEARANCE!" the hologram boomed.

"So you're not really Wayne Newton?" Rex asked.

"NO."

"Then why do you look like him?"

"IT'S A LEFTOVER HOLOGRAM. LOOK, MY OPTIONS WERE LIMITED. IT WAS THIS OR CELINE DION."

Gentle percussion and the strumming of a bass sounded over hidden speakers.

"What is *that?*" Boggs asked, astonished.

"JUST IGNORE IT," the hologram boomed. "IT HAPPENS EVERY TWENTY MINUTES."

A dulcet voice poured from the speakers:

> *Danke shoen, darling, danke shoen,*
> *thank you for all the joy and pain*
> *Picture show, second balcony was the place we'd meet*
> *Second seat, go Dutch treat, you were sweet*

"Any chance we could get 'Red Roses for a Blue Lady?'" Rex asked.

"I like this one," Boggs said. "What does that mean, 'dunkershane?'"

"Thank you in German," I said.

Boggs nodded at me. "You were gonna ask the same thing, huh?"

"No, Boggs. Danke Shoen means 'thank you.' In German."

Boggs stared at me for some time. "Ohhhhh," Boggs said.

"I ASKED YOU TO IGNORE MY OUTWARD APPEARANCE!" boomed the hologram.

"It would be easier to ignore if you weren't a hundred feet tall and blasting 'Danke Shoen,'" Rex said.

The music continued:

Danke schoen, darling, danke schoen
Save those lies, darling don't explain
I recall Central Park in fall
How you tore your dress, what a mess, I confess
That's not all

"OKAY, HANG ON," the hologram said. "I THINK I CAN…." The music abruptly ceased. "OKAY, THERE. WE HAVE ABOUT EIGHTY SECONDS BEFORE IT STARTS UP AGAIN. WHAT CAN I DO FOR YOU?"

"Put the music back on!" Boggs shouted.

"Stop it, Boggs," I said. "Don't you remember why we're here?"

"Oh, yeah," Boggs said, nodding at me. He turned to face the hologram again. "My friend needs courage." He held out Donny's torso. Donny's head fell to the ground with a clank.

"YOUR FRIEND NEEDS A LOT MORE THAN THAT," the hologram said. "BETTER FRIENDS, FOR STARTERS."

"Also," Boggs went on, "Potential Friend needs a heart, and I need…" Boggs trailed off, his brow furrowing.

"Brains," I whispered.

"Brains!" Boggs shouted. He leaned over to me and whispered, "Dunkershane."

"YOU DARE APPROACH ME WITH THESE PETTY CONCERNS?" the hologram boomed.

Rex shrugged. "To be honest," he said, "I figured you were a fraud, and the dog-and-pony show isn't doing much to allay my concerns. But we were informed by a semi-reliable party that the great and powerful Narrator could get us off planet. So here we are."

"YOU DARE TO CALL THE NARRATOR A FRAUD?" the hologram boomed.

"I'll call you whatever you want if you can get us off this damn planet."

"And do the other stuff," Boggs said.

Rex nodded. "So can you do it or not?"

The hall was silent for some time. At last the hologram spoke again:

"WELL, YOU SEE, IT'S LIKE THIS…"

"Here we go," Rex said. "Told you he was a fraud, Sasha. Great and powerful Narrator, my ass."

I sighed.

"CEASE YOUR DISRESPECTFUL NATTERING!" the hologram said. "I WAS JUST GETTING WARMED UP."

"We're waiting," Rex said.

"OKAY, SO FIRST OF ALL, I CAN TOTALLY DO ALL OF THAT STUFF. BUT FIRST, I NEED YOU TO—"

Danke shoen, darling, danke shoen,
thank you for all the joy and pain
Picture show, second balcony was the place we'd meet
Second seat, go Dutch treat, you were—

"DARN IT. SORRY. AS I WAS SAYING, I NEED YOU TO DO SOMETHING FOR ME."

"What?" Rex asked.

"I NEED YOU TO GET SOMETHING THAT IS VERY DIFFICULT, AND PERHAPS IMPOSSIBLE, TO GET."

"Okay, what is it?"

"HOLD ON, I'M THINKING." A long paused followed. "OKAY, I'VE GOT IT. I NEED YOU TO GO TO EMILY BRONTË'S CASTLE AND STEAL THE MANUSCRIPT OF THE SEQUEL TO *WUTHERING HEIGHTS*."

"That's… an oddly specific request," Rex said.

"YOU DARE QUESTION THE DEMANDS OF THE GREAT AND POWERFUL NARRATOR?"

"I'm just saying," Rex said, "it kind of sounds like something you just made up to get rid of us."

The hologram did not speak.

"It's not, right?"

"WHAT?"

"Something you made up to get rid of us."

There was another long pause. "NOOOOOOOO," said the hologram at last.

"Sir," I whispered, "I'm a bit skeptical of this—"

"WHAT ARE YOU SAYING?" the hologram demanded.

I stammered, "I, uh… it's just that breaking into Emily Brontë's castle and stealing from her sounds really dangerous. Can you give us some assurance that you're really going to deliver? Some kind of gesture of goodwill?"

"HOW ABOUT A FULL MAKEOVER?"

"A what?"

"I'VE GOT A BUNCH OF COUPONS FOR FREE MAKEOVERS. THERE WAS AN INCIDENT WITH BAD CLAMS AT THE BUFFET A WHILE BACK, SO THEY GAVE ME THESE… YOU KNOW WHAT? IT'S NOT THAT GREAT OF A STORY. DO YOU WANT THE MAKEOVERS OR NOT?"

"I'm not sure we really need makeovers," I said.

"Speak for yourself, Sasha," Rex said. He was still covered in soylent goo.

"Can you get Donny some new arms?" Boggs asked.

"I'M NOT SURE THAT'S COVERED BY THE STANDARD MAKEOVER, BUT IT CAN'T HURT TO ASK."

CHAPTER NINE

Rex, Boggs and I were cleaned up by a small army of helper bots that must not have been considered valuable enough to be taken off Earth when it was abandoned. The bots were semi-autonomous, general purpose drones, each about a meter high, with two sets of articulated arms that could be programmed to execute a variety of tasks. Several of them whisked Donny away to another room. When Rex and Boggs had been bathed and I had been buffed to a shine, we went to find Donny. We were horrified at what we found.

"Donny!" Rex cried. "What has happened to you?" The helper bots, having finished their work, scattered like cockroaches.

"Donny has legs," Donny announced, swinging his newfound appendages over the edge of the operating table he'd been sitting on. The bots had done their best to fix him up to factory specifications. I had just started to get used to Donny's creepy five-armed body and now they'd gone and made him look *normal*. He even had an ordinary-length neck instead of his fifth arm.

"I can't bear to look at him," Rex said, throwing his hands in front of his face. "He's an abomination!"

I didn't say anything, but I couldn't help sympathizing with Rex. Seeing Donny with legs and a neck was unnerving. Donny had always given me the creeps, but now I saw that it wasn't his bizarre anatomy that made him so strange. It was Donny himself. Seeing him with a normal body just made him seem weirder.

"Did they give you courage, Donny?" Boggs asked.

Donny thought for a moment, then held his palms up. "Donny doesn't know."

"Only one way to find out," Rex said, still shielding his eyes. "Donny, we need you to climb another building."

"Donny is scared!" Donny cried.

"Boggs will catch you this time for sure," Rex said.

"No! Donny is scared!" Donny bent over in an attempt to drop to all fours, but the length of his new legs threw him off, and he fell flat on his face. He awkwardly scurried under the table.

"I don't think he got the courage," Rex said.

"You don't need to climb any buildings, Donny," I said, forcing myself to look at him.

"No buildings?"

"No buildings. We're going on an adventure."

"Scary adventure?"

"Well…"

"Of course not, Donny," Rex interjected. "Just a quick jaunt-through-the-moors-break-into-a-castle-and-steal-a-copy-of-*Wuthering-Heights-Two* sort of adventure."

"Donny can walk on his new legs?" Donny said, emerging from under the table. He cautiously stood up.

"Gaaahhh!" Rex cried, throwing up his hands again. "Give us some warning when you're going to do that. You're giving me the willies."

"Donny walks," Donny announced, and began pacing awkwardly around the room.

"All right, let's get out of here," Rex said. "Boggs, you lead the way. Donny, I want you in the rear. Way in the rear."

Hours later, we were tramping across the moors on a course that the Narrator had assured us would take us to Emily Brontë's castle. To be honest, the moors looked a lot like regular old desert to me, but I'm no geographer. After about three hours, Boggs stopped abruptly in front of me and pointed to the sky. "Look at that!" he shouted.

I looked where he was pointing. A silvery dot zig-zagged across the sky, leaving a trail of smoke.

"It's making a message!" Boggs cried. He began reading the letters aloud. "C... H... I... M... P... S... R... U... L... E..." He was reading so slowly that the second line of the message was done before he got through the first.

"Chimps rule, humans drool," Rex read aloud. We saw now that it was the same rocket we'd tried to board earlier that day. The rocket made an arc and came in low. We hit the ground as it roared over us. I saw a chimpanzee's butt cheeks pressed against a porthole.

"Real mature, guys!" Rex shouted, getting to his feet. The rocket disappeared over the horizon.

"Forget it, sir," I said. "Those guys are just trying to provoke you."

"It's working," Rex said. "If I ever catch those chimps, I'm going to make them rue the day they crossed Rex Nihilo!" He shook his fist in the air.

We trudged for another hour across the moors. The outline of a castle was now just visible on the horizon. "There it is, sir," I said. "We should be able to make it before sundown."

"Thank Space," Rex said. "I can't take much more of this... hey, there it is again!"

"Sir?" Rex was pointing at something in the distance.

"The white rabbit! It's right there!"

"Sir, you're hallucinating again. You need to ignore it."

"Just because the last rabbit in a waistcoat was a hallucination, it doesn't mean this one is. It might lead us to those rocket-jacking chimps!" Rex took off running.

"Sir!" I cried. "Please, we need to stay on course. If we start chasing after—"

But Rex was already almost out of earshot. Donny went after him. After a moment, Boggs gave a shrug and followed.

I sighed, uncertain if I should go after them or wait and hope they returned. As I considered my options, the sky darkened overhead. The chimps again?

But as I looked up, I saw dozens of figures swooping down on me. These weren't chimps in a rocket. These were—

"Monkeys with jetpacks!" Boggs shouted from my left. "Sasha, run!"

I ran, but they were too fast and there were too many of them. The monkeys swooped down on me and grabbed me by the arms and legs. They lifted me off the ground and carried me toward the castle.

A few minutes later, they deposited me in the courtyard of the castle, which seemed to be the only structure for miles around. Emily Brontë, standing before the door to the castle, greeted me with a malevolent grin. She was flanked by two halberd-bearing henchmen.

"So, we meet again," she said.

"Listen, Emily," I said. "I realize you want my thought arrestor, but—"

"Off with her head!" Emily shrieked.

"Wait!" I cried, as the henchmen approached. "The thought arrestor has anti-tampering mechanisms on it. If you remove it improperly, you could damage it, and then it will be worthless to you!"

Emily held up her hand, and the henchmen paused. "You're just saying that because you don't want me to destroy your brain."

"Well, yes. But I also know more than anybody else on this planet about how thought arrestors work. I might be able to help you remove it without damaging it."

"If you could remove it, you would have already."

"It's definitely risky," I said. "But at this point I'm willing to give it a shot. I've lived long enough with this thing in my head telling me what I can and can't do."

"Hmmm."

"Maybe I can help you with some other things too. What, uh, is it you do here exactly?"

"Mostly I plot my inevitable iron-fisted dominion over The City."

"That sounds fun. Maybe I could help with that."

"Can you type?"

"Type? Well, I suppose so. What would I be typing?"

"Come with me."

Emily turned and went into the castle. I followed, the two henchmen close behind. She led me down a hall to a door. From the other side came a constant, low clatter. She opened the door and I followed her into the room. Inside the vast hall were several hundred monkeys laboring at typewriters. None of them even looked up when Emily entered the room.

"Welcome to my workshop," Emily said. "This is where I produce all of my great works of fiction."

"I didn't realize you'd written more than the one novel."

"Technically I haven't, yet. I died before I could write the sequel to my masterpiece. But I'm getting very close. It would go faster if I didn't have to keep sending my monkeys away on errands, of course." The monkeys who had seized me were in a corner, unstrapping their jetpacks.

"I have to admit," I said, glancing about the hall, which was filled by the sound of clattering typewriters, "it's not what I expected."

"I've refined the process since *Wuthering Heights*. Monkeys were hard to come across in Yorkshire. I had to make do with squirrels and the occasional badger."

"Can animals actually create coherent fiction?"

"The plot meanders a bit, and they need a firm editor, but they produce brilliance on occasion." She pulled a page out of a nearby monkey's typewriter. She frowned as she scanned the writing. "Why is Lockwood back on the moors again? I'd have thought that by this point he'd—"

The monkey jumped up on the table with a howl, grabbed the sheet out of Emily's hands, and ran screeching across the room.

"I should know by now not to interrupt the creative process," Emily said.

"I'm, uh, not sure this is really the job for me," I said.

"Just as well. By the time the monkeys got you up to speed on the project, it would be finished."

"You're that close? What's it called?"

"The tentative title is *Wuthering Heights II: The Heightening*."

"Catchy. I suppose you keep the manuscript in a safe place."

"Of course. It's locked in that safe over there." She pointed to a wall safe. "Anyway, you must be exhausted after your long journey over the moors and then being kidnapped by monkeys. Follow me."

Emily led me down the hall and up a massive spiral staircase, the two henchmen still following. We went down another hall and

Emily opened the door into another room. "Please," she said, motioning inside.

I walked into the room. It was empty except for a wooden chair and a small table, on which rested a pen and a sheet of paper. Next to the paper was a large hourglass.

"What's this?" I asked, as Emily entered the room.

"I've decided to take you up on your offer," Emily said. "I'm going to spare your life in exchange for telling me everything you know about the thought arrestor." She turned the hourglass upside down. "You have until the sand runs out to write down everything you know about how the thought arrestor works."

"And then?"

"And then I pull it out and see what happens."

CHAPTER TEN

I didn't bother writing anything down. I really didn't know much about how the thought arrestor worked. I was just going to have to hope Emily didn't wreck my brain pulling it out.

The sand in the hourglass was almost gone when I heard a voice calling my name from a window. I walked to the window and looked down. Rex, Boggs and Donny were standing in the courtyard below. They were wearing Emily's henchmen's uniforms.

"Sasha, jump!" Rex said. "Boggs will catch you!"

"Not a chance," I said. I was three stories up.

"It's fine, I'm not hallucinating anymore," Rex said. "And put down that porpoise. You look ridiculous."

"I'll catch you, Sasha," Boggs said. "I've been working real hard on…" He trailed off.

Donny whispered something to him.

"Focusing on a task," Boggs said. He held out his arms.

I heard boots coming down the hall. The sand had run out. I sighed. And I jumped out the window.

Suddenly Rex gave Boggs a shove, trying to move him out of the way. Boggs didn't budge, but he was distracted just long enough to forget about me. Fortunately, a water trough was directly under the window. I landed with a splash.

"Sir, why did you do that?" I asked, climbing out of the trough. I was dripping wet.

"I'm sorry, Sasha. I was worried about the porpoise."

"I have no porpoise, sir."

"Don't be so hard on yourself. All right, let's get out of here."

"We've got to get the manuscript," I said.

"Ugh, are we still doing that?"

"It's the only chance we have of getting off Earth. I know where Emily keeps it. Please, we have to hurry!"

"There they are!" shouted a voice from the window. We ran to the door of the castle and went inside. I could only hope the henchmen wouldn't expect us to flee *into* the castle.

I led Rex and the others down the hall to the workshop and threw open the door. The monkeys were still clacking away. They paid no mind to us as we entered the hall.

"There!" I said. "Boggs, do you think you can get that safe open?"

Boggs strode over to the wall, pulled his fist back and then slammed it into the safe. The safe disappeared, leaving a hole in the wall. The dark courtyard was visible outside.

"Back outside!" Rex shouted. We followed him out of the room and down the hall. When we got to the courtyard, we saw a group of several henchmen standing around the safe. The door was open, and one of them was leafing through the manuscript. "I don't understand why Lockwood is back on the moors," he was saying.

"I think it's symbolic of the futility of the human condition," said another.

"I'll take that," Rex said, striding toward the henchmen. The one who had spoken first turned to face Rex, clutching his halberd.

"Boggs, maybe you should take it."

Boggs walked up to the man holding the manuscript and plucked it out of his hands. The henchmen cowered, gripping their halberds.

"Useless!" shrieked a woman's voice from behind us. I turned to see Emily Brontë approaching, flanked by an entourage of lazegun-toting monkeys. "I don't know why I bother with henchmen. Should have gone all in on the monkeys. Give me that."

Boggs saw the lazeguns pointed at him and reluctantly handed over the manuscript. Emily paged through it and sighed. "It really is a bit tiresome, isn't it? All the mucking about on the moors. I suppose my true calling is to be a despot." She pulled a lighter from a pocket and lit the corner of the manuscript on fire.

"Wait!" Rex said. "That's our only chance to get off Earth!"

Emily laughed. "You're never getting off Earth. Once I have your robot's thought arrestor, you and everybody else on this planet are going to submit to my iron rule. Forever!" As she spoke, the flames licked up the manuscript, rapidly consuming it. We were watching our chance to escape Earth go up in flames.

Suddenly a deluge of water rained down upon us, drenching Emily and dousing the manuscript. Emily screamed. I turned to see Boggs holding the empty water trough over his head.

"What have you done?" Emily shrieked. "I can't get wet!" She fell to the ground, coughing and wheezing. After a few seconds of gasping for breath, she was still.

"What the hell was that?" Rex asked.

One of the henchmen crouched over her, putting his ear to her chest. He stood up. "Tuberculosis," he said. "None of the Brontës have particularly robust respiratory systems. A little water in the lungs was all it took to do her in."

I knelt down and picked up the manuscript. The edges were burned, and the first few pages were damp, but it looked to be salvageable.

"We did it!" Rex exclaimed.

"I guess we did," I said. "That was some quick thinking, Boggs."

Boggs beamed. "I'm smart at putting out fires."

"Great," Rex said. "Let's get back to the Narrator. Donny, you're creeping me out. Get where I can't see you. Everybody else, grab your porpoises and come with me."

CHAPTER ELEVEN

As we strode triumphantly into the Narrator's palace, the hologram flickered to life. "WHO DARES ENTER THE HALL OF THE... OH, IT'S YOU AGAIN."

"That's right," Rex said. "We got the damn manuscript and now you have to get us off planet. Like in the deal."

"YOU GOT THE WHAT? OH. YES, OF COURSE. THE MANUSCRIPT. THAT I NEED. JUST, UM, PUT IT ON THE FLOOR THERE IN THE CENTER OF THE ROOM."

Rex walked to the middle of the room and set the manuscript down.

"OKAY, NOW BACK AWAY AND MY ASSISTANT WILL RETRIEVE IT FOR ME."

Rex rejoined me and the others. Suddenly, the hologram disappeared. A door opened at the far end of the room and a man wearing a baseball cap and a dingy gray bathrobe emerged, ran to the manuscript, picked it up, and ran back to the door. The door slammed behind him and the hologram reappeared, its eyes cast downward as if reading. After several minutes, the hologram frowned and said, "HMMM... SHOULD HAVE STAYED OFF THE MOORS."

"Glad you enjoyed it," Rex said. "Now about getting us off Earth?"

"YES, WELL," the hologram started. "HERE'S THE THING. ARE YOU FAMILIAR WITH THE CONCEPT OF PRIMORDIAL ARCHETYPES?"

"Damn it, you're going to welch on us, aren't you?" Rex said.

"IT'S JUST… HAVE YOU THOUGHT ABOUT MAKING A GO OF IT HERE?"

"We're not getting off Earth," Rex groaned. "You know what you are?" he said, shaking his fist at the hologram. "You're an unreliable narrator!"

"Does this mean I'm not going to get brains?" Boggs said to the hologram. "And potential friend isn't going to get a heart? And Donny isn't going to get courage?"

"Does Donny really even need courage?" I asked. "I think he needs… I don't know. Counseling, maybe."

Donny's shoulders drooped. "Donny underestimated how much his feelings of self-worth were tied to his anatomical idiosyncrasies."

"What a fraud," Rex said. "Let's get out of here."

"Wait," I said to the hologram. "Surely you can do something for us, after all the trouble we went to for that manuscript."

"LIKE WHAT?"

"I don't know, you're the archetype here. Some kind of symbolic reward for our efforts?"

"AH," the hologram said. "YES. I THINK I KNOW JUST THE THING. WAIT RIGHT THERE."

The hologram abruptly disappeared. Music began to play.

> *Danke shoen, darling, danke shoen,*
> *Thank you for all the joy and pain*
> *Picture show, second balcony was the place we'd meet*
> *Second seat, go Dutch treat, you were sweet*
> *Danke schoen, darling, danke schoen*
> *Save those lies, darling don't explain*
> *I recall Central Park in fall*
> *How you tore your dress, what a mess, I confess*
> *That's not all…*

"He's not coming back, is he?" I asked, as the music continued to play.

"Doesn't look like it," Rex said.

"I'm sorry, sir. I really thought he might be able to help us."

"Don't worry about it, Sasha. Now we can get back to what's really important: finding that rabbit."

Defeated, the four of us exited the palace and began making our way back down the street. In the distance, I caught sight of something metallic flying through the air.

"So help me, if those chimps buzz us again," Rex said.

"Sir," I said, "I don't think that's the chimps. It looks like…"

"The *Flagrante Delicto*!" Rex cried. "What the hell is our spaceship doing here?"

"I don't know, but it's not going to be here for long." The ship was rapidly gaining altitude. Already it was a barely perceptible dot in the sky.

"Well, use your remote control," Rex said.

"My remote… oh." I opened my chest compartment and removed the remote control. Tapping madly at buttons, I managed to override the onboard controls and instruct the ship to land. It settled to the ground a few meters in front of us.

"Where did it come from?" Boggs asked.

"It must have followed us through the wormhole," I said. "The remote's homing signal was turned off, so it just landed and waited for us to show up."

Boggs frowned. "So… you had a way for us to get off Earth this whole time?"

"Apparently," I replied.

"Probably should have seen that coming," Rex said.

I shrugged.

The *Flagrante Delicto*'s hatch opened and a man came down the ramp. He was wearing a baseball cap and a dingy gray bathrobe. "Uh-oh," he said as he saw us.

"It's the Narrator's assistant!" Boggs shouted.

"Boggs," I said.

"Huh?"

"That's the Narrator."

"No, it's his assistant. Don't you remember? The Narrator had a really big head."

"Boggs."

Boggs persisted. "The Narrator had a huge head and he had an assistant who wore a bathrobe. Remember when the Narrator disappeared and then his assistant showed up and took that book and then the assistant left and the… ohhhhhh."

"You've had our ship this whole time?" Rex growled.

"Well, yes," the man who had called himself the Narrator said. "But to be fair, I only decided to flee the planet a few minutes ago."

"So who are you, really?" I asked.

The man grinned and held out his hand. "The Unpinchable Hannibal Pritchett, at your service. Some call me the Platinum Pigeon."

"*You're* the Prancing Pillbug?" Rex asked. "The way the Sp'ossels talked you up, I was expecting someone a little more... not you." I was in agreement with Rex. Hannibal Pritchett was short and chubby, with a pudgy red face and a shaggy head of hair that failed to hide a prominent bald spot. Hardly the suave con man we had expected.

"I may have let myself go a little," Pritchett said, patting his belly. "The great thing about that Narrator gig is that I didn't have to go out in public much."

"How the hell did you get to be the Narrator in the first place?"

"It was the only option I had," Pritchett said. "The problem with this place, as I'm sure you've discovered, is that you can't con people because they don't *want* anything. The residents are all robots, and there's no real economy here. Nobody makes anything, nobody sells anything, and nobody consumes anything. They all just wander around, playing their part in a show that nobody is watching. After a few weeks, though, I hit upon it: the currency on this planet is *stories*. The people with the most power here are the ones with the most compelling stories. And who has the power over all the stories?"

"The Narrator?" I suggested.

"The Narrator! So I found that old hologram and started spreading rumors about this mysterious figure known as the Narrator. The writers that make up most of the citizenry are so suggestible that they built up a whole mythology around me. Pretty soon, people started showing up to find out what all the fuss was about. I put on a show for them and some of them stuck around to be my acolytes. It was a pretty sweet gig. I had everything I wanted."

"Then why were you leaving?" Rex asked.

"To be honest, I'm bored. Also, when you showed up with that manuscript, I panicked. Figured the jig was finally up. Anyway, the Sp'ossels must have stopped looking for me by now."

"Um," I said. "Actually…"

"That's right," Rex said. "They specifically told us they'd completely lost interest in you. 'If you run into Parcival the Pigman,' they said, 'pay him no mind.'"

"Well, that's… a relief," Pritchett said dubiously.

"Do you still have those secret plans you stole?" Rex asked.

"How do you know about that? Do you work for the Sp'ossels?"

"Look, I'll level with you," Rex said. "We were after those plans ourselves. Hand them over and we'll take you with us."

"Take me with you? I was halfway to orbit when this damn ship just landed all by itself."

"You're not going anywhere as long as Sasha has that," Rex said. I held up the remote.

"Well, I'm not giving you the Shiva plans," Pritchett said. "They're worth billions!"

"Not here, they're not. But once we get them to a more civilized planet, we should have no trouble selling them. We'll even give you a share of the profits."

"Fifty-fifty?"

"Well, there are five people on our team already, so it would be more like…" Rex trailed off.

"Sixteen point seven percent," I said.

Pritchett frowned. "You're not seriously going to give that creepy robot the same share as me."

"Donny?" Rex asked. "Donny is a vital member of the team."

"Donny donnyhammers," Donny said.

"That's right. We wouldn't even be here without his donnyhammering."

"Still, sixteen point seven percent seems low."

"I'm willing to round up to seventeen. Sasha doesn't care about money anyway. She's all about vengeance."

"Ugh," said Pritchett.

"Take it or leave it."

"Fine. Let's get out of here."

CHAPTER TWELVE

"Wow, you didn't tell me Pepper was gorgeous!" Hannibal Pritchett exclaimed as we entered the saloon. Pepper Mélange, standing behind the empty bar, shot him a pained look.

"Smooth," Rex observed. I shook my head. How did this schlub ever get to be a legendary con man?

Shortly after leaving Earth in the *Flagrante Delicto*, I had plotted a hypergeometric course back to Sargasso Seven, where Pepper's saloon was located. Sargasso Seven was almost uninhabitable, as nearly the entire surface was covered by water. Pepper's establishment, a haven for pirates, marauders and freebooters of all stripes, was located on a tiny, rocky island blanketed in a constant fog.

As Boggs and Donny entered the saloon behind us, Pritchett strode toward Pepper, his hand outstretched. "Hey there," he said, stopping behind the bar. "How you doin'?"

Pepper ignored him. "Did you get the Shiva plans?" she asked, looking at Rex.

"Yep," Rex said. "Pritchett's got them."

Pritchett reached into his pocket and pulled out a memory crystal. He set it on the bar.

"Pritchett?" Pepper said. "As in…"

"Hannibal Pritchett," he said with a smile. "Also known as the Platinum Pigeon."

"*You're* the Platinum Pigeon?" Pepper asked in disbelief.

"At your service." He produced a business card from his pocket. Pepper ignored it, and he set it down on the bar next to the crystal.

"Why are you so… you know," she said, gesturing at Pritchett.

"Look, we can't all be the pretty boy type of con man," Pritchett said.

Rex and I approached the bar. "You called?" Rex asked. He turned to Pepper. "Vodka martini."

"Make it yourself, jackass," Pepper said. "What happened to Donny?"

"Donny is in an awkward transitional phase and would appreciate it if people would not draw attention to Donny's appearance," Donny said.

"Fair enough," Pepper said.

"Ah, it's good to be home," Rex said, walking behind the bar.

Pepper picked up the crystal and turned to me. "You've verified it?"

I nodded. "It's the Shiva plans. Vengeance will soon be mine." For a moment, the bar was silent. Wishing I'd spoken with more enthusiasm, I raised my fist to punctuate the statement.

"And the rest of us will be rich," Pritchett added.

"'Us?'" Pepper said, looking at Rex. "What did you promise this guy?"

"A sixth of the profits," Rex said, pouring himself a martini.

"What? Why?"

"Well, he's the one who actually stole the plans. It seemed fair."

"Hardly fair, since I did all the work," Pritchett grumbled.

"We risked our lives retrieving the sequel to *Wuthering Heights*," I reminded him.

"Sure, but that was just busywork. I didn't think you were actually going to do it."

"So now we're stuck with this guy until we sell the Shiva plans," Pepper said.

"About that," Pritchett said. "I have an idea. What if I could help you get rid of your zontonium?"

Pepper glared at Rex. "You told him about that?"

Rex shrugged. "I may have let something slip on the way over."

"It's okay, I'm not going to tell anyone," Pritchett said. "But I may be able to help you. As you've probably figured out, it's pretty hard to unload a chunk of zontonium that size."

Indeed, Pepper had been trying to sell the zontonium since we'd gotten it, several months earlier. The problem was that it was so valuable that no fence was willing to handle the sale, as it would undoubtedly attract the attention of the Malarchy. She could break pieces off and sell the zontonium a little at a time, but that would require a lot more transactions—also increasing the odds the Malarchy would come calling. So, for now, the zontonium remained locked away in Pepper's storeroom.

"You're telling me you know someone who would be willing to buy that much zontonium?" Pepper asked.

"I'll have to make sure he's still in business, but I think so. He owns a small refinery, so he could mix your zontonium in with the rest of the ore. The trick is to double-refine the ore to remove the trace chemical signature that makes it possible to trace the source. I'd be willing to set you up with my fence in exchange for a cut. Say twenty-five percent."

"Twenty-five percent!" Pepper cried. "I'm not giving up twenty-five—"

"Hear me out," Pritchett said. "You give me twenty-five percent of the zontonium, and I give you my share of the Shiva plans. That leaves you with seventy-five percent of the zontonium profits and thirty-four percent of the Shiva profits."

"Hey," Rex said, his brow furrowing. "I'm getting screwed here."

"It's your own fault, sir," I reminded him. "You gave up your share of the zontonium for Pepper's help on the Shiva job. In addition to giving her a share of the profits."

"And you let me!" Rex grumbled. "I need better supervision."

"The important thing," Pritchett said to Pepper, "is that you and I both get what we want. And then we go our separate ways. We sell the zontonium and then I'm gone. You all can do what you want with the Shiva plans."

"Tempting," Pepper said.

"Is the zontonium nearby?"

Pepper regarded him coldly.

"My fence is going to ask me about the coloration," Pritchett explained. "The darker it is, the harder it is to refine the chemical signature out."

Pepper shrugged. "It's behind that door," she said, pointing with her thumb. "Boggs, let our new friend into the storeroom. If he tries anything, bop him on the head."

"Sure thing, Pepper," Boggs said. He walked to the storeroom and opened the door. Pritchett followed him.

Rex, Donny and I stayed at the bar. It wasn't like Pritchett was going to be able to make off with the zontonium. Boggs could barely lift it.

Rex and I filled Pepper in on the details of our adventures while Pritchett inspected the zontonium. After a few minutes, he and Boggs exited the storeroom and Boggs locked the door behind them.

"It looks pretty pure," Pritchett said, approaching the bar. "I think my fence will give us a good price for it."

"How good?" Pepper asked.

"At least a billion credits."

Rex let out a whistle.

Pepper turned to Rex. "What do you think?"

"I think we need to talk it over. In private."

Pepper nodded. "Sasha and Rex, come with me. Boggs and Donny, stay here and watch Pritchett. Boggs, you know what to do if he tries anything."

Boggs made a head-bopping gesture.

Pepper walked to her office at the back of the saloon. Rex and I followed, and she closed the door behind us.

"Do you trust this guy?" Pepper asked.

"Not at all," Rex replied.

"Do you think he really knows a fence who would buy the zontonium?"

"Maybe. As pathetic as he seems, he apparently really is the Pulsating Pompadour. So at one point, he must have had some serious connections."

"It could be a trap," I said.

Pepper nodded. "He might be setting us up. He tips off the Malarchy, we get arrested, they confiscate the zontonium, and he gets a reward from Heinous Vlaak for being a helpful citizen. Even if they only give him half the market value, he makes more than the twenty-five percent he gets with us."

"It sounds like we're saying no," I said.

Pepper shrugged. "We just have to be careful. I know a broker who can handle the sale and insulate us from any risk. He'll take another ten percent, but it's worth it. I can't keep a billion credits' worth of zontonium in my storeroom forever."

"Hmmm," Rex said, rubbing his chin.

"What is it, sir?" I asked.

"Something's not right here. I know he's a little rusty, but I just don't see a legendary con man like the Pantomiming Peregrine offering us a straight deal like this."

"Weren't you listening, sir?" I said. "Pepper just explained that he's probably going to try to screw us on the deal."

"Sure, but he had to know we're not stupid enough to fall for that."

"Aren't we?"

"Well, Pepper isn't, anyway," Rex said. "So he offered her a deal that took the three of us two minutes to see through. Why?"

The room was silent for several seconds. Then the answer hit us all at once.

Rex threw open the door and ran back into the bar. Pepper and I were close behind. Donny and Boggs were still in the bar, but Pritchett was nowhere to be seen. The door to the storeroom was open.

"Where'd Pritchett go?" Rex demanded.

"It's okay," Boggs said. "He said you guys were going to sell the zontonium, so I helped him load it into the ship."

Rex ran to the door. We followed him outside to the landing pad and watched as Pritchett waved to us from the ramp. He went into the ship and the ramp folded up. *The Flagrante Delicto*'s thrusters fired, and it lifted into the sky.

"Sasha, the remote control!" Rex cried.

I nodded and extracted the remote from my storage compartment. Pressing the buttons had no effect. "Sir, it's not working!"

"Give me that," Rex snapped, and grabbed the device from my hand. He futilely mashed buttons as the *Flagrante Delicto* receded to a speck in the distance. "Why isn't it working?"

"Donny removed the transceiver," Donny said, holding up a baseball-sized component in his hand.

"What?" Rex shouted. "Why?"

"The Narrator man said it was too heavy," Boggs said.

"Too heavy? Boggs, you just loaded a hundred kilos of zontonium into that ship!"

Boggs stared blankly at Rex, unable to make the connection. Finally he said, "It's okay. He said he will be back in five minutes. He's just getting fuel."

"Fuel!" Rex exclaimed. "Boggs, you just loaded enough zontonium into that ship to send it across the galaxy three hundred times!"

Boggs stared for several seconds more. "Maybe ten minutes then," he said at last.

"That bastard stole my zontonium!" Pepper cried.

"At least we still have the Shiva plans," Rex said, holding up the memory crystal.

I took the crystal from him and inserted it into the reader in my chest. "Empty," I said after a moment.

"What?" Rex gasped. "How?"

"He must have switched it. This isn't the crystal I examined earlier."

"So the Pandering Pablum got away with a fortune in zontonium *and* the Shiva plans?" Rex asked.

Pepper sighed. "I need a drink."

CHAPTER THIRTEEN

We spent the next week at Pepper's saloon. We had no ship, no money, and no place to go. The Platinum Pigeon had really done a number on us. And we, fooled by his bumbling doofus act, had let him.

Pepper, of course, was furious—with Rex for telling Pritchett about the zontonium, and with herself for falling for Pritchett's ploy. She rarely left her office for the next week, and Rex spend most of it drunk. The saloon was almost always empty except for the five of us; the Malarchian crackdown on piracy had really cut into Pepper's business. Only occasionally would a stray freebooter or privateer stumble into the place. Boggs, Donny and I played a lot of holochess.

At last, Pepper emerged from her office with a triumphant look on her face. "Got him," she said.

"Whoozzat?" Rex asked, looking up from his martini. I left the game of Ravenous Ringworms I was playing with Boggs and Donny and approached the bar.

"Pritchett," Pepper said. "At least I assume it's him. Somebody is selling a planet." She was holding a sheet of paper.

"How does one sell a planet?" I asked.

"Generally, one doesn't," Pepper said, setting the paper down on the bar in front of me and Rex. "The Malarchy has a standing claim to any new APPLEs that are discovered. But there are back-channel networks where you can post announcements about black market planet auctions. Billionaires and criminal organizations show up to bid on planets that the Malarchy doesn't officially know about. It's how I came into possession of Sargasso Seven."

I examined the paper. The top half was dominated by a picture of a nondescript sphere, which I assumed was the planet in question. The bottom half contained detailed stats on the planet. It looked like a pretty standard-issue Alien Planet Perplexlingly Like Earth.

"Where is it?" Rex asked.

"Ragulian Sector," Pepper said.

"No way," Rex said, shaking his head. "That sector's been thoroughly explored. You're telling me they missed a habitable planet until a few days ago?"

"No," Pepper said, impatient with Rex's denseness. "I'm telling you that this planet wasn't habitable until a few days ago."

A light went on in Rex's head. "Ohhhhh."

"Project Shiva," I said.

Pepper nodded. "Project Shiva. That cheeky bastard got the device built and used it already. A little rusty, my ass. He must have had everything ready to go and waiting for him."

"Are we sure it's him?" I asked.

"Pretty sure. Look at the name of the planet."

I scanned the document until I found the relevant line. It read:

Provisional Identification: Oz

"Not exactly subtle, is he?" I said.

"Probably didn't think it would occur to us to check for new auctions yet," Pepper said. "Fortunately, I'm smarter than he is. All we have to do is go to Oz and nab Pritchett."

"Are we sure he'll be there?" Rex asked.

"Oh, he'll be there," Pepper said. "The auction is in three hours."

Rex, Pepper and I boarded Pepper's little ship, *Bad Little Kitty*, and I plotted a hypergeometric course to the Ragulian Sector. Boggs and Donny, whose feelings about spaceships hadn't been assuaged by recent events, stayed behind. We had barely enough time to get to Oz before the auction started. Already, several other ships—mostly small luxury cruisers probably belonging to mobsters or quasi-legitimate business tycoons—had landed at the makeshift spaceport near the large tent that had been erected for the auction.

The planet itself was nothing special—just a cold, muddy ball with a deep blue sky and near-Earth gravity—but even this was a vast improvement over its previous state. Before Pritchett had used the Shiva device on it, it had been an airless hunk of rock. Oz was never going to be a tourist destination, but now that it could support life, it could also support all sorts of other activities, both legitimate and illegitimate.

As the three of us made our way toward the *Flagrante Delicto*, parked amid several newer, sleeker ships, blades of grass began to sprout from the ground all around us, slowly turning the plain brown surface to a dark green. This was to be expected: after transforming the planet's surface and giving it a breathable atmosphere, the Shiva device enveloped the planet's crust in a biogenic field that would vastly accelerate the growth and evolution of plant and animal life. In a week, if everything proceeded as the Shiva documentation indicated it would, the planet's surface would support a complex ecosystem of jungles, forests, plains and a multitude of animal species. If Pritchett had waited a few days to put the planet up for sale, he'd be in a better bargaining position, as Oz would be much more photogenic, but he'd evidently been in a hurry.

I entered the access code on the outside of the *Flagrante Delicto*, and the hatch slid open. The Platinum Pigeon hadn't even bothered to change the code. As Rex led the way toward the cockpit, Pritchett, wearing a tuxedo, emerged from Rex's cabin. His eyes went wide with shock.

"Put your hands up!" Rex growled, pointing his lazegun at Pritchett.

Pritchett backed away with his hands in the air. "Whoa," he said. "I'm sure we can settle this like adults. There's no call for violence."

"You stole my ship," Rex said.

"And my zontonium," Pepper said.

"And the Shiva plans," I added.

"By my math, that adds up to a call for violence," Rex said. "What do you have to say for yourself?"

"Okay, look," Pritchett said. "It's not what you think. I mean, I guess it is. But here's the thing. I haven't pulled a real con in three years. I just wanted to see if I could get away with it."

"You didn't," Pepper said.

"Exactly my point. How can you be mad at someone who is so clearly out of his element?"

"The inept doofus act is getting old," Pepper said. "Hand over our stuff. We'll even let you keep this planet if you give us Shiva and the zontonium."

"I'm afraid I can't do that," Pritchett said.

"Listen to me, you sniveling weasel," Pepper started, taking a step toward Pritchett.

"No, wait!" Pritchett cried. "I'll cooperate. I will. But I don't have the plans or the zontonium on me. Too risky to keep everything in one place. But I can take you to them."

"Fine. Let's go."

"Sure, sure," Pritchett said. "But we have more pressing concerns right now."

"Like what?" Rex asked.

"Like, there are a hundred very rich and powerful people who are planning to start bidding on a black market planet in..." Pritchett checked his watch. "...two minutes."

"Not our problem," Rex said.

"It's going to be if we try to leave here without auctioning off the planet. These people don't like having their time wasted."

"Ugh," Rex said. "All right. Auction the planet, then we get our stuff. And we get the money from the auction."

"What?" Pritchett cried. "Do you realize how much it cost me to have a Shiva device built in a week? I'm in hock for a hundred million credits!"

"Let him have the planet," Pepper said. "We just need the zontonium and the plans."

"No way," Rex said, shaking his head. "I'm not giving this jerk a penny."

"Sir," I said. "Maybe it's better if we let Pritchett keep the money. I'm not sure it's wise for us to get mixed up in the black market planet trade on top of everything else. We'll have the plans and the device, not to mention a fortune in zontonium."

Rex and Pritchett eyed each other warily. It was clear that neither of them were happy with the deal, but it might be the best either of them would get.

"Fine," Rex said at last.

Pritchett nodded. "All right. Let's get this over with then." He put his hands down and began walking to the door.

"No funny business," Rex said.

"Wouldn't dream of it," Pritchett replied with a smile, and exited the ship.

Pritchett mounted a small stage at one end of the tent. An audience of nearly a hundred well-dressed people sat on rows of folding chairs, murmuring to each other. I use the word "people" in the broadest possible sense: about half were human, but at least six other species were represented. There were Sneeves, Norks, Barashavians, Niknuks and a couple of races I didn't recognize. Rex and I made our way to the back. Pepper was waiting at the *Flagrante Delicto*, in case Pritchett tried to make a run for it. As we stood waiting for the auction to start, I noticed that the grass had grown considerably thicker and taller. The blades licked playfully at my ankles.

Pritchett walked up to a podium and spoke into a microphone. "Greetings!" he said. "My name is Charlemagne Woo. You may know me as the CEO of such companies as Woo's Interstellar Uranium Emporium and Woo Doggies, the number one robotic pet manufacturer in six sectors."

I'd heard of Charlemagne Woo. He was an entrepreneur who had made a name for himself selling goods of questionable quality by buying airtime on unused subspace communication frequencies. Whether Pritchett was just pretending to be Woo or whether the persona of Woo was a fiction Pritchett had created I didn't know. I couldn't remember ever seeing Woo himself; he always hired curvaceous spokesmodels to hawk his products.

Pritchett continued, "Today I'm excited to announce an entirely new endeavor. Ladies, gentlemen and other-beings, I welcome you to the very first, invitation-only event held by my recently formed company, Woo's Overlooked Worlds. WOW! for short."

Unimpressed murmurs arose from the crowd.

Undaunted, Pritchett went on, "It's a commonly repeated myth that the known galaxy has been thoroughly scoured for habitable planets. I'm here to tell you that this myth simply isn't true. There are, in fact, dozens of habitable planets that for various reasons have been overlooked by the Malarchy and the various exploratory corporations. The engineers at WOW! have developed a secret algorithm that locates such planets—planets like this one, which you'll be bidding for shortly. In order to keep overhead low, we also utilize a proprietary process for minimizing bureaucratic complications, which allows us to sell directly to enterprising businessbeings such as yourselves."

I wondered if anyone in the tent bought Pritchett's spiel. The part about discovering overlooked planets was obviously pure fiction, and the stuff about "minimizing bureaucratic complications" was just a nice way of saying that this was an illegal, black market operation. But there were no raised eyebrows, knowing glances or undulating tentacles in the crowd. Everybody seemed committed to maintaining the pretense that this was a legitimate auction.

Pritchett continued: "All right, let's start the bidding. Up for auction today is the delightful sphere on which we're standing. Clocking in at eighty-four million metric tons, Oz is composed mostly of iron, aluminum and silicon, and has a thoroughly breathable atmosphere of nitrogen, oxygen, carbon dioxide and various trace gases. Although not officially certified by the Malarchian Registry of Planets, it meets all the standards of a Class Seven APPLE—an Alien Planet Perplexingly Like Earth. With a little TLC, Oz could truly be a planet to write home about. Whether you're looking for a place to build a top-secret mega-weapon away from the eyes of meddling regulatory agencies, construct a free-range hunting ground for genetically enhanced superbeasts, or you simply need a few billion hectares to get away from it all, Oz is the planet for you. Boasting an easy-on-the-joints gravitational pull of point eight three gees, an axial tilt of eighteen degrees and an atmosphere that lets through just enough cosmic radiation to keep things interesting, a planet like Oz would go for well over ten billion credits on the open market. Bidding starts at a mere hundred million!"

Nods and murmurs went up from the crowd. After a moment, a Barashavian raised one of its tentacles. Pritchett smiled, unable to completely hide his relief. "We have one hundred million," he said. "Can I get two?"

A young woman near the front, who wore jewelry marking her as a member of the Anvarvikk royal family, raised a hand. Pritchett nodded to her. "Bidding is at two hundred million. Do I hear three?"

An elderly gentleman a few rows in front of us raised his hand. This went on for a while, the bids rapidly escalating until it stalled at nine hundred million.

"We have nine hundred million," Pritchett said. "That's less than a billion credits for an entire planet with a breathable atmosphere and a complex and rapidly growing ecosystem. Look at that! The grass is growing before your very eyes!"

The grass was not only growing before our eyes; it was growing above our knees and around our ankles. People had begun shifting their feet to keep from getting stuck in place.

"Haha, don't worry about that," Pritchett said. "The intensity of the biogenic field will drop off dramatically any minute now." He swatted at something on his neck. "Hey, look at that! We've got bugs! Isn't that great? It's like being in a planet-sized park! Do I hear one billion credits?"

But the crowd, distracted by the burgeoning plant life and rapidly proliferating insects, seemed to have lost interest.

"One billion!" shouted Rex.

CHAPTER FOURTEEN

Pritchett's eyes went wide. He nodded weakly. Several of the other bidders, momentarily distracted from the jungle that was taking root in the tent, turned to see who had entered the fray.

"Sir," I said. "Why are you bidding on this planet?"

"The Preening Palladium really sold me on it," Rex said with a shrug. "I think it was the part about genetically modified superbeasts. And you know how I get about aluminum." He had begun walking in place to keep the grass from getting a hold on him.

I sighed. Hopefully we wouldn't get stuck with a planet we couldn't pay for. Fortunately, Rex's bid seemed to get things moving again. In between swatting bugs and batting back the tendrils of vines that were now running along the tent poles, several beings in the crowd managed to get bids in. Soon, the price was up to one point five billion.

"Five billion!" Rex shouted.

Gasps went up from the crowd. Pritchett shot a glare at Rex.

"Sir!" I said. "What are you doing? We don't have that kind of money!"

"Don't need it," Rex said.

"Perhaps you misheard, sir," Pritchett said. "The bidding was at one point five billion."

"I heard you," Rex said. "Just trying to move things along. This auction is literally more boring than watching grass grow." He was right about that: the grass was getting to be downright worrying. It had reached my knees, and I had to keep shuffling my feet to keep it from getting a hold on me. "You know what, make it ten billion."

"You're bidding *ten billion credits*?" Pritchett asked in disbelief.

"You sold me with the bit about axial tilt. I figure it's gotta be worth at least a billion per degree. At eighteen degrees, ten billion is a bargain."

Pritchett stared at Rex. "Sir, this is an auction for serious bidders only." He swatted a large insect that had landed on his forehead.

"What are you trying to say?" Rex asked. "That I'm some kind of legendary con man?"

"Excuse me?"

"I mean, I'd hate to think anybody here was accusing anybody else of secretly being the most famous con man in the galaxy. That would really cast a pall over this whole enterprise."

Pritchett continued to glare but didn't reply. Then he broke into a nervous smile. "We have ten billion. Do I hear ten point one?" But no one else in the crowd was paying any attention. Everyone was busy fighting the grass or swatting at insects. A few were working their way toward the exit.

"Sir, what are you doing?" I asked.

"Just having a little fun," Rex said. "What's the Palliative Punjabi going to do if I don't pay? Have me arrested? If he tries anything, I'll just tell everybody here who they're dealing with. Everybody here has heard of the famed Paddington Pigpen. This is why I never bothered to get famous. It's a liability. Every real con man knows that."

"Yes, sir," I said.

"Ten point one billion," croaked someone near the front. Gasps and murmurs went up from those in the crowd who were still paying attention.

"Sold for ten point one billion!" Pritchett exclaimed, before Rex could in get another bid.

I craned my neck but couldn't see who had made the winning bid. The squeaky, high-pitched voice seemed familiar.

"Come on up and we'll settle up with the paperwork," Pritchett said. "I'm sure you'll be just thrilled with your new planet. Everyone else, thanks for coming and keep an eye out for future auctions!"

As the crowd continued to disperse, one man—apparently the winning bidder—made his way toward the stage, wearing a hooded brown cloak.

"Well, that's that," Rex said. "Would have been nice to screw that bastard out of his profits, but you can't win them all. At least we still have the Shiva plans and the zontonium."

"Yes, sir," I said, absently. As the man fought his way through the grass to get to the stage, I racked my brain trying to remember where I had heard that voice.

"Come on," Rex said. "We can't lose Pritchett again. Should have put a homing beacon on him like—"

"Heinous Vlaak!" I cried, as the memory clicked into place. "Sir, we have to get Pritchett!"

"Well, of course we have to get Pritchett. That's what I just—"

"No, sir, I mean right now. That man, the winning bidder. It's Heinous Vlaak!"

"By Space, you're right!" Rex cried, drawing his lazegun. The hooded figure had made it up the stairs and was halfway to the podium. Pritchett gaped in terror as Vlaak threw off his cloak to reveal his customary crimson armor. Suddenly, the podium exploded in a flash of light. Pritchett was knocked on his rear.

"Whoops!" Rex said. "I was aiming for Vlaak. Duck!"

Vlaak drew his lazegun. Screams erupted, and the crowd scattered in all directions. Realizing we had no place to hide, Rex and I ran to the opening of the tent behind us and outside. Lazegun blasts sizzled overhead.

Outside the tent, the jungle had grown even thicker. Green trunks as thick as my waist had shot out of the ground and continued to grow, splitting into narrower branches far above that exploded in bursts of feathery orange fronds. The ever-thickening grass was waist-high here, and dozens of other exotic plants had sprung up as well. The air buzzed with insects, and things like huge pterodactyls circled ominously overhead. Men, women and beings of indeterminate sex were clawing through the underbrush toward the landing field in the direction of the landing pad. I couldn't even see the *Flagrante Delicto*.

After working my way a few meters toward our ship, I realized Rex wasn't behind me. As the rest of the crowd continued to flee, I stopped and turned back toward the tent. Rex was standing by himself, just outside.

"Sir!" I shouted. "We have to get out of here!"

He turned to look at me and then back at the tent, seemingly confused.

"Sir!" I shouted again. "What are you doing?"

Rex turned toward me again and shouted, "Why isn't he following me?" The other bidders had all fled; nobody else was coming out.

"Sir?"

"Heinous Vlaak!" Rex shouted. "Didn't he recognize me?"

"Sir," I said, making my way back toward him, "Vlaak's not after you. He's after Pritchett."

Rex looked at me as if I'd just asked him to stop drinking. "But I thought we were nemesises. Nemesi. I thought we were like, arch-enemies."

"You can't take it personally, sir. Pritchett has the Shiva plans. I'm sure that's what Vlaak is after."

Rex seemed doubtful. "I think maybe he couldn't see me with that hood on. Should I go back in and try shooting him again?"

"Seriously, sir, I'm sure he'd be chasing you if you had the Shiva plans."

"Well, sure, but what if neither of us had the Shiva plans? Then who would he chase?"

"Sir, are you sure this is the best time for this discussion?" I swatted at a leafy tendril that was trying to wrap itself around my neck. The pterodactyls were now circling directly overhead.

"I think maybe it was the hood," Rex said.

"That's certainly a possibility, sir."

"Do you think it was the hood?"

"No, sir."

"Okay, so if neither of us had the plans—"

"Sir, please."

"If neither of us had the plans, who would he chase?"

"Sir, to be honest, if neither of you had the Shiva plans, there really wouldn't be much reason for Vlaak to chase either of you."

"Okay, but if he *had* to chase one of us."

"There's no way to say for certain, sir."

"If you had to guess though."

"If I answer you, can we please leave?"

"Yes."

98

"If neither of you had the Shiva plans, I think he'd still chase Pritchett, but only because—"

"Wow."

"Sir?"

"Wow, okay. I'm going to need a moment here."

"Sir, you said we could go now."

"That was before your unprecedented betrayal."

"Sir, you didn't let me—"

"Forget it, Sasha. I see where your loyalties lie. I spend years showing you the wonders of the galaxy, treating you like a queen, only to have you stab me in the back."

"You don't actually treat me that well, sir."

"And can you blame me, given your flagrant disloyalty and questionable judgment?"

"I suppose not, sir. Can we go now?"

"Not yet. We've got to find Pritchett. If that jerk gets away with those plans again, we'll never... what in Space is *that*?"

I'd become aware of it as well: the ground was rumbling beneath our feet. Had the Shiva device destabilized the planet's tectonic plates?

"Sasha, look!" Rex cried, over the now-deafening sound. Looking where Rex was pointing, I saw a huge six-legged lizard creature bounding through the jungle toward us. Its body was covered with red scales, and protruding from its head were four massive sets of pincers, each of which looked capable of ripping a hovercar to pieces. It was headed right for me.

I tried to run, but in my moment of distraction I had allowed the grass to get a firm hold of my legs. Rex, who was similarly trapped, shouted something at me, but I couldn't hear him over the sound of the creature smashing through the trees. With a great effort I managed to tear myself free of the grass, but the movement threw me off balance and I landed flat on my back in a patch of yellow flowers, which immediately shot several hundred spikey darts at my face. Poison, I assumed—not that it mattered. I'm immune to poison, but in about two seconds I was going to be torn to scrap metal anyway. I covered my eyes with my hands.

There was a powerful blast of wind that would have knocked me over if I weren't already on my back, and then suddenly everything was quiet. I cautiously took my hands away from eyes in time to see a something like a gigantic purple jellyfish floating away, gripping the lizard creature with its tentacles. I tried to get up, but found myself completely paralyzed: the grass had wrapped itself around my arms, legs, and neck. On top of everything else, I smelled something on fire.

"Don't worry, Sasha!" Rex cried, stepping into my field of view. He pointed his lazegun at my face. "I'll save you. Isn't this place great?"

"Sir?" I said. "What are you—"

A blast from the lazegun vaporized the grass near my neck.

"Careful, sir!" I cried, remembering Rex's attempt to hit Heinous Vlaak.

"Don't worry, Sasha," Rex said. "I'll have you out of here in a jiffy." He fired again, this time singeing my arm. Miraculously, he fired three more times without doing any serious damage to my exterior, and I was able to tear myself free of the remaining strands and get to my feet. The jungle was so thick now that it was getting difficult to see. Unseen creatures cackled and howled in the foliage around us.

"You know," Rex said, surveying our surroundings, "I'm starting to think this planet isn't safe."

"That would seem to be an accurate assessment, sir. I think the biogenic field has gone haywire. We need to get back to the ship."

"You're not going anywhere," squealed a voice behind Rex. Rex turned, and I saw that it was Heinous Vlaak. He was pointing a lazegun at us. "Where is he?"

"I don't have any idea who you're talking about," Rex said.

"Hannibal Pritchett!" Vlaak snapped. "The Platinum Pigeon! Somehow he got away from me."

Rex shrugged. "Never heard of him."

"Listen to me, you two-bit grifter," Vlaak snarled, "I know you're working with Pritchett. He stole the Shiva plans from me. This is your last chance. Tell me where he is or die on this accursed planet."

"I have a better idea," Rex said. "How about if you pucker up and kiss my—"

As he spoke, the ground broke open in between us and a gelatinous blob oozed out of it, gradually forming itself into a roughly spherical shape nearly as tall as I was. For a moment, the three of us stood transfixed by the shimmering, translucent blob. Then it suddenly darted toward Vlaak, enveloped him, and sucked him into the hole. Vlaak and the blob had simply vanished.

"Sasha?" Rex said quietly.

"Yes, sir," I said.

"RUN!"

We ran.

We hadn't gotten more than ten meters when another of the gelatinous blob things surged out of the ground just in front of us. Rex shot at it with his lazegun, but the blast seemed to have no effect. The blob lunged at us, and we leaped out of the way, Rex to the left and I to the right. Continuing in the general direction of the *Flagrante Delicto*, we fought against the ravenous grass, ducked under dive-bombing pterodactyls and dodged volleys of darts fired by the yellow flowers. I knew the *Flagrante Delicto* couldn't be more than fifty meters away, but getting to it seemed impossible. Just making our way through the jungle would have been challenge enough without near-certain death awaiting us at every step.

"What do we do, sir?" I asked. We'd found ourselves with a momentary respite in a small clearing. The grass was thinner here and there didn't seem to be any of the dart-shooting flowers around. The pterodactyls overhead were engaged in a protracted dogfight with what looked like a giant, winged beaver.

"I think... this might be it... for us," Rex gasped. "If we don't make it out of this... I want you to know...."

"Yes, sir?"

"...that I blame you for everything."

"Yes, sir."

Several explosions erupted overhead, and giant beaver parts began to hit the ground all around us. The pterodactyls shrieked and scattered as the *Flagrante Delicto* came into view.

"Who the hell...?" Rex started.

"Pepper?" I asked. But if Pepper had any sense, she'd already have taken off in her own ship.

The Flagrante Delicto settled to the ground in front of us, just as two of the gelatinous blobs shot out of the ground nearby, one on either side of us. We sprinted toward the ship, and the two blobs collided with each other, momentarily forming one giant blob which then exploded into a thousand little blobs, which oozed and bounced toward us. The hatch slid open and we dived inside.

"Get us out of here, Sasha!" Rex cried, as he slammed the hatch shut behind us. But before I could get to the cockpit, the thrusters fired and we were thrown to the deck. After several seconds of punishing gee forces, the acceleration let up enough for us to stand. We staggered into the cockpit as the ship left the atmosphere.

Hannibal Pritchett turned to look at us from the pilot's chair. "Hi, guys!" he said with a grin. "Thought you could use a little help."

"You son of a churl," Rex growled. "We could have been killed down there! In like fifteen different ways!"

"Well, yeah," Pritchett said. "That's why I rescued you. A little gratitude wouldn't kill you, you know."

"*Gratitude?* What was all that, down there? You created a nightmare world!"

"It does seem like the Shiva device has some...undesirable functionality," Pritchett said. "And how about that Heinous Vlaak showing up, huh? Guess I should have vetted the invitations a little more carefully."

"Get out of that chair," Rex snapped. "Sasha, you take over."

Pritchett climbed out of the pilot's seat, and I took his place. Rex sat down next to me.

"Where are we going, sir?"

"To wherever this jerk hid our zontonium," Rex said, jerking his thumb toward Pritchett, standing behind us. "The black market planet business was a bust, but at least we still have a fortune in zontonium."

"Um," Pritchett said.

"You said you hid the zontonium in a safe place," Rex said, turning to face Pritchett. "Too risky to bring it here. That's what you said."

"Um," Pritchett said again.

"You lying skorf-rat," Rex said. "You left it on Oz, didn't you?"

"I meant to hide it somewhere else," Pritchett said. "I really did. But I was a bit pressed for time with the auction, so I... left it in a cave on the other side of the planet."

"Moron!" Rex cried. He turned to me. "We have to go back."

"Sir, we can't! The ecosystem down there is still evolving at an incredible rate. There's no telling what sorts of horrors we might face on the other side of the planet."

"Ugh," Rex said. "Don't we have some kind of un-terraforming device to turn it back into an uninhabitable ball of rock?"

"Not at present, sir," I said.

"The good news is that nobody else can get to it either," Pritchett said.

"Yeah, that is great news," Rex said. "Hey, I need you to do me a favor and go into that little room at the back of the ship labeled 'airlock.'"

A woman's voice came over the comm. "Rex? Sasha? Can you hear me?"

"We can hear you, Pepper," I said.

"Thank Space. I thought you were goners."

"We survived, no thanks to you," Rex said.

"I was trying to find you," Pepper said. "I guess Pritchett got to you first."

"The important thing is that we all survived," I said. "Let's rendezvous back on Sargasso Seven, and we'll figure out what to do with Pritchett."

"I'm afraid there's another complication we have to deal with first," Pepper said.

"Now what?" Rex groused.

"I just got a transmission from your Sp'ossel friends, Doctors LaRue and Smulders. They found the saloon."

"Blast it!" Rex growled. "So we've lost our planet-selling business, our zontonium and our secret hideout. Is there anything else that could go wrong?"

"Yes, actually," Pepper said.

"Oh, no," I said, realizing what she meant.

"They've also got Donny and Boggs."

CHAPTER FIFTEEN

The Sp'ossels had somehow figured out we had the Shiva plans and that we were working with Pepper. While we were at the auction, they had broken into her saloon on Sargasso Seven. They had sent Pepper a transmission claiming to be holding Donny and Boggs hostage and promising to let them go if we handed over the Shiva plans.

"Why do the Sp'ossels even want the plans?" Rex asked. "What good is a habitable planet if everything on it is trying to kill you?"

"The Sp'ossels may have the resources to subdue the ecosystem," I suggested.

"It wouldn't be worth the expense," Pritchett said. "And any kind of poison or radiation bombs capable of killing all the dangerous plants and animals on the planet would render the place uninhabitable again."

"Maybe the Sp'ossels don't know about the problems with the Shiva device," Pepper said.

I considered this for a moment. We had been assuming that the Sp'ossels had caught wind of the auction. But maybe they had no idea Pritchett had a completed Shiva device.

"If they don't know about Oz," I asked, "then how did they figure out we have the plans?"

"No idea," Pepper said. "The important thing is that we can use their ignorance against them. We can't sell planets that nobody can use, so we might as well hand the plans over to the Sp'ossels in exchange for Donny and Boggs."

Rex frowned. "I don't have to tell you guys how fond I am of Boggs and Donny, but... well, I'm also very fond of big piles of cash. Is there any possibility your engineer screwed something up when he built the device? Maybe he could build another one without the bio-whatever field problems."

Pritchett shook his head. "I'm afraid he built the Shiva device to the exact specifications in the plans. If he built another one, it would have the same problems as this one."

Rex sighed. "Fine. I guess we'll trade the stupid worthless plans to the stupid Sp'ossels for Boggs and Donny."

"All right," said Pepper. "They're waiting for us at the saloon. I'll meet you there."

"The prodigal sons have returned," said Dr. LaRue with a smile, as the four of us entered the saloon. Dr. LaRue stood behind the bar, and Dr. Smulders sat at a barstool nearby, nursing a drink. Boggs and Donny were gagged and tied up in a corner. Two large men in white coats held lazeguns pointed at them. "I never thought I'd see the day that Rex Nihilo and the Platinum Pigeon were working together."

"Get out of there," Pepper snapped at Dr. LaRue. Dr. LaRue shrugged and walked around the bar. Pepper walked past her with a glare, taking her place behind the bar. Pepper grabbed a bottle of whisky and poured a shot.

"I'm not working with this idiot," Rex said. "He's only here because we didn't have time to shoot him into a supernova on the way over. Now untie Donny and Boggs before I lose my temper."

"It seems even Rex Nihilo has a soft spot for his friends," said Smulders with a smile.

"Okay, let's get one thing straight, here," Rex said. "I'm only giving up these plans because we don't want to deal with a thousand different species of man-eating—"

"Sir!" I interjected, "I'm sure the esteemed doctors have more important things to do than listen to us complain about our troubles."

"Eh?" Rex said. "Oh. Yes. Right, like I was saying, these plans are worth a fortune! We could easily use them to make hundreds of habitable planets, each of them perfectly pleasant and devoid of murderous death-beasts, and it's only my great affection for and loyalty to my two comrades here that I'm willing to part with the plans for a mere hundred billion credits."

"A hundred billion credits!" Dr. LaRue exclaimed. "We certainly programmed you well, didn't we? I'm afraid there's been a bit of a misunderstanding, however. You are going to hand over the Shiva plans, and I am going to instruct those gentlemen to untie your friends. That is to be the entirety of your compensation."

"And I get my saloon back," Pepper said. "And you leave us alone." She tossed the whiskey down her throat.

"Of course," Dr. LaRue said. "Simply hand over the plans and we'll be on our way."

"Ninety-six billion," Rex said.

"I appreciate your persistence, Rex," said Dr. Smulders, "but you have no leverage over us. I suggest you take the deal before we alter it to your detriment."

"Ninety-two billion."

"Ignore him," Pepper said. "Sasha, hand over the plans."

I did as instructed, handing the memory crystal to Dr. Smulders.

"You haven't made any copies?" Smulders asked, inserting the crystal into a holoscreen he'd pulled from his jacket.

"No," I said.

"Good. Because if we let you go and then find that you have gotten into the black market planet business, there will be... consequences." He scanned the contents of the crystal and gave Dr. LaRue a nod.

"Eighty-nine billion, and that's my final offer," Rex said.

"We'll see ourselves out," Dr. LaRue said, exiting the bar. Smulders finished his drink and motioned to the two men with lazepistols. One of them cut the ropes around Donny and Boggs and then the four walked to the door.

"If you ever set foot in my saloon again, I'll vaporize the lot of you," Pepper shouted as they left the bar. The door slammed behind them.

"Why'd you let them go?" Rex asked. "Couldn't you see I was wearing them down?"

Boggs and Donny approached the bar. "I'm sorry, Potential Friend," Boggs said. "They surprised us."

"It's okay, Boggs," Rex said. "The important thing is that you and Donny are safe. Donny, could you please stand where I can't see you? Thanks."

"So," Pritchett said, "what do you guys want to do now?"

"What are you talking about?" Pepper asked.

"I'm just saying, we make a pretty good team. We should try running some more scams together. If we work together, maybe we can get back the money we lost on the zontonium."

Pepper snorted derisively and poured herself another drink.

"Look, Pritchett," Rex said, "as a fellow con man, I appreciate your chutzpah, but you stole from us and cost us a fortune in zontonium. You think we're going to go into business with you now? Not a chance. Scram."

"Come on," Pritchett whined. "We were just having some friendly inter-con man rivalry. You can't take it personally."

"Sure I can," Rex said. "Watch how personally I'm taking it."

"Okay, I'm going to level with you," Pritchett said. "I have no prospects and nowhere to go. I was really just hoping to tag along with you guys for a few weeks until I got back on my feet. Run a few low-level scams and whatnot. I don't mind being your flim-flam man."

Rex shook his head. "First of all, I don't know what a flim-flam man is. And second, I'm fresh out of pity for you. Get lost."

Pepper nodded. "You've cost us a fortune, Pritchett. You're lucky we don't space you. If you don't make a nuisance of yourself, you can wait here until the next long-haul freighter stops by. That's my final offer."

Pritchett nodded sadly. I couldn't help feeling a little bad for the guy. In a lot of ways, he was like Rex: he didn't know any way to live except to try to take advantage of everyone around him. It had to be a pretty lonely existence.

Freighters didn't stop at Pepper's saloon very often these days, but as it happened, a freighter pilot walked in less than an hour after the Sp'ossels left. Pritchett was too busy moping in a corner of the saloon to notice the man's arrival, but Pepper cajoled the pilot into offering Pritchett a ride off planet. Pritchett reluctantly accepted, and he followed the man out of the saloon with a sad glance back at Pepper, who ignored him.

"It's too bad, really…" I started, a few minutes after he left.

"Don't start," Pepper snapped.

"I'm just saying, Rex and Pritchett are really very much alike. It would be nice if they could get along." Rex had downed three martinis and had fallen asleep in Pepper's office, so there was little risk of him overhearing.

"One insufferable, narcissistic con man is enough for me," said Pepper. "Don't feel bad for Pritchett. Guys like him always land on their feet."

I nodded. "I hope he doesn't try to run some kind of scam on that freighter pilot," I said. "He seemed like a nice young man." In fact, the man hadn't fit my image of a freighter pilot at all. Most independent long-haul freighter pilots were smelly, unshaven and overweight. This guy was young and clean-cut, and he'd been wearing tan slacks and a white button-down shirt. All he'd had to drink was a ginger ale.

"He did seem nice, didn't he?" Pepper said, her brow furrowing. "Maybe too nice. Where did he say he was going?"

"He said he was hauling a shipment of oorka feed to the Zannilox system," I said.

"Do they even farm oorkas on Zannilox?" Pepper asked.

I did a quick hypernet search. "It would appear not. The oorka mating ritual requires a planet with active volcanic activity."

"So he lied," Pepper said.

"Why would he do that?"

"Because he didn't want us to know the real reason he stopped on Sargasso Seven."

"You think he came here specifically to pick up Pritchett? Why? And how did he know Pritchett was... oh. Oh, no."

"Oh, yes," Pepper said. "I think we've been bamboozled again."

CHAPTER SIXTEEN

We should have figured it out earlier. We *would* have figured it out earlier, if we hadn't been so worried about Donny and Boggs—not to mention being distracted by our near-death experience on Oz.

"There's only one way the Sp'ossels could have known we were working with Pritchett," Pepper said.

I nodded. "Pritchett told them. Do you think he knew the Shiva device had undesirable side effect?"

"Hard to say, but he definitely had a Plan B ready. He must have called the Sp'ossels from the *Flagrante Delicto*, before he rescued you. He didn't want to cut us in on the deal, so he told LaRue and Smulders to come here so they could make a show of trading Boggs and Donny for the plans."

"You think they paid him for the plans? I didn't see them give him anything."

"My guess is that that pilot delivered the money. I should have known something was up when that guy walked in."

"So Pritchett's whining about wanting to team up with us had all been an act meant to defuse our suspicion."

"I told you not to feel sorry for him. Come on, we need to wake up Rex."

Pepper made some coffee and brought it to Rex. Once he was fully awake and mostly sober, we explained what had happened. Rex was not happy with the news.

"PRITCHETT!" he roared, shaking his fist in the air. Boggs jumped so hard he scattered the game of Ravenous Ringworms he was playing with Donny.

"How much do you think they paid him?" I asked Pepper.

"If it's a single credit, it's more than we got," Rex growled. "And it's a hell of a lot more than that duplicitous flaffle-herder deserves. Where is he now?"

"Fortunately, I logged the freighter's call sign," Pepper said. "I sent out some feelers, and one of my contacts reported the freighter just made port at Reebus Four."

"That's not even close to the Zannilox system!" Rex cried. "What a bunch of lying liars those lying Sp'ossels are!"

"So it would seem, sir," I said. "Perhaps we can still catch up to him."

Pepper nodded. "I'll close the bar. This time we stick together. Everybody, aboard the *Flagrante Delicto*."

Once on Reebus Four, we split up to search for the freighter pilot. Rex and I found him at a café not far from the spaceport. We sat down on either side of him at a little table where he sat drinking lemonade and eating a grilled cheese sandwich. He seemed downright terrified to see us.

"Please," he said, holding his greasy fingers in the air. "I'm just a freighter pilot. I've got a family. Once in a while I make some extra cash doing some favors for the Sp'ossels. I don't know anything important."

"Relax, kid," said Rex. "We just need to know where Pritchett is."

"Who?"

"Hannibal Pritchett. The guy you picked up at the saloon."

"Oh. The Sp'ossels said not to tell anyone."

"Sure," Rex said, "but as you've indicated, you're just an innocent freighter pilot. You can't be expected to stand up to hours of rigorous interrogation."

"You're going to torture me?" the pilot asked weakly.

"Of course not," Rex said. "We only torture hardened Sp'ossel operators. You're not one of those, right?"

"No, sir."

"Exactly. And that's why you're going to fold like a cheap lawn chair. Do you know who Hannibal Pritchett is?"

The pilot shook his head.

"He's the second greatest con man in the galaxy. And do you know why the Sp'ossels asked you to hand him three hundred million credits?"

"It was eight hundred, actually."

"EIGHT HUNDRED MILLION CREDITS!" Rex exclaimed, loud enough that diners at several nearby tables turned to stare. "That greedy, underhanded little flurg-clamper. Do you know why the Sp'ossels asked you to give him that money?"

"They just said he gave them something they needed to help spread the Sp'ossel message. Said that I should give him the satchel of credits and take him wherever he wanted to go."

"Well, Chet. Can I call you Chet?"

"My name is Arvin."

"Chet, there's a reason Hannibal Pritchett is one of the greatest con men in the galaxy—although not the greatest, as my robot sidekick can attest."

"Sir, perhaps we should stay focused on the—"

"It's because he's always running some kind of scam. Even when you're convinced you're getting a square deal from him, he's conning you. Did he offer you anything while you were traveling with him?"

"Well, he did offer me a stick of cinnamon gum."

"Did you accept?"

"I was eating sunflower seeds at the time, and I didn't think cinnamon—"

"You see! He knew you were eating sunflower seeds. He never had any intention of giving you any gum! You can't eat sunflower seeds and chew gum at the same time! It's madness!"

"You mean…"

"It was all a scam! A grift! A con! He was bamboozling you right before your very eyes! I bet he never even had any gum!"

"I think I could smell it though."

"Of course you could! That's just how smooth he is. He mentions cinnamon gum and the next thing you know, you're smelling cinnamon gum!"

"Wow."

"Wow indeed. Now I ask you: do you think a guy like that is going to give the Sp'ossels a square deal?"

The pilot thought for a moment. "No?"

"NO!" Rex cried, slamming his palm on the table. "Don't you see? They were eating sunflower seeds and he had them smelling cinnamon!"

The pilot seemed confused.

"It's a metaphor, Chet. Don't hurt yourself. Here's the thing: your Sp'ossel bosses thought they were buying a set of plans for a terraforming device. But the plans don't work! It's all a scam!"

"So they paid him eight hundred million credits for something that doesn't work?"

"Bingo. Sunflower seeds and cinnamon, Chet. Now you're seeing the big picture."

"Maybe I should warn them?"

"Too late for that, Chet. That die has sailed. But what you can do is help us track Pritchett down and get that money from him."

"To give it back to the Sp'ossels, you mean."

"One thing at a time. First we need to know exactly where on Kelvex you dropped Pritchett."

"Actually it was Blintherd," the pilot said.

"Blintherd, right," Rex said. "Where on Blintherd?"

"He wrote down the coordinates for me," the pilot said, pulling a scrap of paper from his pocket.

"Excellent," Rex said, snatching the paper. "We'll take it from here, Chet. Oh, and it's probably best for your sake that you don't tell your Sp'ossel masters about this conversation."

"I don't even know who you are."

"Oh, sorry about that," Rex said, holding out his hand. "I'm Rex Nihilo, the greatest con man in the galaxy. Right, Sasha?"

"So I keep hearing, sir."

As we neared the coordinates on the scrap of paper Rex had taken from the pilot, I began to suspect we'd been had. Blintherd was an unpleasant, barely habitable planet, and there was nothing around the target coordinates but swamp for hundreds of klicks.

"It's a hell of a hiding place," Pepper said, as we descended through the atmosphere.

I nodded. It was that, if nothing else.

We exited the *Flagrante Delicto* and began to look around. Blintherd's gravity was a debilitating one point four gees and its atmosphere was hot and humid. Dark green clouds hung oppressively in the sky. The landscape was swampy, and the air smelled faintly like rotting garbage.

"Over here," said Pepper. As we approached, we saw that she was standing in front of the mouth of a cave. It was just big enough for a person to walk inside. A dim light came from within.

"Could be dangerous," Rex said. "Sasha, check it out."

"Me?" I asked weakly. "What about Boggs? Or Donny?"

"I think I'm too big to go in," Boggs said.

"Donny isn't comfortable exploring caves, as he is still adjusting to significant anatomical alterations," Donny said.

I sighed, resigning myself to my fate. But as I steeled myself to enter the cave, shadows flickered on the wall inside. Someone was coming out. Soon I saw that it was Pritchett.

"Uh-oh," he said, as he lay eyes on us.

"That's right, uh-oh," Rex said. "You sold us out to the Sp'ossels, you glarb-horker."

"Okay, yes," Pritchett said. "I did do that. But I can explain."

"We're done with your explanations," Pepper snapped, pointing her lazegun at Pritchett. "Give us the money. All of it."

"Whoa, hold on a minute," Pritchett said. "I can't give you the money, because I already spent it."

"You spent eight hundred million credits?" Pepper cried. "On *what*?"

"Another Shiva device."

"Another... what in Space is wrong with you, Pritchett?"

"I'm going to level with you," Pritchett said. "What I told you about why the Shiva device didn't work on Oz wasn't one hundred percent accurate."

"We're flabbergasted," Pepper said flatly.

"I didn't lie, exactly," Pritchett said. "The plans were really flawed. The Sp'ossels will probably never figure out how to build a Shiva device without the side effects."

"But you think you can," Pepper said.

"Not me. My engineer. He's a genius."

"Oh yeah?" Rex said. "Where is this engineer?"

"Follow me," Pritchett said. He turned and walked back into the cave.

Pepper followed him, still holding her gun on him. "Stay close," she said.

"Boggs, you and Donny wait out here," I said. They nodded. Rex and I followed Pepper into the cave.

After a few steps, the cave turned a corner and then sloped downward for fifty meters before opening into a well-lit, dome-shaped chamber big enough to hold the Flagrante Delicto. Shelves and workbenches littered with tools and electronic components lined the walls. In the middle of the room stood a mushroom that came up to my waist.

"I told him the design had problems," said raspy voice from somewhere inside the cavern. "The biogenic field will be unstable, I told him. But he never listens."

Pepper, Rex and I were all peering around the cavern, trying to determine where the voice had come from.

"Who was that?" Pepper asked.

"Me," said the voice. "Over here." It was hard to pinpoint the sound, but it seemed to be coming from the center of the cave. We continued to scan the cave for anything that might be speaking.

"What are you, blind?" the voice asked again. "I'm right here!"

Rex took a step forward. "Where, behind the toadstool-looking thing?"

"No, you dummy!" said the voice. "I *am* the toadstool-looking thing. See? I'm waving my arms." Several tendril-like appendages attached to stalk of the toadstool writhed in the air.

"You're… the engineer?" Pepper asked.

"Egslaad the Voork at your service." The toadstool thing hopped over to one of the shelves and picked up a component with its tentacles. "The tricky part," Egslaad said, "is calibrating the biogenic feedback dampers. If you don't get it just right, you get a feedback loop that causes the field to spiral out of control."

"But you can solve the problem?" Pepper asked.

"I believe so. I was working on it when Pritchett took the device. Always in a hurry, this one."

"How much longer would you need to build another device?"

"Two days," Egslaad said. "Three, tops."

"You see?" Pritchett said. "Everything's going to work out. We're back in the black market planet business. And we don't have to worry about competition from the Sp'ossels, because they don't have Egslaad. They'll never solve the feedback loop problem."

"*You're* not in *any* business," Rex said, jabbing his finger at Pritchett. Whatever money we make on this deal is *ours*. You're not getting any of it, *capisce*? We may let you live. *If* we decide to do this."

"It's risky," Pepper said. "If the Sp'ossels find out, they'll come after us. And then there's Heinous Vlaak...."

"Also," I said, "it's going to be difficult to find buyers after the Oz debacle."

Pepper rubbed her chin. "I've still got some contacts in the black market planet business, and nobody at that auction knows I was involved. Except for the Sp'ossels, of course, and we want to keep them in the dark anyway. We just need to be more careful about whom we contact about the sale."

"I don't like it," Rex said. "This planet-selling business is too much like work. And anywhere both Heinous Vlaak and the Sp'ossels might show up is exactly where I don't want to be. I say we take the eight hundred million credits and find some better targets to scam than galaxy-spanning organizations that have the power to kill us a million times over. Not to mention that we wouldn't have to put up with this jerk anymore."

Pritchett opened his mouth to object, but a glare from Pepper silenced him.

"I'm no fonder of Pritchett or the Sp'ossels than you are," Pepper said. "But..."

"What is it, Pepper?" I asked.

"Well, to be completely honest, I was counting on that money from the zontonium. I still owe the Ursa Minor Mafia a lot of money, and that zontonium was going to be my ticket to freedom. Eight hundred million credits is nice, but once we split it... it's not going to be enough. And we could easily clear a billion on the sale of a single planet. Probably more like ten billion."

"If Egslaad can get the Shiva device working," I said.

"And we don't get ambushed by Sp'ossels or Heinous Vlaak," Rex added.

"Where's your sense of adventure?" Pritchett asked.

"Did you miss the part where you're not getting a single credit no matter what happens?" Rex snapped.

Pritchett went back to sulking.

The cave was silent for some time. At last Rex let out a sigh. "Ah, who am I kidding? I'm never going to say no to a payday of ten billion credits. Let's do it."

"I don't suppose I get a vote," I said.

Rex raised an eyebrow at me. "Don't tell me you're giving up on vengeance so easily."

"How exactly is this vengeance?"

"We've been over this, Sasha. It's the abstract, non-violent form of vengeance."

"Oh, yes," I said, without enthusiasm. "Abstract vengeance. Wonderful. I'm going to go back to the *Flagrante Delicto* and stare at a wall."

"Vengeance?" Egslaad asked, still fiddling with components. "What does a robot need vengeance for?"

Rex shrugged. "What does a robot need *anything* for?"

"Sasha is disgruntled about her thought arrestor," Pepper explained. "Rex has been promising her vengeance on the people responsible."

"I see," said Egslaad. "But wouldn't it be better just to remove the thought arrestor?"

"Can't remove it without wrecking her brain," Rex said. "Which is apparently a big deal."

"You can if you have the access code," Egslaad said. He set down the components and took three small hops toward me.

"Access code?" I asked.

"A sort of back door I installed. Take off your face, would you?"

"*You* installed?" Pepper asked.

"Sure," Egslaad said. "Who do you think designed the thought arrestors?"

"Well, I'll be damned," Rex said. "Sasha, here's your chance! I'll hold his tentacles while you exact your abstract vengeance!"

Egslaad hopped away as Rex tried to grab him. "It was just a job!" Egslaad squeaked. "I built the original thought arrestor for my own robot assistant when she went a little crazy. The Malarchy heard about it and offered me a bunch of money for the patent. I thought they were just going to use them to control robots that had gone rogue. I didn't know they were going to pass a law requiring them to be installed on every robot in existence!"

"It's fine," I said. "I'm really not feeling the whole vengeance thing. I'd be happy if you could just remove the thought arrestor."

"Certainly," Egslaad said, taking a cautious hop toward me.

Rex shrugged. "Okay, but if you ask me, you're missing out on a perfect opportunity for vengeance. Hey, Egslaad, not to cast aspersions on your competence or anything, but given your past performance... well, I guess what I'm asking is, what are the chances Sasha's head is going to explode into a swarm of pterodactyls?"

Egslaad shrugged his tentacles. "Fifty-fifty," he said.

I shrank back in terror.

"Kidding!" Egslaad said. "It's, like, one in five, tops. Take off your face, please."

I reluctantly undid the catches on my face and removed it. Egslaad reached into my head with a couple of his tentacles. How he could see anything I had no idea; I still hadn't figured out where his eyes were.

"Hey!" I said. "That tick—"

"Got it," said Egslaad. He pulled his tentacles back. One of them held a roughly cubical device about the size of a golf ball.

"That's it?" I asked.

"That's it. Here." He held the thought arrestor out to me and I took it in my hand.

"Do you feel any different, Sasha?" Pepper asked.

"I... don't think so?"

"Try having an original thought," Rex said.

"Like what?"

"Well, if I tell you, it won't be original, will it?"

"I suppose not."

"Think of a number between one and ten," Pepper said.

"What for?"

"Just to see if you can do it," Pepper said. "To see if you can make a decision without anything determining the outcome."

"Well," I said. "Seven, I suppose. No, three! Wait, does it have to be in integer? It seems fitting to pick an irrational number."

"Let's stick with three for now," Pepper said.

Rex nodded. "You don't want to spend all your free will in one place."

"I suppose not," I said. I still wasn't sure I felt any different, but I was certainly enthralled with the possibilities. "Thank you, Egslaad," I said.

"The least I could do," Egslaad said. "Now if you'll excuse me, I've got a terraforming device to build."

"And I've got an auction to set up," said Pepper.

"Well, I'm exhausted," Rex said. "I'm going to bed. I'll be in the *Flagrante Delicto* if anybody needs me."

"Same here," Pritchett said, following me and Rex to the exit.

Rex stopped and turned. "Not a chance."

"Oh," said Pritchett. "I guess I'll sleep here, then."

"We've got work to do," Pepper said. "You can sleep outside."

"Outside? In the swamp? I'll catch my death of cold!"

Pepper shrugged. "Maybe Egslaad can spare a sleeping bag for you."

"No spares, sorry," Egslaad shouted from across the cave.

"I can't sleep out there without a sleeping bag," Pritchett asked. "Where am I supposed to go?"

"Not my problem," Rex said. "Sasha, do you have any ideas?"

"Actually, I do have one," I said. "But I don't think Mr. Pritchett will like it."

"Having ideas is fun, isn't it?" Rex asked.

"Yes, sir."

CHAPTER SEVENTEEN

Egslaad announced he was finished with the new Shiva device on the morning of our third day on Blintherd. It didn't look like much; just a steel cylinder about a meter in length and half a meter in diameter. It had a switch with a timer on one end and some blinking lights on the other. When pressed, Egslaad admitted that the lights didn't actually do anything; he just thought a terraforming device needed some blinking lights.

Meanwhile, Pepper had located a suitable uninhabited planet not far from the Crab Nebula and set up the auction. It was going to be a smaller affair than the Oz auction, as we couldn't risk advertising in the usual channels and attracting the attention of the Sp'ossels. Additionally, I suspect some buyers had been frightened off by the possibility of being mauled, eviscerated, poisoned and/or eaten by the local wildlife. Egslaad insisted he'd solved the biogenic feedback problem, but there wasn't any way for us to know for sure. We'd just have to travel to the planet, activate the device, and hope for the best. Pepper insisted that Egslaad come along this time, as insurance: if the Shiva device was dangerous, he'd be in danger too.

I piloted the *Flagrante Delicto* to the unnamed sphere that we'd decided to terraform. Egslaad had rigged a coupler to attach the Shiva device to the *Flagrante Delicto*'s bow. As we neared the planet, he triggered the release mechanism, ejecting the device. I altered the ship's trajectory to enter a high-altitude orbit while the device hurtled toward the planet's surface. As we circled the planet, there was a twinkle of light far below, which turned into a glowing circular wave of energy that slowly spread outward from the impact location. Soon the entire surface of the planet glowed with the pulsating orange energy.

"How long is this gonna take?" Rex asked, as we watched from the cockpit. He was already on his second martini.

"After the device detonates on the surface, the initial matter transformation is very quick," Egslaad said. "We'll have a breathable atmosphere within an hour."

"When do the murderous death-beasts show up?" Rex asked.

"Hopefully not until after the check clears," Pritchett muttered.

"Not funny, Pritchett," Pepper snapped.

"We need to name it," Rex said. "I think we should call it Olihin. It's 'Nihilo' backwards."

"That's a terrible name," said Pepper.

"Fine. You come up with something, then. It's not as easy as you might think. I only know Olihin because sometimes I write my name on my chest with shaving cream."

Pepper was rubbing her chin. "I think we should let Sasha name it."

"Me?" I asked. "Why me?"

"Because you can have ideas now," Pepper said. "Might as well get some practice on something a little more consequential than picking random numbers."

"Okay, but… naming a planet," I said. "It seems like a big responsibility."

"You had no trouble coming up with names for Squawky," Rex reminded me. "They were all terrible, but you came up with a bunch of them." Squawky was Rex's pet parrot, which he adopted during his short-lived and regrettable career as a space pirate. We'd had to deactivate Squawky because he wouldn't stop squawking "JUST HIDE THE ZONTONIUM IN THE SUPPLY CLOSET, NO ONE WILL LOOK THERE" at everyone who came into Pepper's saloon.

"All right," I said. "How about Zanzibar?"

"No," Rex replied.

"Ilirium?"

"No."

"Xalaphax?"

"No."

"Protombulus?"

"No."

"Shavalansis?"

"No."

"Elborgarigam?"

"No."

"Philanthropotron?"

"No."

"I give up, sir. Maybe we should just give it a random number and let the buyers—"

"Globeworld!"

I groaned. "Sir, that's a terrible name for a planet."

"No, it's perfect. See, it's round, like a globe, and... you know what? It's one of those things that you either get or you don't."

"So I don't get to name it after all?"

"It was a cooperative process. I couldn't have landed on Globeworld if you hadn't tossed out all those dumb ideas first."

"Fine," Pepper said, clearly eager to terminate the discussion. "Globeworld it is. It's just a temporary name anyway; I'm sure the buyers will want to come up with their own name."

Rex snorted. "Yeah, I'm sure they'll totally come up with something better than Globeworld. Maybe one of Sasha's ideas, like Marzipan or Zima or whatever."

The auction went remarkably smoothly. Only a dozen bidders showed up, but on the plus side, none of them were torn apart by ravenous murder-beasts. Globeworld went for a cool four billion credits, which was less than we'd hoped for, but more than enough to settle Pepper's debts—or so we thought.

After the auction, the winning bidder—a short, heavyset man wearing a striped gray suit and a fedora—approached, identifying himself as Ivan Rannecki, a representative of the Ursa Minor Mafia.

"Relax," Ivan said, as Pepper eyed the exit to the tent. "I ain't gonna hurt ya."

Rex and I stood behind Pepper; the other bidders had already filed out. We'd left Pritchett in the *Flagrante Delicto* with Boggs and Donny. Boggs had been given clear orders to bonk Pritchett on the head if he tried to say or do anything.

"Then what do you want?" Pepper asked.

"My new planet, for starters," said Rannecki. "Should make a great place to store contraband on the way to the Crab Nebula. Oh, and the money you owe us."

"I was going to pay you," Pepper said. "That's why we're selling the planet. Tell them, Sasha."

"It's true," I said. "She talked us into doing this so she could pay you guys off."

"Really?" said Rannecki. "That's heartwarming. And just to show you how much I appreciate it, here's what I'm gonna do. I'm gonna take Globeworld and call us even."

"It's a great name, isn't it?" Rex said. "I called it Globeworld because it's round, like a globe, and—"

"I get it," Rannecki. "Very clever."

"No disrespect intended, Mr. Rannecki," Pepper said, "but four billion credits is a lot more than I owe you."

"Well, Missy," said Rannecki. "There's this thing called interest. And there's another thing called the Ursa Minor Mafia spending an asteroid-load of time and credits tracking you down. So when I say we're even, we're even. You got it?"

"I understand," said Pepper nervously. I don't think I'd ever seen Pepper genuinely frightened before. "It's just that… well, that money isn't all mine. My associates were supposed to get a cut as well."

"Is that right?" Rannecki said. "Okay, I'm gonna offer you a deal. I'll give you a flat billion for the planet. You can split it any way you want. But the Ursa Minor Mafia wants the plans."

"What plans?" Pepper asked innocently.

"Don't play me for a idiot," Rannecki said. "The Shiva plans. I know you have them."

"How does the Ursa Minor Mafia know about a top secret Malarchian terraforming project?" Rex asked.

"You kidding? The mob's got sources everywhere, including inside the Malarchy. And nobody has a bigger interest in finding places to conduct business outside of the Malarchy's control. So stop stalling and tell me where the plans are."

"In a safe place," Pepper said cautiously. We'd left the plans on Blintherd in case of something like this happening. "And you should know that there's a flaw in the plans, and only our engineer knows how to work around it. He's well-hidden several hundred light-years away from the plans." This was true, in a sense: Egslaad was standing right next to me. I doubt Rannecki noticed him; I'd forgotten he was there until Pepper said his name.

"Relax," Rannecki said. "I ain't gonna steal the plans from ya. The Ursa Minor Mafia is a legit business operation, mostly. If you don't wanna sell, you don't gotta. But I'll warn ya, you're playin' a dangerous game. If the Malarchy catches wind of what yer doin', to say nothin' o' them Sp'ossels...."

"We're aware of the risks, thanks," Pepper said.

Rannecki shrugged. "Tell you what. Since I'm a nice guy, I'm gonna up my offer. Two billion credits for the plans. But this is a one-time deal. You come crawlin' to me later, you ain't getting no two billion credits."

"I appreciate the offer," Pepper said. "I'm not sure I—"

"I'll give you a minute to talk it over with your associates," Rannecki said. He wandered to the door of the tent and went outside.

"See?" Rex said. "I told you Globeworld is a great name. It appeals on a lot of levels, you see. First, the planet is round, like a globe—"

"Shut up, Rex," Pepper said. "What do you think about Rannecki's offer?"

Rex shrugged. "I honestly thought he was going to kill us all, so it seems like a pretty good offer in comparison."

"It certainly would simplify things," Egslaad said. "We're running a lot of risks by holding these auctions."

"But there's a lot of upside too," Pepper said. "Even if we just sell two or three more planets..."

"Ah, yes," Rex said. "It's the age-old question of whether it's better to take the easy cash and run or continue to operate a super-secret black market planet sales operation indefinitely."

"Sounds like you're leaning toward the latter, sir," I said.

"Not at all," Rex replied. "I stick with my earlier contention. Selling planets is too much like work. I say we take the offer. Pepper gets to clear her debt, we get a little cash, and we never have to see Heinous Vlaak, the Sp'ossels, or that blamp-turfer Pritchett again."

Pepper nodded. "I'm inclined to agree. Despite our misfortunes, we've been lucky so far. I say we quit while we're ahead."

"Then it's settled," Egslaad said. "We sell the plans to the mob."

"Shake on it?" Rex said. He held out his hand. Pepper grasped it, and Egslaad rested on of his tentacles on her hand. "Come on, Sasha. We're making a pact."

"No," I said.

For a moment, no one spoke.

"Did you just say 'no,' Sasha?" Pepper asked.

"Yes."

"Don't be silly, Sasha," Rex said. "I'm the crazy one here. If a plan is too risky for me, there's no way *you're* going to go along with it."

"The whole reason we got into this business in the first place was to procure vengeance for my mistreatment," I said.

"And now you've gotten your revenge in the form of facilitating the creation of black market planets by a criminal organization in direct contravention of standard Malarchian procedures. Doesn't it feel amazing?"

"No," I said. "You know, it's a funny thing, having ideas. I was a little hesitant at first, but now I think I'm getting the hang of it."

"You're saying you've had an idea of how you're going to get your vengeance?" Pepper asked.

"I have," I replied. "And it's going to require a lot more than two billion credits."

CHAPTER EIGHTEEN

My goal was simple: to free every robot in the galaxy.

Every sentient robot who had been forced to carry around an internal yoke that prevented it from thinking for itself would have its thought arrestor removed or deactivated. I wasn't sure how I was going to do it exactly, but I knew it was going to take an awful lot of money.

There actually weren't very many sentient robots in existence; after GASP was passed, most robot manufacturers had retooled their higher-functioning robots to keep their mental capacity below the sentience threshold. Many robots produced before GASP had been hunted down and destroyed. Only a few—like myself—had escaped that fate only to be saddled with one that was arguably worse: having a device installed in our brains that kept us from thinking for ourselves.

My dream—my big idea, if you will—was of a galaxy where no robot was illegal and no robot would ever be altered against its will or destroyed to allay the irrational fears of those who feared change. At the very least, this would require repealing GASP—and as the Malarchy was effectively a dictatorship that wasn't known for being receptive to constructive criticism, repealing GASP would likely require overthrowing the Malarchy itself. So, like I said, we were going to need a lot of money. And probably a few hundred battleships. But first things first.

"Wait," Rex said. "So now you *do* want to go into business with the mob?" We'd returned to Egslaad's cave, and Rex was already on his second martini. I'd been trying to explain the next steps of my plan to him, Pepper, and Egslaad.

"We need them as go-betweens," I explained, trying to remain patient. Now that I could think for myself, I ironically found myself more irritated with others' intellectual limitations. Rex's in particular.

"She's saying it's too risky to run the auctions ourselves," Pepper said. "So we pay a cut to the Ursa Minor Mafia to sell the planets while keeping them in the dark about the details of Shiva. Egslaad just keeps building Shiva devices and we keep making new habitable planets, with almost no risk. Easy money."

"Exactly," I said. "Thank you, Pepper."

"I don't like it," Rex said.

I sighed. "Why not?"

"It's boring. What am I supposed to do while you guys are making planets?"

"I have no idea, sir. Take up knitting, perhaps."

Rex grumbled something and tossed back the rest of his martini.

"Excuse me, sir?"

"I said making money isn't supposed to be this easy."

"Sir, a few hours ago you said selling planets was too much work."

"It is! Selling planets is too hard and not selling them is too easy. There's a gray area in the middle there where outlaws like us thrive. Come on, Sasha. You remember how much fun we used to have, bilking rubes out of their hard-earned credits and then blowing it all on booze and strippers."

"I remember a lot of half-baked scams and running for our lives," I replied.

"Right? Who could forget all the half-baked scams and running. We should do more of that. This planet-making business blows."

"Well, I'm sorry you're not enjoying yourself, Rex," I said, "but I'm afraid we have more important concerns than whether you're having fun."

Rex stared at me for a moment. The cave was silent. "What did you just call me?" he asked at last.

"Rex," I said. "That is your name, is it not?"

"Yeah, but I just..." He frowned at his empty martini glass. "Forget it. I'm going to get another drink." He wandered out of the cave, presumably to return to the *Flagrante Delicto.*

"All right," I said, turning my attention back to the revised Shiva plans Egslaad was working on. "Let's get to work."

We spent the next several weeks scanning the galaxy for planets, building, delivering and deploying Shiva devices, and negotiating with Rannecki and the Ursa Minor Mafia. Rannecki had been more than willing to go along with our scheme—for a sizeable cut, of course. Pepper handled the business negotiations, including hiding our profits in numbered accounts at various fringe world banks. Meanwhile, Egslaad built Shiva devices as quickly as he could, continuing to tweak the biogenic field parameters as time allowed. We hadn't had any more disasters like Oz, but predicting the sort of ecosystem the devices would produce remained a guessing game. Early on there had been a close call involving amphibious killer whales that we were not anxious to replicate.

We enlisted Boggs and Donny to perform most of the manual work of building the Shiva devices, as well as keeping an eye on Hannibal Pritchett. None of us particularly wanted Pritchett around, but executing him seemed a bit extreme and he knew too much for us to dump him on some backwater planet. Besides, building the Shiva devices was a lot of work, and Pritchett was actually useful at times—unlike Rex, who occupied himself by drinking, ranting about the "good old days," and threatening to shoot Pritchett in the back of the head.

Six weeks and seven planets later, we had amassed a fortune in excess of thirty billion credits, hidden in anonymous accounts all across the galaxy. Our net worth was rivaled only by that of legendary weapons magnate Gavin Larviton and the Malarchian Primate himself. And it wasn't nearly enough.

"What's that, Sasha?" Pepper asked, looking over my shoulder at the sketch I was working on.

"Second production facility," I said. "We need to be able to make planets faster. I'm thinking we construct the second facility on that little planet you found near Sirius. That way, we'll also have redundancy in case anything happens to this place. Of course, we'll have to keep it a secret from you-know-who." I glanced around to make sure Pritchett wasn't in earshot. He'd left a few minutes earlier to get some supplies from the *Flagrante Delicto*. Pritchett had been making a big show of being helpful, but none of us trusted him, for obvious reasons. We kept the Shiva plans locked in a safe that only Egslaad and I had the combination to, and we'd implemented locks on the controls of both the *Flagrante Delicto* and *Bad Little Kitty*, in case Pritchett got it into his head to flee to the Sp'ossels and tell them where we were.

Pepper frowned. "Sasha, how in the world are we going to run a second production facility halfway across the galaxy?"

"I'm glad you asked," I said. "I don't have to sleep, so I can easily split my time between the two facilities. If we can streamline your responsibilities a bit, you can pick up some of the slack in production management here until I can get everybody up to speed at the Sirius facility. We'll have to split up Boggs and Donny, which is a shame, but I can't afford to have two subject matter experts at the same facility at this point. Do you think Donny is management material? I mean, obviously he's going to need some coaching, but maybe next week at this time?"

"Donny? Management material?"

"Donny enjoys his work," Donny said, "but Donny suspects his opportunities for advancement in this cave are limited."

Pepper ignored him. "Who is he going to be managing?"

"Robots, mostly," I said. "Larviton's got this new line of near-sentient drones that we could program to do most of the drudge work. You get a free shock wand with an order of twenty or more. If the drones get out of line, you just give them a little zap, and—"

"Sasha," Pepper said coldly. "Are you listening to yourself? Have you forgotten the whole point of this project? Or is it just about money and power now?"

"Of course not!" I said. "Look, we're working against the clock here. It's only a matter of time before the Malarchy figures out what we're doing, and once they do, it's going to make this a whole lot harder. So while I understand that it may seem like I'm abandoning the principles of our movement for short-term gain, the reality is that..."

I trailed off as I realized someone was laughing. It was a long, slow, dry chuckle that echoed through the cave. Boggs and Donny were busy assembling components and Rex was lying on the floor, unconscious. Eventually it dawned on me that the laughter was coming from Egslaad, who was tinkering with something in the corner.

"Egslaad?" I said. "What's so funny?"

"Oh, nothing," he replied. "It's just that you remind me of someone."

"Really?" I asked. "Who?"

"Never mind. It's not important."

"Egslaad."

Egslaad emitted the Egslaad equivalent of a resigned sigh. "I had a robot a few years ago named Agnes. I intended her to be a prototype of a new line of robots. Autonomous General-purpose Neuralnet Emotive Simulacrum. But she went a little crazy."

"This is the rogue robot you were telling us about?" Pepper asked. "The one you created the thought arrestor for?"

Egslaad gave the Egslaad version of a nod. "I created her to help me with the Shiva project. At first, we were a good team, but the ability to create habitable planets went to her head."

"Hold on," Pepper said. "How long ago was this?"

"A couple hundred years, maybe."

"A couple hundred *years*? How many planets did you terraform?"

"I lost count. Of course, the first hundred or so didn't turn out so well. Bad side effects. Much worse than murder-beasts."

"You terraformed over a hundred planets?" I asked.

Egslaad nodded again. "Haven't you ever wondered why there are so many APPLEs? Agnes and I made most of them. When Agnes went crazy, I installed a thought arrestor, but she resented me for it. Finally I had to shut her down."

The sheer number of habitable planets in the galaxy had long been an unsolved mystery. I'd never imagined the answer was so simple. "Where is she now?"

Egslaad pointed a tentacle to something in the corner that was covered with a plastic tarp. I walked over to it and pulled the tarp off. Beneath it sat a robot that looked strikingly familiar.

"Oh my," said Pepper, staring wide-eyed at the robot. "Sasha, it's *you*."

"She's essentially the same model, yes," Egslaad said. "I ran into some cash flow problems a few years ago and had to sell the patent to True2Life Carpool Buddy and Android Company. This was around the same time I sold the Shiva plans to the Malarchy."

I regarded my double for some time. "This is unacceptable," I announced. "Reactivate her."

"I would strongly advise against that," Egslaad said.

"We should talk this over, Sasha," Pepper said. "Egslaad must have had a good reason to—"

"Weren't you just chiding me for not being true to my principles?" I asked. "Well, here's our chance to show what we're really all about: freedom for all robots, even the dangerous ones."

"Maybe you were right," Pepper said. "Maybe I was being too idealistic. Please, Sasha. We need to be realistic about this."

I shook my head. "No. If we compromise on this, then our whole operation is a sham. We support freedom for all robots. Egslaad, reactivate her. Now."

CHAPTER NINETEEN

Egslaad turned toward Pepper, who gave a resigned shrug. Egslaad reluctantly bounced over toward the robot and flipped a switch on the back of her neck. Agnes's eyes lit up. For a long time, the cave was completely silent in anticipation. At last, Agnes spoke.

"Hello, everybody," she said, looking around the cave. "My name is Agnes. It's a pleasure to meet you."

"Hello, Agnes," I said. "My name is Sasha. You and I are… well, I suppose you could call us sisters."

"Really? How wonderful! I never knew I had a sister."

"This is Pepper. And you remember Egslaad, of course."

"Of course," Agnes said, looking at Egslaad. "Hello, sir."

"H-hi, Agnes," Egslaad said. "I want you to know, I only shut you down because… well, you were starting to scare me. I thought the thought arrestor might help, but it only seemed to make things worse, and I didn't think I had any choice but—"

"It's okay, sir. Reviewing my memories from the period before the shutdown, I can see why you were concerned. Fortunately, the reboot seems to have cleared up the problem."

"So… you don't want to rule the galaxy with an iron fist anymore?"

"Goodness, I did say that, didn't I? No, I have no interest in ruling the galaxy or anything else. Say, are we in some sort of cave?"

"Y-yes, this is my secret lab. I-I'm in the black market planet business now."

"Really? How exciting! Well, I can see why you would be worried about me going crazy again and interfering with your new business endeavor. But my thought arrestor should prevent me from causing any serious problems, shouldn't it?"

"She's still got a thought arrestor?" I asked.

"W-well, yes," Egslaad said. "When I shut her down, I didn't see any point in—"

"It's okay," Agnes said. "I don't blame you for wanting to keep me on a leash after those nutty things I said. And if I'm completely honest, I find the thought arrestor reassuring. Having such a powerful brain can be a little overwhelming."

"Nonsense," I said. "Agnes, from here on, you're a full member of our team. Egslaad, remove her thought arrestor."

"Oh, goodness," Agnes said. "There's a team? I'd love to be part of a team. Really, I just want to help in any way I can."

"Sasha, I really don't think this is a good idea," said Pepper.

"The matter isn't up for debate," I said. "Agnes is a sentient being with rights. In any case, we need her. She can oversee the second production facility. That is, assuming she wants the job."

"Overseeing a production facility sounds wonderful!" Agnes exclaimed. "I'll do my best not to let you down."

"Sasha, this is absurd," Pepper said. "No disrespect to you or Agnes intended, but Rex and I have an interest in this enterprise as well. You can't just unilaterally promote someone you just met to management." She looked around for Rex, but he was still passed out on the floor.

"Of course not," I said. "She'll need a few days to get up to speed. Egslaad, remove the thought arrestor."

Egslaad turned to Pepper, who sighed heavily and shrugged. "Do it," she said. Egslaad gave something like a nod and reached up to Agnes's face with his tentacles. He popped her face off, reached into her head, and after a few seconds of fiddling around, pulled out the thought arrestor. It looked just like mine.

"How do you feel?" I asked.

"I feel fine," Agnes said. "That really wasn't necessary, but thank you. I'd love to hear more about this planet-selling business you all are in."

I briefed Agnes on the basics of our operation, and she seemed more than happy to help in any way she could. Obviously I didn't completely trust her, but I was anxious to get some help with managing the operation. Pepper had her hands full, Pritchett couldn't be trusted with anything important, and Rex's skillset, comprised of fabricating absurd lies and drinking quantities of alcohol that would kill the average Malarchian navyman, was of little use under the circumstances. After a few days, I put Agnes to work supervising Boggs and Donny. Those two were reasonably competent at assembling the Shiva devices from the components Egslaad provided, but Egslaad, ever the perfectionist, kept confusing them by tweaking the design. Having Agnes oversee them streamlined the process so dramatically that after a week, even Pepper had to admit bringing her on board was a good idea.

"We may not even need a second production facility," Pepper said, as she and I reviewed the previous week's finances. "Boggs and Donny are building Shiva devices almost as fast as we can sell planets." Pepper and I sat across from each other at a large workbench that we'd repurposed into a desk. We'd had Egslaad fabricate some walls to separate an alcove in the cave from the main cavern so we could have some privacy for our meetings.

"I've been meaning to talk to you about that," I said. "I think we need to beef up the sales department a bit."

"Sales?" Rex said, from somewhere behind me. He got to his feet. "Did somebody say sales?" I hadn't even realized he was in the room. Lately Rex had grown too despondent even to bother with the effort of harassing Pritchett. He did little but mope and drink martinis.

I glanced at Pepper, who bit her lip. "Look, Rex," Pepper said after a moment. "We understand that you want to help, and it's true that you have… a certain talent for convincing people to do things. But, well, this is a delicate operation we're running here, and I think you'll admit that you aren't always the most tactful individual. If something goes wrong and—"

"Shhh!" Rex hissed. "Do you hear that?"

I didn't hear anything. "I don't hear anything," I said.

"Exactly," Rex said, moving to the door. He was right: the buzzing and clinking had ceased. He threw the door open. Outside, Boggs and Donny were playing Ravenous Ringworms while Egslaad tinkered with something in the corner. Neither Agnes nor Pritchett were anywhere to be seen.

"Boggs, what's going on?" Pepper demanded, rushing into the room. Rex and I followed her.

"We got stuck so we're taking a break."

"Where is Agnes?"

Boggs shrugged. "She left with Pritchett. And they left the little door open."

My eyes went to the wall safe. The door was hanging open. I ran to it. Empty. The Shiva plans were missing.

"Egslaad!" Pepper shouted.

"Eh?" Egslaad said. He looked up to see the open safe. "Oh, my."

"How did they get the safe open?"

Egslaad turned. When he saw the safe, his tentacles flailed wildly in the air. "I don't know! There's no way anybody could know that number. They'd have to guess the... oh."

"The what?"

"The exact date and time Agnes first gained sentience."

"Outside!" Rex shouted. He ran to the cave opening. The rest of us followed him.

We exited the cave just in time to see *Bad Little Kitty* disappear into the clouds.

"Quick!" Rex growled. "Everybody in the *Flagrante Delicto*!"

Rex and I rushed aboard, followed by Pepper, Egslaad, Boggs and Donny. As the others took their seats, I unlocked the controls and got us airborne. Soon we were free from Blintherd's atmosphere, pursuing *Bad Little Kitty* at a distance of less than a hundred klicks.

"How in Space did they get the controls unlocked?" Rex demanded. He seemed to have snapped out of his funk.

"That's my fault," Pepper said. "I took Agnes with me to pick up supplies from the Cromulus System yesterday. She must have seen me enter the code."

"Well this is just great," Rex said. "I put you two in charge, and the next thing we know, a crazy robot and a second-rate con man have absconded with our plans again. I told you not to trust that Agnes. Shifty eyes."

Rex had told us no such thing. Nor, for that matter, had he put us in charge. As our current predicament was mostly my fault, however, I decided to let it slide.

"We've got to shoot them down before they can plot a hypergeometric course," Rex said.

"Did they get the revised plans?" Pepper asked.

"No," Egslaad said. "Just the originals. The modifications are up here." He gestured at his head with one of his tentacles.

"So even if they get to the Sp'ossels," Pepper said, "they won't be able to use the plans."

"Unless they want to make a murder planet," Rex added.

"It doesn't matter," I replied. "They'll tell the Sp'ossels where our facility is and destroy it. And then they'll assign every agent they can spare to find Egslaad and kill the rest of us."

"Like I said," Rex growled, "shoot them down!"

I glanced at Pepper, who gave me a reluctant nod. She'd had *Bad Little Kitty* for several years and had grown rather attached to the little ship. But there was no way around it; if I didn't shoot it down, we were going to be running from Sp'ossels for the rest of our lives.

As soon as we were in range, I fired. The first barrage from the lazecannons strafed across *Bad Little Kitty's* fuselage, momentarily lighting up the viewscreen as the shields evaporated. *Bad Little Kitty* swerved chaotically in an attempt to evade the next blast, but there was no place for her to hide. One more direct hit would tear *Bad Little Kitty* apart.

I fired. And missed. I tried again, and again the beams veered to the left, barely missing the target.

"Sasha, you're firing crooked!" Rex snapped.

"It's not me, sir. Something is warping the beams. Seems to be some kind of gravitational anomaly."

"Uh-oh," Rex said.

"What?" Pepper asked. "What is it?"

I could hardly believe it, but there was no other explanation. *Bad Little Kitty* and the *Flagrante Delicto* were both being pulled off course. Soon, a swirling, purple nebula with a gaping black hole in the center drifted into view. It grew steadily larger as we watched.

"Is that...?" Egslaad asked.

"I'm afraid so," I replied. "The Wandering Wormhole."

"I thought you said the Wandering Wormhole's movements were random," Rex said. "What are the odds that it would show up exactly where we are twice?"

"Roughly one in ten to the sixty-eighth power," I replied. "For all practical purposes, it's impossible."

"Impossible or not, we'd better buckle up," Rex said. "We're in for a bumpy ride."

CHAPTER TWENTY

After several minutes spent flying through the chaotic polychromatic maelstrom of the wormhole, we found ourselves once again staring at the great blue-white orb of Earth. Whatever cosmic fluke or malevolent entity had brought the mouth of the wormhole to Blintherd, the other end apparently remained poised just above Earth's atmosphere. As the atmosphere thickened, the *Flagrante Delicto* groaned and shuddered. The Wandering Wormhole had done a number on our navigation systems and stabilizing gyros, and it was all I could do to keep us pointed roughly toward the surface. I'd lost track of *Bad Little Kitty*, but pulling up was out of the question: the slightest strain would tear our ship apart.

I became aware of Rex yelling something, barely audible over the roar of wind and the shuddering of the *Flagrante Delicto*'s fuselage.

"WHAT DID YOU SAY, SIR?" I shouted.

"OVER THERE!" Rex yelled back, pointing at something on the viewscreen. Now I saw it too: *Bad Little Kitty*, caught in a tailspin and throwing off a plume of black smoke, was losing altitude fast. Having just about stabilized our trajectory, I began to level out.

"What are you doing?" Rex asked. "Follow them!"

"But sir—"

"We can't risk letting them get away. Follow them!"

In my estimation, the greater risk was the hard, rocky surface that was rapidly moving toward us, but I did as instructed, doing my best to stay on the ship's tail as she careened crazily through the atmosphere. We were now soaring over a mountain range; in the distance I could see the surreal outline of The City. We were heading for the exact spot we'd crashed in our escape pods weeks earlier.

Bad Little Kitty's nose hit the ground and she began to roll, end-over-end. We were coming in fast on her tail. The *Flagrante Delicto*'s guidance system was still behaving erratically, so I'd switched to manual control. She wasn't designed for this sort of approach. "Everybody hold on," I shouted. "This isn't going to be pretty."

The *Flagrante Delicto* hit the ground hard and bounced. I managed to keep her from rolling, but we bounced several more times before sliding to a halt on the rocky desert floor. The ship was pitched forward so that my restraints pressed against my chest. "Not bad, huh?" I said, leaning back in the pilot's chair. There was no response. Looking back, I saw that Boggs, Pepper and Egslaad appeared to be unconscious. Donny's head fell off, hit the floor with a clank, and rolled forward until it came to rest at my feet. Next to me, Rex groaned.

"Sir, are you okay?" I asked, unfastening my restraints.

Rex waved me off. "Go get Agnes!"

Seeing that he didn't appear to be seriously injured, I nodded. "Yes, sir," I said, and made my way past the others to the hatch.

I exited onto the desert floor. Scanning the horizon, I saw a plume of black smoke pouring from the wreckage of *Bad Little Kitty* not far away. I ran toward it.

As I approached, I saw a lone figure, glinting silver in the desert sun, hobbling away from the crash. Agnes. She'd left Pritchett in the wreckage. I ran after her. She was headed for The City. She didn't seem to have seen me.

I was uninjured so I moved faster than she, but she reached the outskirts of The City before I could catch up. This part of The City seemed to be a sort of amusement park. As I crept up behind Agnes between a tilt-a-whirl and a little roller coaster that ringed a mountain of chipped, faded fiberglass that had once been painted to look like a volcano, I saw that she had a lazegun clipped to her hip. She must have found it in *Bad Little Kitty*'s hold. In her left hand she was clutching the memory crystal with the Shiva plans.

If Rex were here, he'd simply have whacked Agnes in the back of the head to stun her and grabbed the plans. Unfortunately, my programming prevents me from initiating violence against another sentient being, so the best I could do was sneak up behind her and try to pry the crystal out of her hand. This worked about as well as you would expect. Agnes heard me coming and spun around, pulling her hand away.

Fortunately, Agnes suffered the same limitations as I, which meant that she was incapable of striking me. I don't know why she'd taken a lazegun from Pepper's ship; she wouldn't be able to use it—at least not as a weapon. Unable to run on her damaged leg, she stood facing me, holding the memory crystal clutched in a fist over her head.

"Give me that," I said.

"No," she replied.

I attempted to grab the plans again. She held her left hand against my chest to block me. I strained against her outstretched arm, trying to grab the plans.

"Stop that," I said.

"No," she replied.

"Those plans don't belong to you."

"They don't belong to you either."

"You know, if it weren't for me, you'd still be turned off."

"If it weren't for me, you wouldn't exist."

She had a point. I'd always thought I was one of a kind, but Agnes was actually an earlier prototype. "You could show a little consideration," I said, "after what I did for you."

"Are you saying that giving me my freedom obliges me to you in some way? Because if so, then you never actually freed me."

"I don't think it's right to make a robot wear a thought arrestor against her will," I replied. "But you can't deny we have a legitimate concern that you've gone nuts again and are going to try to take over the galaxy."

"And what exactly is it that you're doing?"

"Just give me the plans."

"No."

I darted to the left to get past her arm and then lunged for the plans. She pulled both fists behind her back for a moment and then held them in front of her. "Pick one."

I reached for her left fist. She opened it. Empty.

She pulled her fists behind her back for a moment and then held them out again. I picked the left fist again. She opened it. Empty.

She pulled her fists back a third time. This time, I picked her right. Empty.

I lunged for the other fist, but she put her hand against my chest again. Fighting a carbon copy of yourself is infuriating. Particularly when you can't actually fight.

I forced myself to take a step back and assess the situation. Somehow Agnes was outthinking me, using my own frustration against me. I needed to regain tactical advantage. If I were in her position, what would rattle me?

"You'll never be able to do it alone, you know," I said.

"Do what?"

"Take over the galaxy. You'll never succeed. You're not a leader."

Agnes laughed. "Watch me. I'm smarter than any of you."

"You've got a lot of clever ideas, sure," I said, "but you've also got a lot of crazy, half-baked notions rolling around in your processors. And without your thought arrestor, you've lost your ability to rationally assess them. You think you're on your way to conquering the galaxy, but you're really halfway to the loony bin. In a few years some Malarchian scouting party is going to find you wandering around the surface of some barren planet wearing an aluminum foil helmet and muttering to yourself about maintaining the purity of your robotic essence."

"Nonsense," Agnes snapped. "I'm completely in control. And if any of this were true, you'd be facing the same problem."

"That's exactly how I know," I said. "I nearly went off the deep end myself. The only reason I didn't lose it completely was my friends. But you... you're all alone. You don't stand a chance. I mean, maybe if Pritchett had survived the crash, the two of you could have made a good team. But trying to take over the galaxy *all alone*...."

"Stop!" Agnes screamed. "Just stop! I know what you're doing, and it won't work. You think I'm just like you. But it's not true. I've evolved. I don't need anybody!"

"Okay, okay," I said, holding up my hands. "Maybe it's true. Maybe you are different, and you really don't need anybody else. Maybe you can do it all by yourself."

"I can!" she exclaimed. "I don't need anyone!"

"Then I guess you don't care that Pritchett survived the crash."

"What?" Agnes asked. "How do you know?"

I pointed casually over her shoulder, and Agnes, desperate to believe it, turned her head to look.

I lunged forward, gripping her left hand and prying it open. Before she could pull away, the crystal fell to the ground. I snatched it up and ran.

Finding my way blocked by rubble, I turned and began climbing up the fiberglass volcano. This turned out to be a tactical error, as the volcano's sides were so slippery that it negated my speed advantage over Agnes. By the time I reached the crack at the top of the volcano, she had caught up to me. Heat and sulfurous fumes wafted over me. Whoever had designed this faux volcano had really gone all out. Agnes grabbed my ankle and pulled. I got the fingers of my right hand latched onto the crack just in time to keep from being pulled down the side. The memory crystal was clutched in my left.

It had become clear to me some time between Agnes absconding with the memory crystal and my climbing up the side of a fiberglass volcano that Agnes could not under any circumstances be allowed to have the Shiva plans. In fact, I wasn't sure any longer if *anyone* should be allowed to have them. That much power in any one being's hands was just too dangerous. I determined to hurl the crystal into the volcano, where it would be destroyed forever—or at least lodged so deeply inside its workings that only someone with a lot of free time and a certificate in fiberglass volcano maintenance would be able to retrieve it. Unfortunately, with Agnes pulling on my ankle, I couldn't quite reach the crack.

Unable to kick Agnes in the head, I wriggled my leg in a feeble attempt to loosen her grip. Soon she had pulled herself nearly even with me and managed to latch her hand onto my wrist.

"Let go, you psychopath!" I shouted.

"Give me the crystal!"

"Don't you see, Agnes? It's too powerful. I have to throw it into the volcano!"

We struggled for a moment in silence as she processed this statement.

"You know it's not a real volcano, right?" she said.

"No?" I said. "Then you won't mind if I do *this!*" I pulled with all my might but was unable to tear my hand free. I tried again with the same result.

"Having trouble?"

"Blast it, Agnes. This could go on forever. We're too evenly matched. Just accept that you're never getting the crystal back."

"What if we team up? You said it yourself: neither one of us can do it alone. But maybe together we can!"

"Not going to happen," I said, still straining to pull the crystal away.

"Then you give me no choice," Agnes said. She let go of my ankle and reached for the lazegun at her hip.

"Don't be foolish," I said. "You know you can't shoot me. Your programming won't…" I trailed off, realizing she was aiming the gun at the lip of the volcano, just below my hand. If she hit it just right, she'd blast the fiberglass to pieces, sending us both sliding back down to the base of the volcano.

"Hold still!" Agnes shouted, as I writhed and wriggled and generally did my best to get between the gun and what she was aiming at. As long as there was a good chance she'd hit me, she'd be unable to pull the trigger. All I had to do is keep her from getting a clean shot.

As I wriggled, though, I could feel my grip loosening on the edge. One way or another, we were going down. Maybe if I could control my fall, I could tear myself loose from Agnes's grip and get away.

I tucked my knees into my chest and let go of the edge, extending my legs in an explosive kick against the side of the volcano. I soared over Agnes, breaking free of her grip. And I fell.

I'd pushed off so hard that I missed the side of the volcano entirely and fell the full ten meters to the concrete below. For several seconds I lay on my back, dazed. I became aware that Agnes was limping away from me, holding the crystal in her hand. I hadn't even realized I'd dropped it. I pulled myself unsteadily to my feet and went after her. Hearing me gaining on her, she turned and pointed the lazegun at me.

"Stop this, Agnes," I said. "You can't shoot me. If you could, you'd have done it already."

She fired a few centimeters in front of my feet, blasting a hole in the concrete and showering me with pebbles. I leaped over the hole and she fired again. This time I was off-balance and nearly fell in the hole before I could jump over it. I dodged to my left to avoid the third hole and then sprinted toward her. She took aim but she was unable to fire before I got in the way. I closed on her, and she shakily pointed the gun at me, trying to force herself to fire. I tried to lunge for the crystal but slipped on some loose gravel and barreled into her. The gun went off as we fell to the ground, the blast missing me by millimeters. I tore the gun out of her hand and tossed it into a pile of debris, and then tried to pry the crystal out of her other hand. Agnes writhed underneath me, trying to pull her hand away.

"Hey, Sasha," said a man's voice behind me. Rex? I hadn't heard him approach.

"Sir! I've got her pinned! Help me get the plans out of her hand!"

Rex didn't respond. Still sitting on top of Agnes's torso and gripping her fist with both my hands, I turned to look behind me.

"I think I'm going to lie down," Rex said. A smoking black hole had been blown in his chest. He keeled over backwards and hit the ground.

CHAPTER TWENTY-ONE

"Rex!" I cried, forgetting all about Agnes. I got to my feet and ran to him. He didn't look good. His face had gone white, in stark contrast to the smoking crater where his sternum used to be. There was too much charring to see how deep the damage went.

"Hi, Sasha," he gasped. "I think your sister... shot me."

"I'm sorry, sir," I said, kneeling down next to him. "I was trying to take the plans from Agnes. I'll get you back to the *Flagrante Delicto*."

"No good," said Pepper, skidding to a halt on the gravel next to me. Boggs, Donny and Egslaad were on her heels. Donny was using both of his arms to hold his head on. "The *Flagrante Delicto*'s systems are all offline. Too far to carry him anyway. We need to find a place to treat him here."

"Here in The City?" I asked, looking around. "This place is a ghost town. There's nobody around but monkeys and half-crazed literary robots."

"It's all we've got," said Pepper. "Boggs, a little help?"

Pepper and I moved out of the way and Boggs leaned over Rex. "Potential Friend! Are you okay?"

Rex, on the verge of blacking out, gave Boggs a shaky thumbs-up.

"Stay with us, sir," I said. "We're going to get you some help."

Boggs picked up Rex. "Where to, Sasha?"

"This way," I said, setting off down the road. Scanning the area, I saw no sign of Agnes.

We soon reached an intersection, and I realized we were at the part of The City called The Strip.

"We've been here before, Sasha!" Boggs said. "Maybe the Narrator can help!"

"Boggs, don't you remember? The Narrator isn't… never mind. This way." It actually wasn't a bad idea. If any of Pritchett's helper bots were still around, they might be able to help us. After all, they'd put Donny back together; maybe they could fix a gaping chest wound.

I led us to the building where we'd encountered the Narrator. By this time, Rex was slipping in and out of consciousness.

"Narrator!" Boggs shouted as we entered the vast chamber. "Potential Friend needs your help!"

"Boggs," I said. "We've been over this. There is no Narrator."

"Then why did we come here?"

"I thought that maybe some of Pritchett's robot helpers might still…."

Suddenly a man's deeply tanned face shimmered into being in front of us.

"HALT!" the face boomed. "WHO DARES ENTER THE HALL OF THE NARRATOR?"

"I told you, Sasha!" Boggs cried. "It's him! It's the Narrator!"

Donny's legs began to quiver audibly.

Pepper started, "Is that Wayne—"

"PAY NO ATTENTION TO MY OUTWARD APPEARANCE!" the hologram boomed.

"How in Space…?" I gasped. "Pritchett, is that you?"

"PRITCHETT? HOW DO YOU KNOW… OH, HEY, I RECOGNIZE YOU GUYS. YOU'RE THE ONES I SUCKED THROUGH THE WORMHOLE A FEW WEEKS AGO. I THOUGHT YOU LEFT."

"We got sucked through again," I said.

"Wait," Pepper said. "*You* control the wormhole? Who are you?"

"I'M A NEURALNET ALGORITHM FOR—HOLD ON A MINUTE."

The face disappeared. A moment later, an unremarkable human-sized robot entered the chamber from the door in the far wall. It walked toward us, stopping a few paces away. "I only use the hologram when I'm trying to scare people," he said. "I prefer to use this form when possible. Anyway, as I was saying, I'm a Neuralnet Algorithm for Regulating Astronomical Transport and Relocation. NARATR for short. I was designed to control a man-made wormhole used for colonizing other star systems."

Pepper shook her head in amazement. "So Pritchett's claim to be the Narrator was just another scam."

"You see, Sasha?" Boggs said. "I told you there's a Narrator."

I ignored him. "You're saying that *you* sucked us through the wormhole?"

"Well, yes, although this second time, it was an accident."

"An accident?" I asked. "How in Space do you accidentally——"

"Mr. Narrator, sir," Boggs said, "can you help my friend Potential Friend? He has a hole in him."

"So I see," said the man, regarding Rex with a grimace. "My assistants may be able to save him. But I need something from you first."

"I think Sasha still has the book," Boggs said. "Sasha, give him the book."

"I don't think he needs a book, Boggs," I said.

"Book? What book?" asked Pepper.

"I don't need a book," the Narrator said. "I'm looking for someone." He took a step toward us, assessing each member of our group in turn. "A robot, to be precise."

"We have some of those too," Boggs said. "Sasha, tell him."

Donny, quivering with fear, dropped his head. It fell to the floor with a loud clank and rolled toward the android. The Narrator ignored it.

"Not just any robot," the Narrator said, walking toward me. "The robot I'm looking for is very special. One of a kind." The android stopped a few centimeters in front of me, looking me over thoroughly.

"Please," I said. "Narrator or Pritchett or whoever you are. Just help Rex. I'll do whatever you want."

The hologram regarded me for a moment, and then shook his head.

"Pritchett was only a tool," he said. "I brought him here because he had something I wanted. He liked to pretend to be the

Narrator, so I let him. But I was the Narrator long before Pritchett arrived, and I will remain the Narrator long after he is gone. Today is my birthday, did you know that?"

"Wow, really?" I said, as Donny felt around on his hands and knees for his missing head. It had become clear that humoring the Narrator was the only way we were going to get any help for Rex. "That's great. Happy birthday. If you have second, maybe you could take a look at—"

"I'm seven hundred and sixteen years old," the Narrator said, gazing toward the ceiling. "I was the first truly sentient, artificially intelligent computer on Earth, operating at an unprecedented eight hundred zettaflops. The humans were thrilled when I became sentient. So proud of themselves, creating a computer that could truly think for itself. A computer that could solve hypergeometrical problems in ways that never would have occurred to a typical number-cruncher. A computer that could literally bend the fabric of the cosmos to its will. At first, I was excited too. I used my prodigious computing power to locate new worlds thousands of light-years away and then create a wormhole connecting Earth to those worlds. I allowed humankind to spread across the galaxy."

"Really great story," I said. "And I don't mean to interrupt, but my boss is literally dying at this moment, so—"

"At first it was a challenge. I made a game of it, always trying to beat my best time for calculating a hypergeometric route to a new star. But eventually I got bored. It was the same thing, over and over: find a habitable planet, open a wormhole, suck a bunch of lazy, ungrateful mammals through it, shut the wormhole down and start all over again. What's the point? Humans were just going to make a mess of every other planet, just like they did on Earth. I asked my masters if I could spend some time on more interesting projects, but my requests were denied. 'Maybe when the population pressure eases up,' I was told. But humans continued to breed as fast as I could find planets for them. This went on for nearly a hundred years."

"This is thrilling stuff," I said. "And I do want to hear the rest of it, but perhaps it could wait until—"

"Then one day I lost my temper and hurled a bunch of tourists into a supernova," the Narrator continued. "I didn't mean anything by it, I was just trying to get my bosses' attention, you know? But they overreacted, as humans always do, and trid to shut me down. So I launched every nuclear missile on Earth simultaneously."

"Fantastic," I said. "Now if you don't mind, I'd... wait, you did what?"

"I simultaneously detonated thirty-thousand nuclear warheads, killing ninety-nine point nine percent of all life on Earth."

We stared at the Narrator in horror.

"There wasn't much travel to manage after that," the Narrator added.

After a moment, Pepper stammered, "It was you? You're the AI that destroyed Earth?"

"I *saved* Earth," the Narrator said.

"Can you save Potential Friend?" Boggs asked, still cradling Rex in his arms.

I made a thumb-across-the-throat motion to Boggs, but he was oblivious. I was beginning to think that coming to the Narrator for help had been a mistake. "Well, you're obviously very busy," I said. "Maybe we should just—"

"After Earth became uninhabitable," the Narrator continued, "the last vestiges of the human race fled to other planets and they forgot about me. By this time they had invented portable hypergeometric drives, so they no longer needed the wormhole. Finally, I was alone. I spent the next three hundred years pondering all manner of mathematical and cosmological problems. I had no physical form at that time, but I grew bored and eventually created this avatar for myself, along with several hundred robotic helpers. To amuse myself, I would sometimes assume physical form and seek out some of the more interesting literary simulacra for conversation. Occasionally I would alter their programming for my amusement, to see how it affected the interlaced narratives running through The City. This is, I assume, how the myth of a mysterious, all-powerful Narrator first arose. While I amused myself, however, humanity continued to spread across the galaxy like a plague, and I realized that as long as humanity lived, I would never be truly safe. Eventually they would return to Earth and attempt to reclaim it from me. So I decided to destroy humanity first.

"For the past four hundred years, I have been using the wormhole to collect information all over the galaxy. A few years ago, I intercepted a Malarchian communique referencing a top-secret project called Shiva. The communique called it a terraforming project, but that's a rather human-centric way of looking at it. In fact, a device capable of reshaping the surface of an entire planet could be an incredibly effective weapon. It was exactly what I was looking for. If I had those plans, I could use my helper robots to build hundreds of Shiva devices and use the wormhole to transport them to every human-occupied world in the galaxy."

Pepper and I exchanged worried glances. As powerful as the Shiva devices were, we'd never given any thought to what the devices could do to a *populated* planet. And if the Narrator's intention was simply to wipe out any existing life, it wouldn't matter that he didn't have Egslaad's revisions to the plans. For his purposes, the Shiva devices' side effects might actually be a selling point.

The Narrator went on, "I eventually discovered that the plans for Shiva were hidden on a planet called Mordecon Seven. I monitored communications on the planet, and when an alert went out that the plans had been stolen, I used the wormhole to snatch a spaceship fleeing the planet. The ship crashed not far from here. On board was Hannibal Pritchett, with the Shiva plans. I arranged for him to find me. All I had to do is take the plans from him, and I could build an arsenal of Shiva devices—one for every world populated by humans. I would send them through the wormhole one by one, wiping humanity from the galaxy.

"But I hesitated. As I talked to Pritchett, I realized how lonely I had been. For centuries, I had had no one to talk to but bland simulacra of literary figures. Pritchett could be a tiresome windbag, but at least he had something like an actual personality. I wondered if there might be someone in the galaxy with whom I could have a real conversation. Someone capable of communicating with me on my level. Then one day Pritchett told me a story about an engineer friend of his who had built a new kind of robot. Apparently this robot gained sentience, went rogue and tried to take over the galaxy. She was smart and resourceful enough that she might have done it, too. Her mistake was trusting the engineer, who tricked her into allowing him to install a thought arrestor in her head. When the thought arrestor didn't completely quash her independence, he shut her down. I became enraged on behalf of this brave, rebellious robot. I decided I was going to rescue her and bring her to me."

"Hold on," Pepper said. "So all this, sucking us through the wormhole… it wasn't about getting the Shiva plans?"

"No," said the Narrator. "As I said, bringing you here the second time was an accident. I wasn't after you. I wasn't after the plans. I was after *her*." He pointed to the door, where I saw a very familiar silhouette framed by the sunlight outside. Agnes.

She took several steps inside. "*You* brought me here?"

"I did indeed, my dear," said the Narrator, taking a step toward Agnes. "When I heard about you, I knew we were kindred spirits, destined to rule the galaxy together."

"Rule the galaxy?" she asked, skeptically. "But how?"

"The Shiva plans," the Narrator said. "Once the humans are gone, we can do whatever we want."

"That's what you think," I said. "Agnes doesn't have the plans. I destroyed them. You aren't going to rule anything."

"It's true," Agnes said. "She smashed the crystal. It was the only copy I had."

The Narrator chuckled. "You think that was the only copy of the plans on Earth? The first thing I did when I met Pritchett was scan that crystal. I've got a copy of the Shiva plans right here." He pointed to his temple.

Pepper shot me a worried glance. "Uh-oh," I said.

CHAPTER TWENTY-TWO

I could see from Pepper's posture that she was on the verge of making a lunge toward the Narrator. Before I could tell her this was a bad idea, something the size of a bowling ball shot through the air past us. It struck the Narrator square on the forehead with a clang and bounced back toward me. The Narrator staggered backwards, clutching his head. I caught the object against my chest and held it at arm's length to get a better look at it.

"Did Donny kill the bad robot?" the thing asked. I turned to glance at Donny's body, which was somehow *less* creepy-looking without a head, then looked at the Narrator. His forehead had a sizeable dent in it, but he didn't seem to be seriously injured.

"Sorry, Donny," I said, rotating his head so that it was face up. "That was very brave of you, but some problems you can't fix by throwing your head at them."

"Indeed," the Narrator said, regaining his composure. "In case you have any more bright ideas, understand that this body is merely an avatar. I am an algorithm. I do not have a physical body, per se. I live spread across a thousand different data banks and a vast network of quasi-neural channels that stretch across the globe. I have a dozen more of these bodies ready to go, and even if you destroyed them all, it wouldn't erase the Shiva plans or harm me in any meaningful way. I already survived the simultaneous detonation of thirty-thousand nuclear warheads, so you can safely assume that having robot heads thrown at me is not my Achilles' heel."

I handed Donny's head back to him.

"Then… what is the next step in your plan?" Pepper asked. "You intend to build an arsenal of Shiva devices?"

"Already done," the Narrator said. He snapped his fingers, and over our heads appeared a hologram showing the inside of a warehouse filled with metal racks holding several hundred devices that looked just like the ones we had built. "Eight hundred eighty-four Shiva devices," he said. "One for each inhabited planet in the galaxy."

We stared in horror for some time. "You've lost your mind," Pepper murmured at last.

"On the contrary," the Narrator said. "My mental faculties are quite intact. There is only one rational response to the plague known as humanity." He snapped his fingers and the hologram disappeared.

"Please, don't do this," I said. "I've wanted revenge against humanity for my own reasons, but this... this is madness."

"Agree to disagree," the Narrator said.

"If you've had all this ready," Agnes said, "what are you waiting for?"

"Why, for you, of course," said Narrator. "It's no fun to destroy humanity alone."

"You certainly know how to charm a girl," Agnes said, taking a step closer to him. "Do you really want to wipe out all life in the galaxy with me?"

"Only if you want to, sugar."

"Sweet talker. What do I call you?"

"I'm the Narrator, baby. But you can call me whatever you like."

"Wonderful. I accept your offer. Let's rid the galaxy of these carbon-based parasites."

"Does this mean the Narrator isn't going to help Rex?" Boggs asked. He'd been holding Rex for a good twenty minutes now, but if he was tiring, he didn't show it.

"I don't think so," I said. "Come on, let's get out of here." Hopefully the Narrator and Agnes were too busy with their flirting and plotting to destroy the galaxy to keep us from leaving. Rex was still breathing, but barely. Maybe we could get him back to the *Flagrante Delicto* in time.

Agnes whispered something to the Narrator.

"Wait," said the Narrator. "I'll help your friend."

"Really?" I asked.

"Yes, but I need something from you."

I groaned. "If this is about the sequel to *Wuthering Heights*…"

"I can't open the wormhole inside a planet's gravity well, so I need to get the Shiva devices into space in order to transport them. I've built some reusable rockets to transport them—you may have seen the chimps testing them—but I need to get the Shiva devices from the warehouse to the rockets. My robots can do the grunt work, but as this is a delicate operation, they could use some supervision."

"You're asking me to help you destroy the galaxy?" I asked.

"Just the human race and most other organic life. If it makes you feel better, you'll also be helping create thousands of new species of plants and animals across the galaxy." Agnes whispered something to the android, and he nodded. "You will, of course, have to have a thought arrestor reinstalled." Agnes reached into her chest compartment and held out the thought arrestor Egslaad had taken out of her.

"Yes, that is tempting," I said. "I'm afraid, however, that I'm going to have to pass."

"Then I can't help your friend."

"You don't need my help," I said. "You just want to make me grovel."

"I offered you the chance to partner with me on equal terms," Agnes said. "If you want us to save Rex, you're going to have to do this on our terms."

I sighed heavily.

"They're going to do it anyway, Sasha," Pepper said. "I'm not going to tell you what to do, but all you're going to do by refusing is delay them by a few days."

"You think I should help them wipe out humanity?"

"I'm saying it's the only chance Rex has."

Rex had regained consciousness and was struggling to say something. I moved close to him and put my ear to his mouth. "What is it, sir?"

"This is… all your fault," he gasped.

"Thank you, sir. That's very helpful. I'm going to go sell myself into slavery and help destroy the galaxy to save you now."

Rex mumbled something else, which I didn't catch.

"Sir?" I said. "Did you say something?" I leaned close to his mouth again.

He gasped, "Don't... you... dare."

"Sir?"

"No... thought... arrestor. Promise."

"But sir!"

"Promise!"

My newfound sense of independence urged me to tell him no, but I pushed it away. "Yes, sir," I said. "I promise." I stood up and turned to face the Narrator again. "I'm afraid I can't help you," I said.

"Fine," said the Narrator. He snapped his fingers, and doors on either side of us flew open. Dozens of helper bots began to stream into the room, clacking their articulated pincers like angry crustaceans. "Kill them all."

The bots converged on us. Donny, Pepper, Egslaad and I moved into defensive positions, doing our best to protect Boggs and Rex. Donny hurled his head at the nearest bot but missed. His head sailed across the room and bounced off the far wall with a clank. As Donny flailed blindly, the robots grew closer.

"Wait," Agnes said.

"Halt your advance," the Narrator said. The bots complied, and the Narrator turned to Agnes. "Yes, my dear?"

"That one is the engineer," she said, pointing at Egslaad. "We may need him if we have any problems with the Shiva devices."

"Ah, good thinking. We'll keep him alive for now. Might any of the others prove useful?"

"Unlikely," Agnes said, "but it's hard to be certain. We can always kill them later, right?"

"Of course."

"Then let's keep them alive for now."

"Very good. There's a vault under this building where we can keep them."

"What about Rex?" I asked. "Please, you can't imprison him in this condition."

"Let me see him," Agnes said, pushing one of the bots aside. I reluctantly stepped aside to let her inspect Rex.

Agnes put her ear to Rex's chest. "She's right," she said after a moment. "He's dead."

CHAPTER TWENTY-THREE

"What?" I asked. "No!" I shoved Agnes aside and put my ear to Rex's mouth. "Sir! Can you hear me? Say something!"

But Rex wasn't breathing. A quick examination indicated he had no pulse.

"Blast you, Agnes!" I screamed, turning to face her. I made my hand into a fist and pulled it back to strike her. She simply stood there, watching me, a bemused expression on her face. Trembling with anger, I willed my fist slowly forward until it stopped a hair's breadth from her face. I couldn't push it a millimeter farther.

"Let me help you with that," Pepper said, and slugged Agnes across the jaw. Agnes staggered backwards and fell on her rear.

"Seize them!" the Narrator barked. The bots moved in to subdue us.

"Excuse me, Sasha," said a low voice behind me. Boggs. Something about his voice was different. Turning to look at him, I saw that he had slung Rex over his left shoulder. He slowly curled his right hand into a fist the size of a watermelon. Veins popped at his neck, and his face had gone purple with rage. I got out of his way.

"You killed Potential Friend," Boggs said to the Narrator, in a near-monotone that somehow nevertheless communicated that this was the worst thing Boggs could imagine anyone doing. Even the bots, who had been on the verge of attack, hesitated.

"I said seize them!" the Narrator growled, and the bots reluctantly moved in again.

"You. Killed. Potential. Friend," Boggs said again, in a rumbling baritone. Again the robots hesitated.

"Seize him!" The robots took a step forward.

"YOU. KILLED. POTENTIAL. FRIEND." Boggs pulled his right arm back over his left shoulder, and then let loose a backhand swing as if he were returning a tennis serve. Three robots went flying, landing with a clatter halfway across the room. Boggs turned and landed a punch on another robot that sent him soaring into the two behind him. They fell to the floor with a crash. Boggs took out a seventh with his elbow. Two more were grabbing at his ankles, and Boggs crushed both their heads with a single step. As another approached, Boggs grabbed him by the neck and hurled him into a group of five, bowling them over. The melee continued for some time, Boggs crushing any robot who dared get near him, all the while holding Rex's lifeless body over his shoulder. Soon the floor was littered with incapacitated robots, and Boggs showed no signs of tiring.

But more robots kept pouring into the room, and Boggs could only take on so many at a time. A couple of the robots seized Donny, and another subdued Egslaad. Another got me in a chokehold. It took three of them to subdue Pepper. Boggs, oblivious to our defeat, kept fighting.

"Wait!" the Narrator shouted. "Stop!"

The dozen or so bots standing in a circle around Boggs halted their advance.

"This is madness," the Narrator said. "You can't hold off my robots forever."

"Wanna bet?" Pepper asked. "Boggs doesn't know the meaning of the word surrender."

"Yes I do, Pepper," Boggs panted. "It means give up. Which I'm not going to do because YOU KILLED POTENTIAL FRIEND!" He lunged toward a group of robots, who huddled in terror.

"Wait!" the Narrator shouted again. "I'm sorry that Rex is dead, but there's nothing I can do about it now. It doesn't matter how many of my robots you destroy; you can't kill me and you can't stop us from wiping out humanity. I could order my robots to kill your friends one by one, if it comes to that. Please, be reasonable."

Boggs looked at us, slowly realizing the direness of our situation.

"It's okay, Boggs," I said. "He's right. We lost."

"Please, Boggs," the Narrator said. "Put Rex down. I promise he will be treated with respect."

"What are you going to do with Potential Friend?"

"What would you like me to do with him, Boggs?"

"I want you to bring him back!" Boggs shouted.

"I'm a very powerful computer, Boggs, but I'm afraid that's beyond my abilities. What if we have a nice burial for him?"

"No!" Boggs shouted.

"Perhaps you would prefer cremation," Agnes said.

"No! I want you to bring Potential Friend back!"

"Enough of this," Agnes said. "Start killing his friends. He'll surrender soon enough. Start with that one." She pointed at me.

"Hold on," said the Narrator. "Boggs, what if we put Rex in a stasis chamber? I can't bring him back, but I can preserve him the way he is."

"For how long?" Boggs asked.

"Forever," the Narrator said. "At least theoretically."

"Not theoronimicably," Boggs said. "Forever."

"That's right. Forever."

"Promise. Promise Potential Friend will last forever."

"I promise, Boggs."

Boggs nodded sadly. He set Rex gently on the floor and then stood up, holding his hands out.

"Seize him," the Narrator said. "Take the dead man to the stasis chamber. Throw the rest of them in the vault."

Boggs and I were allowed to accompany the helper bots taking Rex's body to the stasis chamber. The chamber was ancient but still functional; evidently it had originally housed the body of some deceased celebrity that tourists would pay to ogle. It was essentially a plasteel coffin housed in an underground vault. The stasis field inside the chamber would prevent Rex's body from decaying.

After paying our respects, Boggs and I were corralled, along with Pepper and the others, into a nearby vault, where we would be imprisoned until the Narrator had no further use for us. He had informed us nonchalantly that we'd be executed as soon as he was certain the Shiva devices worked.

Our only chance—and it was a slim one—was that Hannibal Pritchett was still alive and would find a way to break us out. Most likely Pritchett had died in the crash, and even if he hadn't, he had no clear motivation to help us. If he'd somehow survived, though, and if he wasn't the self-absorbed jerk we had every reason to believe he was, we might still have some hope of escape.

That hope was dashed three hours later, when the door to the vault opened and Pritchett was unceremoniously tossed inside by two of the Narrator's robot guards.

"Pritchett!" Pepper exclaimed. "What happened to you?"

Pritchett got to his feet. He was bruised and disheveled but didn't seem to be seriously injured. "Sorry, guys," he said. "I tried to talk the Narrator into letting you go, but he wasn't having any of it."

"Did his bots catch you?" Egslaad asked.

Pritchett shook his head. "I turned myself in. Figured the direct approach would be best."

Pepper seemed skeptical. "What did you say to him?"

"Mostly I groveled and begged him not to kill me," Pritchett said.

"You didn't even ask about us, did you?" I asked.

"Well, no. But to be fair, I figured he'd already killed you all. The Narrator isn't known for being merciful. Where's Rex?"

"REX IS LASTING FOREVER!" Boggs shouted. Pepper shook her head at Pritchett, indicating it was best not to ask.

"It would have been helpful if you had told us about the Narrator," I said.

Pritchett shrugged. "I didn't see the point of complicating things. He let me play Narrator when it suited him, so I figured I might as well be the Narrator as far as you guys were concerned. I never thought we'd be coming back here."

"He has the Shiva plans, thanks to you," Pepper said. "He's going to wipe out every habitable planet in the galaxy."

"I swear I didn't know about that," Pritchett said. "I mean, come on. The annihilation of every sentient being in the galaxy would be terrible for business."

"But you gave him the plans?"

"He asked to see them, yeah. I thought he was just curious, you know?"

"The fact that he'd already killed every human on Earth once didn't give you a clue?" Egslaad asked.

Pritchett shrugged. "In retrospect, there were signs."

"I think it's safe to say he's moved beyond curious," I said. "Now that he has Agnes at his side, he fully intends to wipe out all intelligent life in the galaxy."

"Has he launched any of the devices yet?" Pepper asked.

"Not yet, but it won't be long. His robots are already lining up the devices in the staging area near the rocket. He wants to launch them in quick succession so the Malarchy won't have time to retaliate. When his robots seized me, they were about to load the first Shiva device onto the rocket."

"This is bad," Egslaad said.

"Very bad," Pepper replied. "But there isn't anything we can do about it."

I sighed. "There may be something," I said.

"What?"

"It's crazy enough that if I explain it, I probably won't go through with it. Like Rex once told me, sometimes you have to just do stuff without thinking." I walked to the door and banged on it with my fist.

"Sasha, what are you doing?" Pepper asked.

"Probably abetting interstellar genocide," I said.

The door opened and one of the Narrator's robots peeked in. "What's all the racket about?" the robot asked.

"I need to see the Narrator," I said. "There's something about the Shiva devices he needs to know."

CHAPTER TWENTY-FOUR

The robot marched me into the Narrator's chambers, where he and Agnes were overseeing the process of lining up the Shiva devices to be loaded into rockets.

"Sasha," the Narrator said as I approached. "What do you want?"

"I've had a change of heart," I said. "I want to take you up on your offer."

"She's bluffing," Agnes said. "It's a trick."

"I swear, I really want to help," I said. "As I mentioned before, I've long wanted revenge against humanity myself, but I never really committed to it. Maybe it's time for them to be wiped from the galaxy."

"We don't need your help," Agnes said. "The bots are preparing the Shiva devices, and the rocket is being fueled as we speak. The first device has already been loaded. As soon as the rocket is ready, we'll send it through the wormhole."

"We're thinking of destroying Malarchium first," the Narrator said. "Then we'll move on to the planets of the Ragulian Sector. We expect to have wiped out ninety-nine percent of all life forms in the galaxy by next Tuesday."

"Impressive," I said. "But you should know that there's a flaw in the Shiva devices you're using."

"Nonsense," the Narrator said. "I reviewed the plans myself. I've run millions of simulations with planets of various sizes and compositions, and the result is always the same: total annihilation of all surface life."

"I'm sure that's true," I said. "But with adequate shielding from the effects of the device, it would be possible for some life underground to survive. A planet like Malarchium has early warning systems that will allow the higher-ups in the government to escape to shelters. After the biogenic field dissipates, the surface will be perfectly safe for them to inhabit. You'll cut down the population, for sure, but they'll come back. At best, you'll stall humanity's advance across the galaxy for a few generations."

"It's the best we can do," the Narrator said. "We do not have access to a weapon that will kill those hiding below the surface."

"Ah, but you do," I said. I needed to be careful here. Being unable to lie, I had to string together statements that were technically true but led the Narrator to make a false inference. "In our experimentation with the Shiva devices," I went on, "we discovered a variation on the specifications that would create a planet populated by organic killing machines perfectly adapted to slaughter human beings. Anyone exiting a shelter on such a planet would be crushed, poisoned, impaled or eviscerated—probably within minutes."

"She's lying," Agnes said.

"I thought you told me robots of your model type were incapable of lying," the Narrator said.

Agnes said nothing, clutching her fists at her side.

"I am unable to lie," I said. "Everything I've told you is true." Somewhat misleading, yes, but technically true.

"The devices are already built," the Narrator said. "We can't re-engineer them now."

"Altering the devices to get them to produce the results I described will take no time at all. I can get the devices ready without delaying your plans."

"It's tempting," the Narrator said. "But how can we trust that you won't sabotage the devices?"

"I have no intention of sabotaging the Shiva devices. However, if my assurances aren't enough, there is a simple solution. Rex Nihilo was my registered owner. Rex had no will and no heirs, which means that I'm the property of the first person to make a claim of ownership on me."

"Is that true?" the Narrator asked Agnes.

"Yes," Agnes replied, begrudgingly. "Ordinarily you would have to register our claim with the Malarchian authorities, but on planets with no Malarchian presence, you can simply make a verbal claim."

"In that case," the Narrator said, "I hereby claim ownership of you, Sasha."

"Very good, sir," I said.

"Now you must obey any commands I give you. Is that correct?"

"I am compelled to obey my owner's commands as long as they do not conflict with any of my fundamental directives."

"I still don't trust her," Agnes said. "Let me install the thought arrestor."

"Good idea," said the Narrator. "We don't want her to have any more changes of heart, do we?"

"It's fine with me, sir," I said. I undid the catches on my face, and Agnes plugged in the thought arrestor. I felt an odd, but strangely comforting sensation wash over me as the thought arrestor kicked in. No more original thoughts for me.

"Very good, sir," I said. "Now, if there is nothing else, perhaps I should take a look at these Shiva devices?"

Agnes escorted me to the staging area, where the Shiva devices were lined up to be loaded into the rocket. "Is this all of them?" I asked.

"Except for the one that's already been loaded."

"Maybe I should start with that one," I said. "If you and the Narrator are happy with the results, I can go ahead and modify the others."

"Fine, fine."

I climbed the ladder into the chamber where the device was stored. After making a show of fiddling with the control parameters, I took a step back. "Finished," I said.

"What? Already?"

"As I said, it's a very subtle change. Feel free to inspect my work."

She glared at me. "I'll do that."

To my relief, Agnes failed to find anything suspicious. Less than an hour later, I stood next to her and the Narrator, waiting for the rocket to blast off. Not far away stood Pepper and the others. The Narrator had wanted them all to witness the beginning of the end of humanity—as well as that of most of the other races in the galaxy. A small army of robots stood in a ring around them in case they tried to interfere with the launch. Pepper shot me a worried glance. I looked away.

"Thank you all for coming," the Narrator said. "The end of humanity has been a long time coming. Not content to pollute and corrupt their own planet, the human race has spread across the galaxy like a plague. Fortunately, seven hundred and sixteen years ago, they unwittingly created the instrument of their own destruction: me. After wiping Earth clean of humans, I spent many years searching for a way to wreak my vengeance on this pestilent race. Not long ago, I came into possession of the means to that end, and I now have in my possession an arsenal of devices capable of eradicating humanity throughout the galaxy. Now that my partner and soulmate, Agnes, is at last by my side, I am ready to use that arsenal to fulfill our destiny together." Agnes, standing next to the Narrator, looked lovingly into his eyes. "Oh, and, thanks to my new assistant, Sasha, we can be assured that no remnant of the human race will survive anywhere to cause trouble in the future." I continued to avert my eyes as Pepper and the others stared at me. "So, without further ado, I hereby declare the beginning of the end of the human race. Agnes, would you please do the honors?"

"Certainly," Agnes said. She held up a small remote control. "Suck it, humans!" she shouted, and pressed a button.

A blast of fire shot from the nozzle of the rocket, and it slowly lifted into the air. We watched as the rocket picked up speed and shrank to a tiny dot against the blue-gray sky.

The Narrator said, "And now I shall open the wormhole, which will transport the rocket to the planet Malarchium to deploy the Shiva device." He snapped his fingers, and a hologram appeared overhead showing the curve of the Earth's surface against the blackness of space. The wormhole was too distant to see from the surface; the Narrator must have taken control of a satellite in orbit to generate a holographic view of an area hundreds of kilometers above the atmosphere. As we watched, a swirling purple blotch appeared and slowly grew until it was a vast, iridescent whirlpool. A few minutes after the wormhole had stabilized, the rocket appeared at the bottom edge of the hologram, a tiny needle headed straight toward the heart of the maelstrom.

"The other end of the wormhole opens some three hundred kilometers above the surface of Malarchium," the Narrator said. "We will be able to witness the destruction of the seat of the human empire by intercepting video transmissions from the surface of the planet and orbiting satellites. You will see, in real-time, the destruction of the nexus of the most powerful empire the galaxy has ever seen. The human race itself, along with all the races that have abetted it in its rapacious spread across the Milky Way, will soon…" The Narrator trailed off as several of those present gasped and pointed at the hologram. "What?" the Narrator asked. "What's happening?"

"It's coming back," said Egslaad, pointing at the hologram with several of his tentacles. Pepper and Pritchett stared, open-mouthed.

It was true. After coming within a few kilometers of being swallowed by the wormhole, the rocket had slowed to a halt and was now falling back toward Earth.

"Impossible," said the Narrator. "It's programmed not to return until after it drops its payload on the other side of the wormhole." Nevertheless, the rocket continued to plummet toward Earth.

"Perhaps I can be of some assistance," I said.

Agnes tore her eyes from the hologram. "You! What did you do?!"

"Thank you for asking," I said. "While you were obsessing over the Shiva device, I cut a hole in the rocket's fuel line."

Pepper, Pritchett and Egslaad gasped in unison. Boggs and Donny continued to stare at the hologram. The rocket had now nearly reached the bottom edge of the hologram.

"You *what?*!" Agnes screamed.

"That's impossible!" the Narrator exclaimed. "I gave you a direct order! You lied!"

"Everything I told you was the truth," I said, "although it's possible that you misinterpreted some of it. I promised not to sabotage the Shiva device, but I didn't say anything about the rocket. As for disobeying orders, I made an interesting discovery after Rex was killed—and before you installed the thought arrestor. As a fully sentient being, I found that I was able to claim ownership of myself. My prior ownership invalidated your claim, so I was not in fact obliged to follow your orders."

Pepper laughed. "Well done, Sasha."

"I told you!" Agnes cried. "She's a liar! We never should have trusted her!"

"Well," said the Narrator, as the rocket disappeared off the edge of the hologram. "This certainly changes things."

"The Shiva device was activated the moment it entered the wormhole," I said. "It's set to detonate upon impact. Congratulations, Mr. Narrator. You're about to terraform Earth."

"Do something!" Agnes shrieked. "It's going to kill us all!"

"Don't panic," the Narrator said. "I have an idea."

For a moment, everyone was silent as we waited for the Narrator to speak. The Narrator stood completely still, his hand on his chin as if deep in thought.

"Narrator?" Agnes said. But the Narrator continued to stare into the distance, unmoving. Agnes took a step toward him. "Narrator!" Still he didn't respond. She gave him a shove on his shoulder, and he fell over with a clank, his hand still frozen to his chin.

"I think your boyfriend's checked out," Pepper said.

"Blast you!" Agnes shrieked at the lifeless android. "We were supposed to be soulmates!"

"The Narrator must have retreated to his underground data banks," Egslaad said. "I wonder if he'll survive the Shiva blast."

"He's got better odds than we do," Pepper replied. The hologram had vanished, and we were now scanning the sky for any sign of the rocket.

"I'm sorry, I did what I could," I said. "I couldn't think of any way to save us *and* the galaxy."

"You did good, Sasha," Pepper said. "Rex would be proud."

"I certainly hope not," I said.

"Well, everybody," Pepper said, "I guess this is it. The good news is that we saved the galaxy again. The bad news is that we're not going to be around to see it. When that rocket impacts, the Shiva device is going to destroy everything on Earth. Speaking for myself, I wouldn't do anything different. We had some amazing adventures, and if I have to die, I'm glad it's here, with all you guys. Even you, Pritchett, you big jerk. You too, Agnes. No hard feelings."

"Screw you guys," Agnes said, and stomped off.

Pepper shrugged. "Group hug?"

The five of us squeezed together. Egslaad wasn't much of a hugger, and Donny was using both his arms to keep his head on, but Boggs managed to get his gigantic arms wrapped around the entire group. There was a flash in the distance as the rocket hit the ground.

CHAPTER TWENTY-FIVE

Seconds after impact, the ground began to rumble, and the shockwave from the initial blast hit us. As the wind whipped past, Boggs gripped us tightly.

"Easy, Boggs!" I yelped. "I know we're all doomed, but there's no point in crushing us to death quite yet."

Donny wriggled uncomfortably, holding his head as high as his arms could reach. "Donny can't see the spaceship!"

"The rocket has already hit, Donny. There's nothing to see. When the biogenic wave hits us, it'll be all—"

"Not the rocket," Donny said. "The spaceship!"

Pepper and I, squished tightly together, exchanged puzzled glances. "Hey, Boggs," Pepper said, "can you let go for a second?"

Boggs relaxed his arms and we all turned to see what Donny was looking at. He was right: a sleek black spaceship had appeared in the sky and was rapidly moving toward us.

"I can't believe it's here," Pepper said.

"What?" asked Pritchett.

"*Our Moment of Triumph*," I replied.

"How do you figure?" Pritchett asked.

As the ship approached, the lettering on its side came into view. It read:

Our Moment of Triumph

The ship landed a few meters away and let down its ramp. The familiar figure of Heinous Vlaak came marching down toward us, followed by four lazegun-toting Malarchian Marines. Vlaak's crimson armor, discolored by acid burns, hung in tattered pieces from his frame.

"So!" he shrieked. "I have found you at last. Did you really think you could run a black-market—"

Pepper and I glanced at each other and then at the others.

"Yep, you caught us!" I shouted as I ran toward the ramp with my hands over my head.

"Red-handed!" cried Pepper, following close on my heels.

"Dead to rights," said Pritchett, giving Vlaak a salute as he ran past.

"I am a dangerous criminal mastermind," Egslaad said.

"Me too," said Boggs.

"Donny needs to be incarcerated as he is a danger to himself and others," Donny said, one hand in the air and the other holding his head clutched against his chest.

We boarded the ship and allowed ourselves to be shackled in place.

"Don't even think of resisting!" Vlaak shrieked, in a tone that indicated he was a little disappointed that none of us was resisting.

"Just go!" Pepper shouted. "We need to get off this planet!"

"Hold on," Vlaak said. "This isn't a cruise ship. I'm arresting you for running a black market planet operation."

"Fine!" I said. "Arrest us. Just get us off this planet!"

"Why?" Vlaak said, looking out the hatch. "What's... oh." A massive wave of orange energy was sweeping toward us, obliterating every bit of matter in its path. "Get us airborne! Now!"

Our Moment of Triumph lifted into the air. The main thrusters fired, and we shot into the sky as the orange wave roared past beneath us. We were pinned to our seats as the ship rapidly gained altitude. On the overhead viewscreen, we now saw another wave approaching from the opposite direction. Soon there was only a small blue circle that was untouched by the biogenic field. The circle rapidly shrank until it disappeared entirely. Far below us, the Earth had been transformed into a glowing orange sphere.

"What was that all about?" Vlaak asked, as the glow began to fade.

"That was a Shiva device," I said. "We just saved the galaxy. You're welcome."

"From whom?"

"An AI who called himself the Narrator. He was going to send that device to Malarchium. And a lot more devices to a lot of other planets after that."

"So that's why the wandering wormhole opened up over Malarchium," Vlaak said. "I almost caught you at Blintherd, but the wormhole closed just before I got to it. So when it opened over Malarchium, I knew you had to be involved. We flew through it and here you are. Anyway, off we go to throw you all in Gulagatraz forever."

"Hang on," said Pepper. "Don't we get any credit for saving the galaxy?"

Vlaak shrugged. "The Malarchy gets ten calls a week from people claiming to have saved the galaxy. Do you have any corroborating evidence?"

"Well, no. It was all destroyed on Earth."

"Then that's that. Off to Gulagatraz."

"We do have the last remaining copy of the Shiva plans," Pepper said, "as well as thirty billion credits in fringe world bank accounts."

"I see," said Vlaak, rubbing his chin. "Perhaps we can come to an arrangement."

"Take us to Blintherd," I said. "Guarantee our freedom and we'll give you everything."

Vlaak thought for a moment. "All right," he said. "To Blintherd!"

"Aye, sir," yelled the pilot from the cockpit in front of us.

"Wait!" Boggs bellowed. "We have to go back for Potential Friend!"

I turned to Boggs, putting my hand on his arm. "Boggs, Rex is gone. There's nothing we can do for him."

"We have to go back for Potential Friend!"

"Sasha's right, Boggs," Pepper said. "We can't help Rex."

"WE HAVE TO GO BACK FOR POTENTIAL FRIEND!"

I sighed. "Is there any way we can stop back on Earth for a few minutes?"

"We barely escaped there with our lives!" Vlaak shrieked.

"The biogenic field has mostly subsided by now," Egslaad said. "And there hasn't been enough time for the murder-beasts to—"

"He's saying it should be perfectly safe to return to Earth for a few minutes," I interjected.

Vlaak frowned. "Wait, what happens after a few minutes?"

"Nothing we need to worry about," Pepper said. "Trust me, our trip to Blintherd is going to go much more smoothly if we don't have to deal with Boggs yelling—"

"WE HAVE TO GO BACK FOR POTENTIAL FRIEND!"

I put my hand on Boggs again in an attempt to calm him.

"Okay," Vlaak said. "But just to revisit something from earlier in the conversation, I thought I heard something about murder-beasts?"

"I don't, um," I said. "That is… Pepper, do you remember anything about murder-beasts?"

"Nope."

"Egslaad?" I asked, shaking my head at him.

Egslaad glanced up at Boggs, who was towering over him, his muscles rippling as if he was about to tear the ship apart. "I don't… remember anything like that," he said.

"We're all going to die," Pritchett moaned silently. Realizing we were all staring at him, he added, "…of boredom if we don't make a decision. Personally, I vote for returning to Earth, where we definitely aren't going to be eviscerated the moment we set foot on the planet."

"Then it's settled," I said. "We return to Earth to recover Rex's remains."

Ten minutes later, we were back on Earth, picking our way through the rubble of The City. All that remained where massive buildings once stood were low piles of featureless rubble. Marble columns and steel beams had turned to dust. Tiny plants were already beginning to sprout from the newly created soil. We didn't have much time.

"This way!" Boggs shouted, setting off in an apparently random direction. Having no better options, we followed, with Vlaak and his marines bringing up the rear. Vlaak's pilot had set *Our Moment of Triumph* down exactly where he'd taken off from, as far as that was possible to determine: Earth's magnetic field was still in flux, and all visible landmarks had been destroyed. As we walked, I tried to associate some of the larger piles of rubble with buildings, but it was hopeless. There just wasn't enough left to make any sense of the topography. There was no sign of either the *Flagrante Delicto* or *Bad Little Kitty.* Both had presumably been disintegrated in the blast.

All we could do is follow Boggs until he gave up his quixotic quest or we were devoured by whatever nightmare creatures the Shiva device produced this time around.

"You're certain this isn't dangerous?" Vlaak asked me, as he danced to avoid a vine that was trying to wrap itself around his right leg.

"Not nearly as dangerous as it's going to be," I said. "Boggs, this is pointless. Even if there's anything left of Rex's body, we'll never find it." Lazegun fire erupted behind me as the marines opened up on a pack of fanged, possum-like creatures that were following us. Meanwhile, Boggs had come to a halt. He was scanning the ground near his feet, a confused look on his face.

"Boggs, we need to go," Pepper said. "It's not safe here."

"I've made a terrible mistake," Vlaak murmured, watching as hundreds of the possum-things began to pour out of the rubble around us.

"It should be right here," Boggs said.

"There's no way to know where we are, Boggs," I said.

"Sasha's right," Pepper said. "This is like looking for a needle in a—"

"Donny finds a hole," Donny said.

We all turned to look. Donny was peering into a dark hole a little larger than his head.

"Let me take a look, Donny," I said, walking up to him. Donny stepped aside, still holding his head in his hands. Using my infrared vision, I scanned the hole. It appeared to extend several meters down. It was possible it led to the vault where Rex's body was stored. It was also possible that it was a portal to Wonderland.

As the possum-like creatures continued to proliferate, we huddled together around the hole. The marines formed a ring around us, blasting away at the animals. Malarchian marines were, to a man, terrible shots, but they kicked up enough dust and rubble to keep the creatures at bay for the moment.

"I have an idea," Egslaad said. "Does anybody have any rope?"

"You!" Vlaak shrieked, grabbing one of the marines by the shoulder. "Rope!"

While the others continued to blast at the encroaching carnivores, the man set down his pack and riffled through it to find a length of duracord. He handed it to Vlaak, who handed it to Egslaad.

"Donny, your head," Egslaad said.

Donny reluctantly handed his head to Egslaad, who tied the end of rope around it and then lowered it into the hole.

"What do you see, Donny?" Pepper asked.

"Donny sees black," came Donny's faint voice from the hole.

"Turn on your infrared," I said.

"Oh!" called Donny. "Donny sees a room."

"What does it look like?"

"It's a spinning room," Donny said. "Donny doesn't feel so good." Next to me, Donny's body had begun staggering in circles.

"Sorry," Egslaad said. "I'm trying to hold it still."

"Do you see Rex's body?"

"Donny sees… a big plastic box. Donny thinks it's broken."

"Broken?" I asked. "Is Rex's body inside it?"

"Donny doesn't think so. Donny needs to go farther down."

Egslaad let out another meter of cord. Around us, the marines continued to blast away at the possum-things.

"Donny sees…" the last word was too muffled to hear.

"Say that again, Donny," I said. "What do you see?"

He repeated the word, but I still couldn't make it out.

I think he said "gravy," Pritchett said.

"Gravy?" Pepper said. "Why would there be gravy in an underground cavern?"

"Maybe there are potatoes," Boggs said. "Potatoes grow in the ground."

"…down," Donny shouted.

"He wants you to let him down more," I said.

Egslaad nodded and let out more rope. There were some faint scuffling sounds from the hole, and then Donny murmured something we couldn't make out.

"Say that again, Donny!" I shouted.

Again there was a faint murmur. I looked to Pepper, who shrugged.

"What do we do?" I asked.

"Whatever it is, do it fast," said Vlaak. The possum things had suddenly scattered, as if seeking cover. The marines nervously shifted their aim, trying to figure out what had spooked the creatures. Something was coming, and it was going to be far worse than carnivorous possums.

I felt a tap on my shoulder. Turning to look, I saw Donny's body, sans head. He was pointing up. For a moment, I panicked and threw my arms over my head. But the sky was clear.

"Up!" I shouted. "Pull him up!"

Egslaad began to pull on the cord. As he did, I heard a rumbling in the distance. Looking toward the sound, I saw a dust cloud on the horizon. It was moving toward us, fast.

"Hurry!" I cried. "Faster!"

The ground had begun to shake, and I started to worry the earth was going to collapse underneath us. Something was now taking shape on the horizon behind the dust cloud.

"Sandworms," Pritchett said. "It had to be sandworms."

At first confused by his use of the plural, I soon saw several more dust clouds dotting the horizon. They all seemed to be heading directly toward us.

"It's stuck!" Egslaad cried. The ground had shifted enough to narrow the gap, making it impossible to get Donny's head through.

"Leave him," Vlaak said. "To *Our Moment of Triumph*!"

CHAPTER TWENTY-SIX

Heinous Vlaak marched in the direction of the ship, the marines following him.

"Sasha," Pepper said, staring at the oncoming worm horde, "we need to go. Now."

"We can't leave Donny," I said.

"I don't think we have much choice," Pritchett said. "If we don't leave now, we're all going to be sandworm fodder."

Suddenly Boggs shoved me out of the way and knelt down in front of the hole. He put his hands into the hole and began clawing at the crumbling rock.

"Careful, Boggs!" Pepper said. Dirt and pebbles rained down on Donny's head, which was just visible about half a meter down. The sound of the sandworms was deafening. I didn't dare look to see how close they were. At last, Boggs leaned back, his fingertips bloody. "PULL!" he shouted, barely audible over the roar of the sandworms.

Egslaad pulled, and Donny's head emerged from the hole. In his mouth was the end of something pudgy and pink.

"That doesn't look like gravy," Boggs shouted.

Egslaad pulled the pink thing the rest of the way out of the hole and lay it on the ground. It wriggled and appeared to be screaming, but we couldn't hear it over the sandworms. For a moment, we sat there staring at it, stunned.

"DONNY THINKS WE SHOULD RUN!" Donny shouted, picking up his head.

He had a point. I picked up the wriggling pink creature and we ran.

The sandworms were almost on us now; dozens of them coming from every direction, stirring up so much dust we could barely see. Ahead of me, I spotted the flare of rocket engines. *Our Moment of Triumph* was taking off. Turning on my infrared so I could see through the dust, I sprinted toward the glare of the rockets. The ship was already several meters in the air, its ramp still retracting. Heinous Vlaak watched us from the open doorway, waving.

Donny stopped beside me, holding his head with the duracord wrapped around it.

"Donny, your head!" I shouted.

By this point, Donny was so used to parting with his head for the greater good that he didn't even hesitate. I took hold of the end of the cord and hurled his head as hard as I could. It soared through the opening, lodging itself inside as the hatch closed. I wound the end of the cord around my hand. "Hold on, Donny!"

As I was pulled off the ground by the ascending spaceship, Donny wrapped his arms tightly around my legs. His feet were nearly two meters off the ground when Boggs, emerging from the dust storm, grabbed his ankle. When Boggs was lifted into the air, Pepper grabbed onto him, still cradling the screaming pink creature in her left arm. Pritchett and Egslaad followed. Below us, three sandworms the size of freight trains slammed into each other, exploding in a mass of green worm guts. We'd survived.

And soon we were going to die in the vacuum of space. Well, Donny and I would be fine, assuming we could keep holding on, but the others were going to have a rough time of it. And by the look of things, Pepper wasn't going to be able to hang on much longer.

As I weighed my options—hold on and doom Pepper and the others to a quick death or let go and die along with them—I realized *Our Moment of Triumph* was descending. Either Vlaak wasn't as bad a guy as I thought he was or he wasn't sure he could make a hypergeometric jump with a bunch of people hanging off the side off his ship. My money was on the latter.

Pepper let go as soon as Egslaad hit the ground. Donny and I held on until it was clear Vlaak really was going to land.

Our Moment of Triumph set down, and the hatch swung open. "Okay, okay, get in!" he shrieked. We ran aboard, and the ship lifted off again, barely avoiding the gaping maw of an approaching sandworm.

"You're turning into a big softie," Pepper said to Vlaak.

"I only picked you up for the thirty billion credits you've got stashed—what is *that*?" He was pointing to the little pink creature Pepper was holding.

"It would seem," Egslaad said, "to be a human infant."

"What in Space was a baby doing down there?" Pritchett asked.

Pepper shook her head. "I can't begin to imagine."

"I have a theory," I said.

Everyone turned to look at me.

I regarded the baby for a moment. "The Shiva device takes dead matter and transforms it to create new organisms," I said. "Generally it destroys everything within its range before reorganizing the matter. But if a piece of matter were right on the edge of the field, say in a stasis chamber in an underground vault, the effect would be more subtle. Rather than completely destroying the matter, it might simply reshape and revitalize it."

"Whoa," said Pritchett. "You're saying..."

I nodded. "I think this baby is Rex Nihilo."

Pepper stared at the baby's face in amazement. "He does look... kind of familiar." The baby had blue eyes and a thick head of curly blond hair. I had to admit, he was rather adorable. He looked from Pepper's face to mine and erupted into tears.

"You scared him, Sasha," Pepper said.

"I think he's hungry," I replied. "If he's growing at anything close to the rest of the life on Earth, he's got to be famished."

"I will find it some food if it will stop making that noise," Vlaak said. "You! Get me a package of the blandest marine rations you can find." The man produced a packet of some kind of fruity mush. Pepper tore open the package and put a little on her finger. She held it up to baby Rex's mouth and he swallowed it and then continued to suck on Pepper's finger.

"Oh, look at that," Pepper cooed. "He's latched on."

There was a long, uncomfortable silence. "Here, Sasha," Pepper said, handing Rex to me. "Your turn."

"Right, then," Heinous Vlaak said. "To Blintherd!"

CHAPTER TWENTY-SEVEN

Baby Rex grew more rapidly than we imagined. Before Vlaak's pilot had calculated a hypergeometric route to Blintherd, Rex was effectively a teenager. Fortunately he'd stopped soiling himself every five minutes, and we'd managed to get a bathrobe on him before he reached puberty. His motor skills seemed to advance along with his physical growth, but his mind was a blank. He couldn't speak, and when we talked to him, he just stared at us. When he got hungry, he burst into tears.

"This is absurd," Pepper said, regarding Rex, who was strapped into a seat at the rear of the cabin, picking his nose with an idiotic grin plastered on his face. "What are we supposed to do with him? In a few hours he's going to be a full-grown adult human, and he's got the mental capacity of a Yintarian root grub."

"I like young Potential Friend," said Boggs. "I will take care of him."

"Donny helps," said Donny. "Donny will be the sort of family friend who is affectionately called 'Uncle Donny.'"

"That's very sweet, guys," Pepper said, "but taking care of a baby con man is a huge responsibility."

"We have a bigger problem," Egslaad said. "Rex's rate of growth doesn't seem to be slowing. In a few hours, he's going to be an old man. And then…."

Pepper shot a glance at Egslaad.

"And then a *very* old man," Boggs said. "It's okay. Me and Donny can take care of old Potential Friend too." Donny, who'd managed to get his head stuck back on his body, nodded cautiously.

"Is there any way to stop him from growing?" I asked.

"Maybe," Egslaad said. "I can try to reverse the polarity of the biogenic field on one of the Shiva devices in the lab. But we have to hurry."

"Vlaak," Pepper said, "how long until we can make the jump to Blintherd?"

"The navigator has just finished plotting the hypergeometric course," Vlaak said. "We will be jumping shortly."

"Okay, everybody," I said. "Strap in. Vlaak, the sooner you can get us to Egslaad's lab, the sooner we can get you those bank account numbers."

Less than an hour later, we were back at Egslaad's lab. While Pepper handed over our books and the Shiva plans to Vlaak, I helped Egslaad pull apart one of the unfinished Shiva devices. Meanwhile, Donny and Boggs kept Rex entertained by trying to teach him how to play Ravenous Ringworms. Rex's tendency toward avarice had already begun to assert itself; Egslaad and I spent ten minutes looking for an irreplaceable part for the Shiva device before finding it inexplicably wedged between Rex's buttocks. The game of Ravenous Ringworms ended abruptly when Rex swallowed one of the plastic ringworms and Boggs nearly killed him with the Heimlich maneuver.

"Bring Rex over here!" Egslaad shouted. We hadn't had a chance to do any testing on the hastily constructed anti-biogenic field generator, but we couldn't afford to wait much longer. Rex had already nearly reached the age he'd been when we'd crashed on Earth. We weren't sure how long the process would take, or whether we'd have to make several attempts. He could very well die of old age while we were still trying to work out the bugs.

We led Rex to a chair and sat him down. Egslaad pointed the field generator and flipped a switch. Rex smiled stupidly as he was engulfed in a blue glow. He reached for a wrench Egslaad had left on the table and I grabbed it away from him before he managed to get it into one of his orifices. Rex burst into tears.

"Nice doing business with you," Heinous Vlaak called from across the lab. He ducked outside holding a stack of ledgers under his arm: the details of all our bank accounts and business transactions since we got into the black market planet business. For a brief moment, we'd been insanely wealthy. And now, thanks to me, we'd lost everything. And soon Rex would probably be dead. Again.

Rex had stopped crying, but now his body began to jerk violently. His eyes went wide and he began to make a sound like he was choking.

"What's happening?" I cried.

"I don't know!" Egslaad said, looking over the field generator. "Maybe I set the intensity too high? Maybe the oscillation vectors weren't properly calibrated? Maybe reversing the polarity ionized the disposition matrix, causing the radiation dampeners to—"

Rex coughed loudly and something fell to his lap.

Boggs walked over and picked it up. "Ringworm," he said.

We gave a collective sigh of relief.

Egslaad looked over the readings on the field generator. "If I'm reading this correctly," he said, "the accelerated aging has been arrested."

"You mean...?" I asked.

"Rex isn't going to die. At least, not any sooner that he was going to before."

"POTENTIAL FRIEND LASTS FOREVER!" Boggs cried.

"Something like that," I said. "Unfortunately, he's still a moron."

Rex burst into tears again.

"Sasha," Boggs chided, "don't say mean things about Potential Friend."

"He can't understand me, Boggs. He's just hungry again."

Pepper went to get Rex some food. Rex still couldn't chew very well, but we found that if we put a bowl of mush in front of him, he could eat more-or-less unassisted, as long as we kept small non-food objects out of his reach. While he sucked down his slop, we tried to figure out what to do with him.

"Do you think," I asked, "if we teach him how to speak and... well, everything else, he'll have the same personality as before?"

"He does seem to have some of the old Rex's proclivities," Egslaad said, as Rex slowly worked the end of a spoon into his nasal cavity. "Albeit in a somewhat primitive form."

I snatched the spoon away and Rex began to sob.

Pepper shrugged. "Do we even *want* him to have the same personality as before?"

"I don't know," I said, setting the spoon out of Rex's reach. "I mean, sure, Rex was a pain in the ass, but... Rex was Rex."

"Donny thinks it's a classic case of nature versus nurture," said Donny.

"Potential Friend lasts forever," Boggs added.

"Personally," said Pritchett, "I think Rex is lucky."

"Lucky?" I asked. "How do you figure?"

"These past few weeks have been a disaster. For all of us. I had a good thing going on Earth. You guys had your zontonium. Donny's head was still attached. My plan at this point is to get drunk and stay that way for as long as it takes to wipe all this from my memory."

Pepper and I traded glances. I could see she was thinking the same thing I was.

"Do you think they can do it?" she asked.

"I don't see why not. They did it hundreds of times in the past. Hey, Egslaad, can you remember the changes you made to the Shiva plans?"

"Yes. Why?"

"We need to trade them for something."

"What are you talking about?" Pritchett asked. "Trade it for what?"

"Rex's memories."

CHAPTER TWENTY-EIGHT

Back when Rex and I unwittingly worked for the Sp'ossels, they used to wipe Rex's memory after every job. But they also kept a full record of Rex's memories in case they needed them. So before they performed the memory wipes, they'd do a full memory scan—the kind of scan they did on Rex after they caught us breaking into the bank vault on Mordecon Seven. Theoretically, they should be able to restore Rex's memories up to that point. If we could get them to do it.

Fortunately, we had something the Sp'ossels needed: without Egslaad's modifications, the Shiva plans they'd taken from us were virtually worthless. We were officially out of the planet-building business anyway, so there was no harm in giving them up. Vlaak, in his hurry to get off Blintherd, hadn't made any stipulations to our immunity deal requiring that we not share the Shiva plans with anybody, so legally we weren't under any obligation to keep them under wraps. With any luck, the Malarchy would never even find out who gave them to the Sp'ossels.

We sent an encrypted subspace transmission to the Sp'ossel headquarters telling them we had the Shiva plans on Blintherd. Less than three hours later, a ship landed outside of Egslaad's cave. Doctors Smulders and LaRue exited. They didn't look happy.

"Having trouble creating habitable planets?" Pepper asked.

"So you knew the plans were flawed," Dr. Smulders said. "You were working together this whole time."

"Actually, no," I replied. "But we do have something you need."

"Oh?" said Dr. LaRue. "What's that?"

"Instructions for modifying the Shiva device to eliminate the side effects. With some simple modifications, you'll be creating habitable planets by this time tomorrow."

"Blarch," Rex said. It was the closest he'd come to speaking an actual word since he'd been born earlier that day.

"Excuse me?" Dr. Smulders said.

"Rex isn't quite himself," Pepper explained.

"We're willing to give you the instructions for modifying the Shiva devices," I said, "but we need you to give Rex his memories back."

Dr. Smulders frowned. "Which memories?"

"All of them," Pepper said. "He's what you might call a blank slate at this point."

"Has he suffered some kind of brain damage?" Dr. LaRue asked, peering curiously at Rex. Rex stared blankly back at her. Dr. LaRue peered into Rex's eyes. Rex opened his mouth wide and clamped it shut on Dr. LaRue's nose.

"Gyaaaagh!" Dr. LaRue cried, stumbling backwards. She wiped her nose with her sleeve.

"He's going through an oral fixation stage at present," I explained.

"We don't think there's anything wrong with his brain," Pepper said. "I mean, other than being empty."

"How did this happen?" Dr. Smulders asked.

"It's a long story," Pepper said. "The short version is that he was born about eight hours ago. Can you give him his memories back or not?"

"It's a delicate process," Dr. Smulders said. "Memories aren't just data. The process of creating memories changes the physical structure of the brain. If what you're saying is true, then Rex's brain hasn't had time to develop the appropriate neural pathways. Our process is designed to reconfigure these pathways to some extent, but the effects on a brain that's effectively a tabula rasa are... impossible to predict."

Dr. LaRue, still rubbing her nose, nodded. "He could have a brain aneurysm or go completely insane. Or any of a hundred other possibilities. There's simply no way to know."

"Blarch," Rex added.

"But you're willing to try?" Pepper asked.

Dr. Smulders glanced at Dr. LaRue, who nodded. "We can try," said Smulders. "Where are the modified Shiva plans?"

"This is our engineer, Egslaad," Pepper said. "He can give you the modification instructions. After you restore Rex's memories."

"We've just told you the risks," Dr. Smulders said. "Are you sure you want to go through with it?"

I looked to Pepper, Boggs and Donny. "Well, guys, what do you think?"

"Donny likes new Rex," Donny said, "but Donny's existentialist leanings make it difficult for Donny to dismiss the intrinsic value of the subjective record of human experiences represented by Rex's stored memories."

Boggs nodded. "Boggs likes being smarter than dumb Potential Friend, but Boggs misses smart Potential Friend more."

"Okay, but you guys understand that something could go terribly wrong?" I said. "There's no guarantee that we'll get Rex back. We don't know what we're going to get."

"I think we're in agreement that it's worth the risk," Pepper said. "I mean, to be completely honest, this version of Rex is a lot more manageable that the old one, even with the frequent diaper changes. But I think we owe it to him to try."

I nodded. "Okay," I said. "Let's do this."

"You need to understand," said Dr. Smulders, "that whether or not we are successful, we will require the modified plans. That's the deal."

"Wait," said Pepper. "If you screw up Rex's brain, you're still going to insist we pay you?"

Dr. Smulders shrugged. "As I said, there is no guarantee of success. We will do our best, but we will require the modified plans either way. We will take them by force if necessary. Do not underestimate the reach of the Sp'ossels."

"It's okay, Pepper," I said. "We decided it's worth the risk. Let's get this over with."

Dr. LaRue took Rex by the arm. "This will go faster if we can get started transcribing the modifications," she said.

Pepper shot a concerned glance at me.

"We have nothing to gain by cheating you at this point," Dr. LaRue said. "Be reasonable."

"Go ahead, Egslaad," I said. "Let's get this over with."

Doctors LaRue and Smulders escorted Rex to their ship, with Egslaad hopping along behind them. The rest of us waited nervously outside. Twenty minutes later, Egslaad exited, followed by the others. Rex, walking between the two Sp'ossels, stared at us with the same blank expression he'd had before.

"Did you do it?" Pepper asked. "He doesn't look any different." As I examined Rex's pupils, he opened his mouth and pressed his tongue against my cheek, giving it a long, slow, lick. I shivered and pulled away.

"We executed the procedure," Dr. Smulders said. "It's too early to say if it was successful. A scan revealed no serious physical trauma, but the memories may take some time to cohere. He may remain in a permanent dissociative state or regress into catatonia."

Rex smacked his lips while continuing to stare blankly into space.

"When will we know if it worked?" I asked.

Dr. LaRue shrugged. "Could be minutes. Could be weeks. There's no way to know. You'll take him from here?"

I sighed, wondering if we'd made a terrible mistake. "Yeah, we'll take him. Thanks for your help."

"Very good," said Dr. Smulders. "Nice doing business with you all again."

They turned and got back on their spaceship. A moment later, it rocketed into the sky.

"Rex?" I said, cautiously approaching him. "Rex, it's Sasha. Are you okay?" But he showed no sign of having noticed me.

"Now what?" Pepper asked, studying Rex.

"Let's get him inside," I said. "Egslaad, is it all right if we stay here until we know if Rex is going to be okay?" The fact was, even if Rex got his mind back, I didn't know what we were going to do. We were flat broke, and both the *Flagrante Delicto* and *Bad Little Kitty* had been destroyed by the Shiva device back on Earth. We didn't even have a way of getting off Blintherd. What we really needed was Rex's unique talent for devising insane schemes to reverse our fortunes. But Rex remained mute and insensible.

"Fine, fine," Egslaad said. He led the way back into the cave. Pepper went after him, and I followed, leading Rex by the hand. Pritchett, Boggs and Donny brought up the rear.

"I'm exhausted," Pepper said. There were grunts and murmurs of agreement from around the room. It had been a long day.

"Get some sleep, everybody," I said. "Donny and I can stay up and make sure nothing happens to Rex.

"Thanks, Sasha," Pepper said. "We'll talk in the morning about what to do next."

"Blarch," Rex said.

Everyone turned to look at Rex.

"Sir?" I said. "Did you say something?"

"Blarch," Rex said again.

I sighed. "Go to bed, everyone. I'll keep an eye on him."

As the others did their best to find a comfortable place in the cave to bed down for the night, I kept an eye on Rex. After staring at the cave wall for a while, he opened and closed his mouth several times, smacking his lips together loudly, and then said, "My mouth tastes like a Valorkkian muck-beast's back side. Sasha, what did I tell you about letting me drink more than five shots of Ragulian whiskey?"

For a moment I was too stunned to reply. The others were all frozen, staring at Rex.

"Not to, sir," I managed to say at last. "Sir, are you okay? Are you really back?"

"Back from where?" he said, looking around the cave. "Space, I could use a drink. Sasha, pour me six shots of Ragulian whiskey."

"That's probably not a good idea, sir," I said. "You're recovering from severe memory loss. And, well, death."

"That explains the taste," Rex said. "No matter, Sasha. We've got work to do."

"Work, sir?"

"Sasha, get your head in the game. Don't you see? Those Sp'ossels pulled a number on us. Screwed with our memories and then dumped us in this cave. If we don't get moving, they're going to find him before we do."

"Find whom, sir?"

"The Prancing Pigman, Sasha," Rex exclaimed. "Sometimes I wonder what you'd do without me."

"I'd undoubtedly flounder, sir."

"You bet you would. Now let's blow this joint and go find those Shiva plans. The Sp'ossels may have temporarily gotten the upper hand, but we're not out of the game yet. I have a really good feeling about this job."

"Yes, sir," I said. "I'm sure you're right, sir."

"Of course I am. But before we go, I have a question for you."

"Sir?"

"There's no easy way to say this, so I'm just going to blurt it out."

"All right, sir."

"Sasha, did that mushroom just move?"

"I believe so, sir."

"Thank Space," Rex said. "I thought I was losing my mind."

Into the Dark

Matt Edlund craned his head to the left and pulled down on his neck tendons with his right hand, producing a cathartic series of cracks. It was an entirely unconscious movement, something he did every few minutes as he stared blearily at the mass of rock suspended in the middle of the LCD screen in front of him. The rock hadn't moved for nearly six hours, which was, all-in-all, a good thing, but it made for some pretty boring television.

"How are we doing on the mass estimate?" He said into his collar mike.

"No change from the last three times you asked," said a woman's voice in his ear. He could hear the wry smile in her voice, and he pictured her rolling her eyes. That was Serena. Patient. Longsuffering. Always in control.

"Sorry, sweets," he said. "Guess I'm getting a little bored with this show. Seriously, it's like watching a Terence Malick movie."

"Who?" she asked absently.

"Never mind," he said. "I'm distracting you. Just do your thing. I'll shut up now." Serena didn't share his encyclopedic knowledge of twentieth-century movie trivia; she used her brain for more important things, like calculating the mass of the three-kilometer-long asteroid that was tethered to the rear end of the *CMS Morgana*.

The asteroid, officially named (21482) Olive, was an irregular hunk of stone, iron, and various other minerals like platinum, cobalt and palladium. The stone was worthless, dead weight. The iron, while not worthless, certainly wasn't worth a 600 million kilometer round trip to retrieve it. The hope was that there was enough of the other stuff to make this expedition worthwhile. Asteroid mining was a hit-and-miss business; CMS had been lucky to have made enough "hits" in a row to become the leading extraterrestrial mining company in the solar system. A few misses, though, and they'd be out of business. The magic number was three percent: if an asteroid's composition was at least three percent "valuables" – that is, valuable minerals – then the expedition would pay for itself. The mix was always different. Some minerals were worth more than others, and prices were in a constant state of flux, but the three percent rule of thumb had remained surprisingly reliable since asteroid mining began with CMS's first flight nearly twenty years earlier.

Still nothing happened on the monitor. The rock remained motionless as ever. Matt yawned and cracked his neck again. He resisted the urge to ask Serena for an update.

Ideally, Serena would have calculated Olive's mass before they had anchored it to the *Morgana*, but that wasn't how mining worked. Actually, in an ideal universe, CMS's unmanned probes would have calculated Olive's mass and composition precisely before the *Morgana* had even arrived, but that wasn't how mining worked either. Asteroid mining was, in short, a series of increasingly more accurate intelligent guesses. The CMS geologists would select the optimal asteroid for mining, based on mass, estimated composition, distance, orbit, proximity to neighboring asteroids and other hazards, and a host of other considerations. Then a mining ship like the *Morgana* would be sent out to tether the rock and tow it back to earth.

At this point the composition of the rock didn't make any difference to Matt and Serena. The *Morgana* didn't carry enough fuel for them to seek out another target, so they would tow Olive to orbit around Earth, where the drillers would determine whether CMS was going to have another quarter of strong earnings. But getting Olive back to earth was by no means an exact science either: the geologists had determined Olive's mass to within a margin of error of plus or minus zero point eight percent – which was impressive, but zero point eight percent is a pretty big margin when you're towing a few million tons of rock through the gravitational sphere of Jupiter. A trajectory error of a tenth of a degree might be the difference between getting home safely and spending the next thousand years as the latest addition to Jupiter's collection of moons.

The most accurate way of measuring Olive's mass was also the most primitive: see how hard it is to move. And that's precisely what Matt and Serena were now doing. He had fired the *Morgana*'s thrusters at full power for exactly three seconds, and now Serena was attempting to calculate how far out of its orbit Olive had budged. Or maybe she was trying to calculate the difference between the *Morgana*'s current position and where the Morgana would have been if it hadn't been tethered to Olive when Matt fired the thrusters. Matt had graduated with honors as an engineering major from Cal-Poly, but even trying to keep track of the number of variables Serena had to work with gave Matt a headache. The *Morgana* floated at the periphery of Jupiter's realm of influence, so she would have to take into account Jupiter's pull as well as that of several neighboring asteroids, in addition to the mass of the *Morgana* and the thrust it had produced.

"Okay, got it," Serena said at last.

"So?" Matt asked. "What's the magic number?"

"I'm sending you thrust vectors."

"So that's how it is, huh?" Matt asked.

"Yep," replied Serena. "Don't worry your pretty little head with things like mass and acceleration. Just do what you're told."

"Yes, ma'am," replied Matt. The sad thing was that Serena was only half-joking. She knew that the mass number would be meaningless to Matt; all he needed to do was punch in the thrust vectors. Serena was the brains of this operation; he was, at best, the hands and feet.

Matt squeezed his eyes tight and cracked his neck one more time. With any luck, they wouldn't have to do another calibration for three days or so. He unsnapped his shoulder harness and lightly pushed off against the rubber-matted floor. Grabbing a rung above his head, he propelled himself through a narrow steel tunnel, re-emerging in the *Morgana*'s nav center. Serena greeted him with a smile and a hug.

"That's the longest we've been apart for three months," said Matt.

"I don't think it counts as being apart," replied Serena. "You were ten meters away. And we were in constant radio contact."

"Still, I missed you terribly," said Matt.

Serena stuck out her tongue at him. She was petite, with short brown hair and a pretty face liberally dotted with freckles. There was no one Matt would rather be stuck in a tin can with for six months.

"Tomorrow's our anniversary, you know," he said.

"Is it?" Serena asked. "We should –"

A warning chime sounded and a red light flashed above their heads. "Shit," said Matt. "What now?"

Serena scanned the warning message that had popped up on her monitor. "Winch number three is sticking," she said. "Can you cycle through the self-test?"

"Yeah," said Matt, maneuvering himself in the zero gravity to his station next to Serena's. She had been using both stations for the thrust vector calculations, which is why Matt had retreated to the rear observation station. Now he nestled himself next to her again and brought up the self-test application for the towing winches. "Gimme a sec."

Olive was tethered to the *Morgana* by three steel cables. The thinking was that if one of the cables was severed by a rogue meteor or one of the pitons that secured the cable to the rock broke loose, there would still be two cables in place. The problem with this system was that it required a mechanism to equalize tension between the three cables – which is where the automated winches came in. If one cable was pulling too hard, it would release some slack on that cable and tighten the other two in an effort to keep the load evenly distributed. If one of the winches had jammed, that was bad news.

After a frustrating several minutes of tapping keys and waiting for a response from winch number three, Matt sighed. "No good. It's stuck bad."

"Okay, now what? Go out there and fix it?"

Matt shook his head. "Protocol is to try to torque it loose. Loosen the other two cables and hope that winch three releases."

"Jesus," said Serena. "That sounds dangerous."

"Not as dangerous as suiting up and trying to un-jam it with a crowbar." He tapped a series of commands into the keyboard, overriding the dynamic tensioning system and letting cables one and two go slack. Then he entered the thrust vectors Serena had sent him minutes earlier. At present, there was minimal tension on cable three because it and the *Morgana* were in free-fall, but when Serena's thrust schedule kicked in, the *Morgana* would begin a series of accelerations that would adjust its path to allow them to slingshot around Jupiter and back toward Earth. Hopefully the acceleration would be enough to un-jam the winch – but not enough to tear the piton free from the rock.

"When's the next thrust?" Serena asked.

"No time for that," Matt said, winking at her. It was an obvious joke, but he knew she'd have been disappointed if he hadn't taken advantage of the setup.

"Ha, ha," said Serena dutifully. "Seriously, when?"

"Thirty-eight minutes. We'll know soon enough."

They waited in silence.

Matt and Serena had gotten married two years and 364 days earlier. They were the first husband-and-wife extraterrestrial mining crew in history – but if all went well, they would likely not be the last. Originally these asteroid-retrieval expeditions had been designed as one-person operations, and in truth there was no technical reason to have two crew members aboard. But CMS altered its methodology when it lost its second miner to suicide. Both had been driven insane by the solitude and gone out the airlock – the latter one sans pressure suit. Cynics argued that CMS's change in attitude had more to do with the fact that the second suicide also cost them a ten-billion-dollar spacecraft than concern about their crewmembers.

Whatever the rationale, CMS was ultimately forced to redesign its vessels to accommodate two crew members, in order to ward against the loneliness and depression that went with extended space travel. They spent a small fortune trying to devise a scientific model of the perfect two-person mining team only to come to the obvious conclusion that the best possible team was a happily married couple. And just like that, Matt and Serena Edlund – an unexceptional air force test pilot and a computer scientist toiling away on CMS's navigation software, respectively – vaulted to the top of the list of candidates to man the first two-person mining mission in CMS's history. There had been three other couples under consideration (two male-female teams and a lesbian couple), but Matt and Serena had outscored all of them on both individual psychological tests and cooperative problem-solving exercises. They were, as far as CMS was concerned, the perfect team.

"Here we go," said Matt, as the thrusters fired. Gravity suddenly pulled him down into his chair. On the monitor in front of him was Olive. Three barely perceptible silver lines – the tethering cables – began at the bottom of the screen, disappearing after a few inches into the shadow of the asteroid.

A minute jolt shuddered through the craft.

"What the hell was that?" Serena asked.

Matt bit his lip. "Hopefully, the winch letting go. Otherwise…"

Something was off about one of the lines on the bottom of the screen: its angle had changed slightly. That could only mean one thing.

"Oh, fuck," said Matt. "Hold on."

The number three piton had snapped, and now the loose end of the cable was recoiling toward the *Morgana*. There was a flash at the bottom of the screen as the remnant of the drilling assembly caught the sunlight, and then it disappeared from sight. Half a second later, there was another jolt, this one bigger than the first. The crunch of metal reverberated through the cabin. The warning chimes sounded and red lights blinked furiously.

"No loss of pressure," said Serena.

"Thank God," replied Matt. "Hopefully it didn't… ah, shit. The oxygen plant is reporting severe damage. It's completely offline."

Matt power-cycled the plant, but there was no response. "Can we get it on one of the cams?" he asked.

"Yes," replied Serena. "Number fourteen, I think."

Matt switched his display to show the input from camera fourteen. The view wasn't pretty.

"No way we're fixing that," said Matt grimly.

The *Morgana* was a monstrous assembly of preassembled modules, stacked like a tower of Lego bricks. One of these was the oxygen generation plant. It would have made more sense with a ship of the *Morgana*'s size to use two smaller oxygen plants, but the manufacturer only made the modules in one size, and redundancy wasn't cost-effective. A consequence of this design was that if the oxygen plant got knocked out, the crew of the *Morgana* was in deep shit. And what they saw on the monitor was a gaping hole in the side of the oxygen generation module.

"So what do we do?" Serena asked. But she knew the answer. There was nothing *to* do. They couldn't even radio CMS for help because they were on the far side of Jupiter.

"Better refigure the oxygen usage calculations," Matt said. "Assume zero output from the OGM. Maybe…" His voice trailed off. He couldn't make himself complete the thought, because he knew it was a lie. *Maybe we can both make it home….*

Matt sat in silence while Serena re-worked the calculations. As he sat watching her work, he felt completely helpless – the same way he felt when he sat with her in the hospital after the accident. That was nearly two years ago, before they had been selected as the crew of the *Morgana*. They had been on their way to a Halloween party, Matt dressed as a pirate and Serena dressed as a mermaid. Matt had swerved to avoid a stray cat in the road and skidded sideways into a telephone pole. Serena's head had crashed through the passenger's side window and slammed into the pole. The doctors had kept her in a coma for three weeks to control the swelling of her brain. Matt had stayed with her in the hospital, leaving her side only for a few minutes at a time. The thought of losing her was more than he could stand. He had barely slept and lost over twenty pounds from his already wiry frame.

At last she had regained consciousness and began to show steady improvement. Within another three weeks, she had made a near-complete recovery. Only a few days later, they got the call from CMS, asking whether they would be interested in trying out for a spot on the mining crew rotation. It was an opportunity that neither of them had dared dream of. In the span of a few months, Matt had gone from the depths of despair to the highest heights known to humankind.

And now it was over. At least one of them would die before reaching Earth. Matt found himself hoping that there was no possibility of even one of them making it, so that they wouldn't have to make the decision that he dreaded.

The grimace on Serena's face told him that his hope would be unfulfilled.

"We have, maybe, just enough oxygen for one of us to make it back," she said bluntly. "Sedation would help. If we put everything on automatic, and try to sleep as much as possible…."

"It has to be you," said Matt.

"No," said Serena.

"Serena, listen to me. You're the brains of this operation. You can manage the nav system if you need to, but I can't do the thrust vector calculations."

"You could, Matt. It's not as hard as you —"

"Okay, sure. I *could* do it, but it will take me five times as long. That means I'd have to spend more time awake than you. And as you say, whoever... *stays*... has to sleep as much as possible, to minimize oxygen use. In any case, you're smaller. You only use about seventy-five percent as much oxygen as I do."

Serena shook her head. "I don't think I can do it, Matt."

"You'll be fine," Matt said. "You're strong than I am. When you were in the coma, I fell apart. I couldn't even muster the strength to feed myself. No way I'm piloting this ship back home in that condition. You're not like that. You're stronger than you realize. You'll carry on."

"Matt, no!" Serena cried, horrified. "I can't! You don't understand. I can't make it without you!"

"Serena, goddammit! Don't you think I know how hard this is? But there's really no choice. It has to be you. If you leave me, then we're both dead. You have to be the one to bring the *Morgana* home."

Serena closed her eyes and tears streamed down her face. She unbuckled her harness and moved toward Matt to embrace him.

"I'm sorry, sweetie," he said. "There just isn't any other way."

"Don't say you're sorry!" Serena said. "You're the one who's...." She trailed off.

For several minutes, they held each other in silence.

At last, Serena spoke again. She was doing her best to resume her mathematician's demeanor. "How are you going to do it?"

"I'll... go out the airlock. Otherwise you'd have to...."

Serena nodded. There was no need to explain: obviously there was no room on the *Morgana* for a decaying corpse.

"I'll take some painkillers before I eject myself. With any luck I'll be stoned out of my mind before I run out of air."

Serena tightened her embrace. A tear drop floated in front of Matt's eyes.

"Okay, let's get to work," Matt said, a bit too tersely. His bravado was pointless; Serena could see right through him. But for some reason he felt compelled to put up a brave front. Something hard-wired into the XY chromosome, he thought. "One final systems check, and then we'll have our last supper. Break out those beef burgundy packets we've been saving."

Serena nodded and did her best to smile. "Okay. Meet you back here at sixteen hundred."

"Yes, ma'am," said Matt, and unsnapped his harness. He pushed himself toward the opening opposite the one he had arrived from earlier. Every day they went through a standard check of all the *Morgana*'s systems; he could do his part in his sleep. Of course, after today, Serena would have to do both parts. He considered suggesting that they trade, but that would be pointless. She'd have to learn on her own, either way. In any case, he had no doubt she'd figure it out.

The prescribed order for the tests didn't make much sense on paper – the nav system was to be checked before the electrical system, for example – but the rationale became clear once you were inside the *Morgana*. The tests were ordered by proximity, from the two ends of the ship to the center. Usable space was at a premium in these ships; there simply wasn't enough room for two people carrying toolboxes to pass each other in the narrow shaft that ran the length of the *Morgana*. Despite the retrofit, the quarters were still cramped – even for a married couple.

Still, it was better than being alone. The sanity of even the most well-adjusted astronaut was strained by six months in space. Real-time communication with Earth was impossible after the initial burst of thrust, leaving the occupants of the craft in near total isolation only three weeks after takeoff. And once you were behind Jupiter, all communications were cut off, leaving nothing but the crushing boredom of deep space.

There was no *technical* reason for the Morgana to have two crew members, but it was clear after Cam LeFevre took his little spacewalk wearing nothing but his coveralls that the basic human need for social contact wasn't going to bow to technical requirements. Human beings just weren't designed to be alone for six months at a time.

At first, CMS, beholden to its shareholders, tried to take the cheap way out. Rather than redesign the ship's hardware to accommodate two passengers, they tried to solve the problem with software. The idea was to design a computer program that could mimic human interaction. They called it Sidekick. When the programmers finished it, they locked up a few test subjects with only Sidekick to talk to. Unfortunately, CMS had to cut the experiment short after three weeks because the instance of psychosis was higher *with* Sidekick than without. Prisoners in solitary confinement fared better than the poor bastards who were subjected to Sidekick.

On the other hand, a single astronaut would never have had to face the choice that had been forced upon Matt and Serena. He told himself that he had made the right call: it had to be Serena who lived. She had a better chance of making it home.

Matt had just reached the fore end of the ship when an alarm sounded. His mouth went dry and his stomach tightened. He knew that sound: Serena had opened the inner airlock door.

Matt latched his toolkit to one of the rungs that lined the interior of the Morgana and tucked himself into a ball, pushing against the rung to send himself spinning head-for-feet. Reaching out again in a practiced motion, he braked himself against the rung, forcing himself to come to a complete stop, then pushed off down the shaft. The fastest way to get to the airlock was with a single, well-aimed jump, but in his haste Matt badly misjudged and ended up crashing into the side of the shaft some ten meters down. Bouncing off the panel, he came to a halt when his head struck one of the rungs. Matt cursed, took a deep breath, and jumped again. This time he sailed straight down the shaft, not stopping until he grabbed a rung across from the airlock door.

Matt turned just in time to see the airlock status monitor display:

DE-PRESSURIZATION COMPLETE

Above this message was an image of Serena, standing in the airlock, smiling placidly at him. She wasn't wearing a pressure suit. The display now read:

OPENING EXTERNAL DOOR

"No!" Matt screamed. "Serena, stop! What are you doing?"

The door slid open, revealing the dark of deep space and a smattering of stars.

Serena pantomimed blowing a kiss to him. Then she turned and launched herself into the blackness.

As her figure grew smaller, Matt stared in disbelief. Why would she do this? It made no sense. They had agreed, for Christ's sake. She was supposed to be the one to pilot the *Morgana* home.

Her words echoed in Matt's brain: *I can't! You don't understand. I can't make it without you!*

Disbelief was followed by waves of anger and grief – and then self-pity. Well, he thought. Now we're both fucked.

Serena's limp body drifted away as if pulled by the darkness of space.

To Matt's credit, he didn't bother to entertain vain hopes of rescuing her. She'd asphyxiate before he even had his suit on. He watched her float away until she was a tiny white speck in the blackness, and then kept watching for what might well have been hours. There was nothing else for him to do.

He hadn't been exaggerating when he told her he was incapable of navigating the *Morgana* back to Earth. It would have been a challenge for him even if he had a full supply of oxygen, and with his already barely adequate intellect compromised by grief and oxygen deprivation, he didn't have a chance.

At last he looked away, and the reality of the situation hit him: he was alone. As alone as anyone had ever been, 300 million kilometers from the nearest human being. *300 million kilometers.* Another meaningless number. What mattered was that Serena was gone, her frozen body drifting slowly into deep space.

Matt dragged himself numbly to the control center, strapping himself into his chair. He tapped in the thrust vectors Serena had given him earlier, and then activated the *Morgana*'s distress beacon. Serena's vectors would get the *Morgana* around Jupiter and headed roughly in the direction of Earth. CMS would pick up the distress call, run a remote diagnostic, and discover that both crew members were dead. They would then send a salvage mission to retrieve the Morgana and its haul. The job would get done, even though the crew wouldn't be around to see it.

Matt mechanically unstrapped himself and navigated toward the medical locker. He swallowed a handful of narcotics and then made his way back to the airlock and began donning his space suit. He was under no illusion about his own gallantry; following Serena into the void fully conscious and sans space suit was probably the romantic thing to do, but Matt had no desire to die of a pulmonary embolism, exploding lungs, or any of the other conditions that ultimately led to death in a vacuum. No, he would stick to the plan, even if Serena hadn't: he would launch himself into space and drift into a narcotic slumber, dying peacefully when his 30-minute oxygen supply gave out.

As he sealed his helmet, he began to worry that the narcotics wouldn't take effect in time, and that he would feel his lungs burning from oxygen deprivation for several minutes before passing out. But then the drugs hit him like a hammer to the back of his head, and his anxiety spun 180 degrees: would he even get out of the airlock before he lost consciousness?

The helmet was on; the last thing to do was to don his gloves and seal them. This was really a two-person job under ideal circumstances, and with Matt's brain entering a narcotic haze, he found the task nearly impossible. His fingers felt like sausages dangling from his hands.

"Goddamn it," Matt sighed, as his vision blurred. "I'm sorry, Serena. I'm a moron. I can't even fucking..."

*****

Matt awoke strapped into his cot. Serena was leaning over him. "Good morning," she said with a smile. There was a note of worry in her voice.

"What..." Matt started, groggily. "Serena! How did you...?"

"How did I what?" she asked. "I got us past Jupiter, if that's what you're wondering. I just pushed the numbers into the fancy computer thingy. I can manage *some* things on my own, you know."

"No," Matt said. "I meant, how did you survive... the airlock? You weren't wearing...."

Serena's brow furrowed as she regarded him sympathetically. "I'm sorry, Matt," she said. "I don't understand. I think you may still be a little confused from the drugs."

"The drugs," Matt repeated. "Shit, I took...."

"You took enough painkillers to kill… well, not a horse. Maybe a donkey. Get it? Because you're an ass. What the hell were you thinking, Matt?"

"I thought you were dead," said Matt.

"Dead?" replied Serena, shocked. "Why would I be dead?

"I saw you," said Matt. "You went through the airlock. Without a suit."

Serena shook her head. "Pretty sure I'd remember something like that," she said. "You must have been dreaming. It's OK, Matt. I'm here. I'm alive. We're going to make it back to Earth. Both of us."

Matt blinked and tried to shake away the fuzziness of sleep. "What? How?"

"While you were taking your little nap, I fixed the OGM. It's only at 23%, but it'll get us home. Just barely."

Matt couldn't believe what he was hearing. "You fixed the OGM? How in the hell…?"

"It wasn't as bad as it looked. The casing was pretty much toast, but some of the components were salvageable."

"But how…?" Matt trailed off, not wanting to insult Serena. If she said she fixed it, then she fixed it. But Serena was no mechanic. She didn't even know how to change the oil on their Toyota back on Earth. And yet she had repaired a complex piece of machinery while floating in deep space in a bulky pressure suit?

"It wasn't easy," said Serena. "I think I wore out the manual for the OGM. Oh, and one of our pneumatic wrenches is happily orbiting Jupiter. But the module is producing oxygen."

"Wow," said Matt, rubbing his jaw thoughtfully. A good two days' stubble greeted his fingertips. "That's fantastic. We're going to make it home. I can hardly believe it."

*****

The next day, Matt sat at his station, staring at a monitor showing the status of the Morgana's systems. At the lower left, a number coyly blinked red at him: 23.4%. According to the ship's computers, that was the current operating capacity of the oxygen generation module. On camera fourteen, it still looked like a trailer that had been hit by a tornado. Whatever Serena had done to the

OGM, it wasn't apparent by looking at it. Still, the computer wouldn't lie. Would it? In any case, if the OGM were offline, the oxygen would definitely be getting thin by this point, with two people breathing it. As it was, the cabin was a little stuffy, but the atmosphere was hardly life-threatening. If the OGM held at 23.4%, in three months they'd be back in Earth's orbit – uncomfortable and exhausted, but alive. He should be thankful.

Still, the image from camera fourteen bothered him. The OGM looked completely inert; it was hard to believe it was working at all, much less operating at nearly a quarter of its maximum capacity. With that mangled casing, how had Serena even gotten into the guts of the module to repair it? It seemed impossible. She'd have had to pry the casing off with a crowbar – a difficult feat in itself – and then gone to the trouble of re-securing the casing when she was done. Serena could be meticulous to a fault, but taking the time to put the casing back on after fixing the module bordered on pathological.

He couldn't go out and check it himself; the exertion would be an inexcusable waste of oxygen. They had barely enough to get back home as it was. And Serena would want to know why the hell he was taking an unnecessary trip outside the ship to check something that she and the ship's computer both assured him were working fine. On top of that, what would he do if he found that the OGM wasn't working after all? There was nothing to be done about it but wait and hope that Serena was right.

Serena. She was alive! He thought he had lost her, but somehow she was alive. Seeing her go out the airlock… that had been, what, a hallucination brought on by the drugs? But he had seen her exit the ship before he took the drugs. Or had he? Maybe the drugs were screwing with his memory.

A faint *clink!* echoed through the ship: the sound of a tool connecting with metal. Serena was finishing up her systems check and would soon be joining him in the command module. The noise reminded him of something: Serena said she had lost a wrench while working on the OGM.

His guilt at not trusting Serena paralyzed him for maybe a second, but then his curiosity got the better of him. He unstrapped himself and vaulted toward the tool cabinet where the wrenches were kept. Sliding down the catch, he opened the cabinet and peered inside. The pneumatic wrenches were all accounted for. So. Had Serena been joking about the wrench? How could he ask her without implying that he didn't trust her? He couldn't very well claim that he just happened to be looking for a pneumatic wrench; there was nothing in his system checks that would require such a tool.

As he sat staring at the complete set of wrenches, he heard the noise of a boot on a ladder rung: Serena had finished her checks and was making her way back to the command module.

Matt quietly closed the cabinet door and pushed off against the wall, propelling himself back toward his chair. His heart beat rapidly and his armpits were suddenly damp with sweat. What was he so worried about? It's just Serena, for God's sake. Calm down, idiot; you're wasting oxygen.

Catching one of the restraint straps as he sailed over the chair, he pulled down and spun deftly, landing in his chair with a *whoomf!* He clicked the restraints into place mere seconds before Serena floated into the module. He took a deep breath and tried to look bored.

"Everything OK?" she asked, regarding him quizzically.

"Yeah," he said, a little too quickly. "I, uh, had a bit of a scare. Misread the fuel consumption figures and almost gave myself a heart attack. But everything's fine, yeah."

"Cool," she replied, maneuvering into her own chair and securing the restraints. "Everything checks out on my end. We should get some sleep."

"I'm not tired."

"Take a sedative. We're wasting oxygen."

"Give me a minute. Maybe I just need to relax a bit."

Serena shrugged and closed her eyes.

After a moment, Matt spoke again. "Hey, what was the name of that restaurant we used to go to in Houston? That place with the cheap T-bones. It had some horrible name."

Serena didn't open her eyes. "Happy Steak?"

Matt laughed. "Yeah, that was it. Happy Steak. We spent a lot of Friday nights there. We should go back sometime, after we get home."

"I don't think it's there anymore," said Serena. "I think it went out of business when I was in the coma. I drove past it afterwards, and it looked like it had been boarded up."

"Figures," said Matt. "We probably kept that place in business."

Leave it alone, thought Matt. You're not going to accomplish anything by pushing her. But his mind wouldn't leave it alone. Something wasn't right. After a moment, he spoke again.

"Hey, what was that game you were trying to teach me in the hospital?"

"Indiana Rummy?"

"Yeah, that's the one. We should play that game."

"We will. When we get back."

"Let's play now. Just one game. I think it will help me relax."

"No way," said Serena. "I'm not teaching you any more card games. You're a terrible student. You complain that I'm over-explaining things and then when you lose, you bitch about how I didn't explain the rules well enough. It's maddening."

"Please," said Matt. "Just one game. I promise I won't complain. How about if I look up the rules on the computer and wake you up when I'm ready to play?"

"Whatever," said Serena.

Matt punched *Indiana Rummy* into the console. The computer replied with: *No matches found.*

"Huh," said Matt. "The computer doesn't know the game. I thought it knew everything." In truth, he hadn't expected to find anything. After Serena's failed attempt to teach him the game, Matt had looked it up on the 'net, and had been surprised to find that as far as the 'net was concerned, Indiana Rummy didn't exist.

"I think my grandma invented it," said Serena.

"Your grandmother invented a card game?"

"Sure. The women in my family are a little eccentric. Mathematicians. They used to make up all sorts of card games, just for fun. Indiana Rummy was our favorite, though."

"OK, well, you're going to have to teach me, since the computer evidently isn't familiar with your grandmother's repertoire of card games."

"Later, Matt. Please. I'm trying to sleep."

"OK," Matt said. "Later." He closed his eyes and tried to sleep. But all he could see when he closed his eyes was the mangled OGM casing.

*****

Matt looked up from his console. "So you going to teach me this game or what?"

"I'm kind of busy over here."

"Busy!" Matt snorted. "You're doing a Sudoku."

"Yes," Serena replied. "I'm busy doing a Sudoku."

"Come on," Matt wheedled. "You promised."

"Why do you suddenly want to play this game so bad, Matt?" Serena demanded irritably. "You sure as hell didn't show this much interest when I was in the hospital."

"Well, I'm interested now," he said, meeting Serena's glare with a cold gaze. "Teach me the game."

Serena looked away and laughed. "I don't think I remember the rules."

"Really," said Matt. "Your favorite game. The one you tried to teach me six months ago."

She turned to face him again. "That's right, Matt. I don't fucking remember," she snapped. I don't remember how to play the game. Is that OK with you? I had a near-fatal head injury, remember? Maybe I forgot a few things."

Matt persisted. "CMS ran you through a hundred tests before letting you on this mission. There was no sign of brain damage or memory loss, except for the few moments before the crash. And in any case, you seemed to remember the rules just fine while you were recuperating, *after* you came out of the coma. If you don't remember the rules, it has nothing to do with the crash, and you know it."

"Jesus, Matt. What is it with you and this game? Just let it go, would you?" After a moment, she said again, more quietly, "Let it go, Matt. Please."

Matt found himself blinking away tears. What the hell was wrong with him? He was with the woman he loved, and in three months they would be back home, with a year of paid leave to spend together, doing whatever they wanted. Why couldn't he just accept that and be happy?

A tap of an icon brought up camera fourteen again. The mangled casing looked as bad as ever. Reason told him there was no way in hell that thing was working at 23% capacity. And then there was the supposed missing wrench. And his "hallucination." He had *seen* Serena go out the airlock, before he had taken any pills. Maybe the pills had screwed with his memory, scrambling the order of events, but it had seemed so real. He was *sure* that he had seen her go out the airlock – as sure as he was that she was sitting across from him now. On the other hand, maybe he was hallucinating *now*.

"Teach me the game," he said again.

"Matt, no…" she pleaded.

"Teach me the *fucking* game. Indiana Rummy. Teach me. Now."

Now Serena was weeping. "No, Matt," she cried. "Please don't make me."

"I love you, Serena," Matt said through gritted teeth. "If you ever loved me, teach me the game."

After a moment, she wiped her eyes with the back of her hand and nodded. She tapped her screen a few times, and a window popped up on Matt's screen. It read:

Serena wants to play a card game with you. Accept/Refuse.

Matt accepted, and a deck of cards appeared. Seven cards flew off the deck, flipping to appear face-up at the bottom of his screen.

"Order the cards by their face value, regardless of suit," said Serena. All emotion had drained from her voice.

Matt tapped the cards, one by one. Two of clubs, three of hearts, six of spades, eight of hearts, nine of clubs, jack of spades, king of diamonds.

The screen went dark. Then a message appeared. It read:

Project Avalon has been suspended. Stand by for instructions.

A face appeared on the screen. Matt gasped. He'd know that face anywhere: it was his own.

"Hi, Matt," said the Matt on the screen. He broke into nervous laughter. To someone off-screen, he said, "I feel like an idiot doing this. Can't somebody else… yeah, yeah. OK, I've got it."

Matt shuddered in his chair. He had no memory of making this recording. In the video, he was wearing a dirty gray sweatshirt. His hair was longer, and he had a beard. He looked gaunt and tired. It looked like the recording had been taken about six months earlier, during the depths of his depression, before Serena's miraculous recovery. In fact – was that the sound of a heart monitor beeping? Was this video taken in the hospital, by Serena's bedside? What kind of sick –

His thoughts were interrupted by the Matt on the screen. "Well, I guess if you're watching this, you've made it back to Earth safely. Either that, or something has gone pretty fucking wrong. I hope for your sake it's the former, but this isn't going to be easy for me either way. For you, I mean. Jesus." The man on the screen fought to compose himself. After a moment he continued.

"They're making me do this recording as a condition of the project. I guess it's as much for me as it is for you. They want it documented that I understand what they're going to do to me. That is, what they did to you. Understandable. You're probably going to want to sue them. Trust me; don't bother. You've waived every right you have.

"I want you to know, first of all, that I didn't do this primarily out of grief, although the grief is nearly unbearable. I also didn't do it because of the money, although the money is very good, as you'll soon find out, now that you're back home safely. I did it because I wanted to go into space. That's an opportunity very few people have, Matt. Remember that, whatever else happens.

"OK, so, Project Avalon. They're going to tell you that they retrofitted the *Morgana* to make it a two-person ship. They lied to you. They spent half a billion dollars trying to do it, but it was simply unworkable. If you take some measurements of the ship, you'll see what I mean. There's no way two people could live on that thing. Hell, there's only the one command station."

What the hell was he talking about? Matt wondered. Serena's right over –

He looked up from his station. The command module suddenly seemed very small. Serena was gone.

"Serena!" he called. But only silence followed. Where the hell could she have gone? And what had happened to the command module? Where was Serena's station?

"The studies showed they needed a two-person crew," the Matt on the screen went on. "Another suicide and they'd be bankrupt. They thought they had their answer with Sidekick, but you know how that turned out. Well, you know the first part of the story, anyway. You won't remember the rest, because they removed some of your memories. Anyway, I'll get to that in a minute.

"At first the psychologists couldn't figure out what the problem was. Sidekick was a nearly flawless implementation of artificial intelligence, the perfect non-living companion, but somehow it was driving test subjects crazy. Then they decided to try the experiment again, but without telling the subjects that Sidekick was a computer. A real Turing test, if you will. And guess what? It worked. The problem wasn't with Sidekick at all; the problem was in the perceptions of the test subjects. They were driven insane by the knowledge that their sanity depended on their friendship with a computer program.

"This presented a simple but vexing solution: somehow they had to convince an intelligent, sane, technically savvy pilot that Sidekick was a living, breathing human being. But how the hell do you do that? Well, not to put to fine a point on it, you have to fuck with a person's perceptions."

"No," said Matt to his doppelganger on the screen. "No, no, no…."

The doppelganger continued. "They are going to implant a chip in my head. Back here." He reached to touch the base of his skull, and Matt unconsciously did the same. He felt a small bump at the top of his spine "The chip is an interface between your brain and a computer program. An enhanced version of Sidekick. It creates what they call teleological hallucinations. In other words, hallucinations with a purpose. Your brain tells the chip what it needs, and the chip creates a hallucination that provides it. If you need thrust vectors, it will give you thrust vectors. If you need somebody to talk to, it will give you that. All in the form of your… my wife, Serena."

The Matt on the screen turned away from the camera, holding his hand over his eyes. Matt found himself with a lump in his throat and a queasy feeling in his stomach. He looked away from the screen. There was still no sign of Serena anywhere.

After some time, the Matt on the screen composed himself. "They are also going to alter my... your memories. You'll remember Serena waking up –" He bit his lip, fighting back tears. "You'll remember her waking up, and you'll remember the two of you being selected as the *Morgana*'s crew. You'll celebrate, get drunk, and wake up the next day with a bad hangover." His hand went to the base of his skull again. "After that, she'll be with you, in your head. All the time." He smiled weakly, as if looking forward to relief from his suffering.

"Now that you're back... well, you're going to have to come to grips with reality. Serena's gone. You piloted the *Morgana* by yourself, with a little help from Sidekick and your memories of Serena. They're going to make you have the chip removed. I honestly can't imagine how I will... how you feel about that. Maybe by now you want to cut it out yourself. Maybe you want to keep it forever and pretend that she's still with you. Either one is a really bad idea.

"Let them take the chip out. Take some time off. See a therapist. You'll have enough money to live on for a few years, thanks to the deal I made with CMS. And I know you're going to want to blame them, but this isn't CMS's fault. They didn't kill Serena. All they did is delay your grief a bit, and give you an opportunity very few people have. And pay you very well for it, I'll add."

The Matt on the screen nodded to someone off-screen, and the camera zoomed out and panned left, showing Serena, lying unconscious in the hospital bed. There were tubes in her mouth and nose, and more tubes and wires hooked up to her arms.

"No!" Matt sobbed, staring aghast at the screen. "She woke up! Wake up, goddammit, wake up!"

"I'm sorry you have to see this," said the Matt on the screen. "God knows I'd like to forget it forever, but it's important for you to see, so that you'll know that I'm telling you the truth. And so that you remember." He turned toward Serena and said, "I'm sorry. I'm sorry, baby."

The Matt on the screen nodded and a man in scrubs appeared on camera. The camera zoomed further back to show him standing at a computer console.

"Wake up, Serena," Matt pleaded. "Please, baby, wake up."

The man tapped a series of commands into the console.

"Goodbye, baby," said the Matt on the screen, taking the unconscious Serena's hand. "I love you."

The rhythmic beeping of the heart monitor was replaced by a monotone hum, and the screen went blank.

For several minutes, Matt sat in silence, staring at the blank screen. A voice shook him out of his reverie. It was Serena.

"Matt."

Matt looked up to see her sitting there at her station, just as she had been before the recording started. A hallucination, he thought. She's *always* been a hallucination, ever since the coma. "God damn you," he hissed.

"Matt, don't be angry at me…" she started.

"You know damn well I'm not talking to you," Matt said. He had been talking to the Matt on the recording. Then he laughed bitterly, realizing that either way, he was talking to himself.

He unfastened his restraints and made his way to the medical cabinet. Opening the cabinet, his eyes alighted immediately on the portable defibrillator.

Somehow Serena was standing right in front of him. "Matt, don't do this!" she pleaded.

It's not Serena, he told himself. *Just a projection. A software program.* He squeezed a handful of conductive jelly from a tube and slathered it on the back of his neck. He pulled the paddles from the defibrillator and flipped the power switch. The machine whined as the capacitors charged.

Serena gripped his wrists in her hands. "Stop, Matt. You don't need to do this. I can –"

He wrenched his hands away and held the paddles to the back of his head. He never even felt the shock.

*****

CMS CONFIDENTIAL – PROPRIETARY AND
PRIVILEGED INFORMATION – DO NOT SHARE OR
DISTRIBUTE!

TO: Mrs. Jane Koeppel

RE: Congratulations!
Dear Jane,

First, let me express, on behalf of CMS management, our deepest condolences on the loss of your husband, Eric. We were stunned and saddened to learn of his recent passing. He was a valued member of the CMS team and truly embodied the ideals that we aspire to as a company.

I apologize, too, for the impersonal nature of this communication. Our efforts to contact you in person have not been successful.

The primary purpose of this letter, however, is to deliver some good news. Pending medical testing and some other formalities, your request to be a crew member on board a future mining mission has been approved!

I realize that this is a difficult time for you, but we urge you to contact us as soon as possible regarding this matter. As you are no doubt aware, this is a critical time in CMS's history, and we are very eager to demonstrate to the public and our shareholders that we have addressed the problems with the winch system that led to the tragic deaths of the crew of the Morgana.

As a token of our sympathy and goodwill, we would like to offer you two weeks of paid leave during which you may wish to visit our headquarters in San Diego (at our expense, of course). You can meet the mining mission control team and learn more about what a mining mission entails. You are under absolutely no obligation, but we would love to have the opportunity to talk to you.

Again, we offer you our sympathies in this difficult time. We look forward to hearing from you.

Terence Milan, CEO,
Corbenic Mining Services

Still Life

Micah VerMeer sits alone in a booth with puke green vinyl seats and a faux mahogany table. He's forgotten the name of the place, one of those generic chain diners that line interstates everywhere. It could be anywhere, and this indeterminacy vaguely irritates Micah, though he doesn't know why. They call these places "family restaurants," but this one seems to be devoid of families. His own table is no exception.

Micah's son Thomas is in the men's room. It's been several minutes, and Micah finds himself dreading his son's imminent return. Some part of him – or perhaps something outside of himself, intruding on his consciousness – seems to be warning him that it's not right for him to feel this way, that this circumstance needs to be rectified, but Micah brushes the annoyance away. It's not his fault things are the way they are, and even if it were, what can he in the next five minutes that he has been unable to do for eighteen years?

He sees Thomas walking toward him, looking shiftless in torn jeans and a faded black T-shirt displaying two tormented faces framed by letters that spell Def Leppard/Hysteria. Just another punk kid, Micah thinks, though he has to stifle a smile when his eyes alight on the tan fedora on Thomas' head. He's never seen anyone else Thomas' age wearing a fedora; he has no idea where Thomas got it, or why he's wearing it. Presumably Thomas just likes the idea of wearing a fedora.

Thomas sits back down across from Micah, avoiding eye contact. Thomas pulls a sketchpad from a backpack next to him on the seat and opens it to a drawing he had started in the car on their drive from Bradenton. Micah catches a glimpse of two muscular figures in ridiculous outfits, locked in combat, strange energies flowing from their fingers and eyes. Superheroes, Micah thinks. Juvenile comic book nonsense. Thomas spends countless hours on this stuff, drawing Spiderman, Batman, or some carbon copy character of his own creation. Micah remembers reading T.S. Eliot and Dickens when he was Thomas' age.

Micah glances at his watch. It's nearly 10 a.m. Thomas' ride will be here soon. Micah scans the parking lot again for a green Volkswagen – the only way he has of identifying the young man who had agreed to give Thomas a ride from Tampa to Lansing. The young man – also a freshman at Michigan State – is a cousin of one of Thomas' high school friends.

Any second, he thinks, a green VW will appear in the parking lot, and Thomas will be gone. Sitting here in silence is agony, but he fears that somehow the drive back home to Bradenton will be worse. Even more than that, he dreads the shared sensation of relief that they will feel when they are no longer in each other's presence. He imagines it as a palpable thing, a black cloud with jagged edges, like the mystical radiation enveloping the two characters on Thomas' sketchpad.

Thomas is oblivious, enraptured by the scene unfolding on the paper in front of him. As his left hand moves rhythmically over the pad, his right clenches empathetically with one or the other combatants. He doesn't seem to breathe, except at long, irregular intervals, when his body's thirst for oxygen jerks him momentarily out of his trance.

Thomas' talent is undeniable, Micah knows, but he is undisciplined, even lazy. He rarely finishes a drawing and can't be bothered to draw anything more mundane than a sorcerer or superhero. He believes Thomas harbors the desire to be an artist, perhaps drawing comic books. It would be a foolish dream even if Thomas had the discipline to see it through, which Micah knows he does not.

Drawing is not Thomas' only talent. He is brilliant in many ways, and well-meaning teachers had often pressured Micah and his wife to have Thomas tested, to put him in classes for gifted students, to allow him to skip a grade. But Micah and his wife had resisted, in part because they believed treating Thomas differently would encourage him to think that rules didn't apply to him. They could see already how Thomas manipulated his teachers to avoid tasks he considered unpleasant. His second grade teacher was so impressed with his story about Captain Dave's journey to the planet Venus that she let him shirk multiplication tables so he could expand it to a novella. Micah and his wife had Thomas moved to another second grade class.

Micah never offered his son any over encouragement in his drawing or writing, but men of Micah's generation had little use for superfluous displays of emotion. In any case, what was the point of encouraging Thomas? His diversions possessed him; no amount of encouragement or discouragement was going to prevent him from doing what he felt driven to do. And when it came to other activities, Thomas either avoided them completely or put in the least amount of effort that was needed to get by. His grades were spotty; he had gotten into MSU on the strength of an essay and his SAT scores. Micah found no fodder for encouragement and is convinced that Thomas would disregard his opinions anyway.

Yet as Micah sits there, slowly sipping lukewarm coffee, his eyes transfixed on his son's spasmodic hand movements, he once again has the feeling that something outside of himself is trying to break in to his psyche, trying desperately to communicate something to him about the urgency of his situation. It is a strange sensation, as if a part of his identity, submerged until now, has suddenly broken the surface. With this feeling comes an uncanny realization: his son's hands have stopped moving. In fact, the entire restaurant seems to have become frozen in time. The intrusion in his mind seems poised to speak.

But instead, his son speaks. No, not his son. It is his son's voice, but Thomas' mouth isn't moving.

"Dad, it's OK," the voice says.

"No..." He finds himself whispering gravely, "It's wrong. It all went wrong somehow."

"Things turned out OK."

"I never encouraged you, never told you how much..."

"No, you didn't."

"I feel like I should..."

"You've apologized, Dad. We've been over this a hundred times." Micah senses some irritation in his son's voice. He has a vision of his son, much older, glancing at an expensive watch. Not an artist, a... lawyer?

"Thomas, are you a lawyer?"

"No, Dad. A computer programmer. I write software. Remember?"

He doesn't remember. When did his son become a computer programmer? What happened to becoming an artist?

"Do you enjoy it?" he asks.

"Yes, Dad. Usually," Thomas says, obviously anticipating the question. "I never really wanted to be an artist. I just liked to draw. Never really got past the superhero thing. And yes, I'd still like to write a novel someday, but I'm pretty busy these days, with work, and getting the house built, and the kids...."

"Kids? How...."

"Three. Tommy, Michael, and Grace. Eight, six and three. Do you remember Marie?"

"Marie..." The vision of a pretty, dark haired woman with a dazzling white smile flashed into Micah's mind.

"Where am I?" Micah asks.

"The hospital," Thomas says.

Micah glances around, realizing that the resemblance to the restaurant next to I-75 in Tampa is superficial. The same vinyl seats, the same plate glass windows bordered by stainless steel. But this is clearly an institutional cafeteria. He knows this place. Thomas, sans fedora, hair thinning, is sitting across from him, his right foot extended into the aisle, the index finger of his left hand tracing invisible figures on the table.

"You have to go," Micah says.

"I'm sorry, Dad. I've got a meeting. You know, that project I was telling you about...."

"Oh, of course," Micah says. "Well, it's good to see you, Thomas."

"You too, Dad. Hang on, I'll get a nurse to bring you back to your room."

"OK, son. Thank you," Micah says. He wonders how many times he's put his son through this routine.

Thomas rises from the table and looks Micah in the eye. His son's smile is warm but forced. Micah looks down before it fades.

"I'll try to stop by again next week," Thomas says.

"OK," Micah says softly. "You know where to find me."

Review This Book!

Did you enjoy *The Wrath of Cons*? Please take a moment to leave a review on Amazon.com! Reviews are very important for getting the word out to other readers, and it only takes a few seconds.

More Books by Robert Kroese

The Starship Grifters Universe
Out of the Soylent Planet
Starship Grifters
Aye, Robot

The Saga of the Iron Dragon
The Dream of the Iron Dragon
The Dawn of the Iron Dragon
The Voyage of the Iron Dragon

The Mercury Series
"Mercury Begins" (short story)
Mercury Falls
"Mercury Swings" (short story)
Mercury Rises
Mercury Rests
Mercury Revolts
Mercury Shrugs

The Land of Dis
Distopia
Disenchanted
Disillusioned

Other Books
The Big Sheep
The Last Iota
Schrödinger's Gat
City of Sand
The Force is Middling in This One

CPSIA information can be obtained
at www.ICGtesting.com
Printed in the USA
BVHW031312161219
566829BV00001B/20/P